CAST OF CH~

Tommy Hambledon. A British intellige~

Herr Goertz. An unlucky German who ~

Isidore Skutnas, Lukas Olgar, and **Moritz Wenezky** (aka **Erich Sachsen**). Three very dangerous Middle European communists who desperately want that packet.

Captain Dirk Gielink. Skipper of the *Melicant Myrdal* out of Rotterdam.

Johannis. A Dutch passport forger and piano teacher, an old friend of Tommy's.

Horaz Kenrade, aka **Stefan Kalvag.** A former SS officer of some notoriety.

Nilsen and **Peycke.** Two former Nazis living with Kenrade in Rotterdam.

Kirk Rougetel. An anxious middle-aged German living in Paris.

Antoine Marillier and **Frolich.** Rougetel's brothers in exile and his bodyguards.

Charles Denton. Tommy's longtime friend and colleague at the Foreign Office.

James Hyde. An Englishman with a recently acquired taste for adventure.

Anatole Brihou and **Jean le Mari.** French black market lorry drivers.

Jules Arcache. A taxi driver in the village of Ste-Marie-en-Marais.

Etienne. A guide.

Jeannot of the Goats. The village innocent.

William Forgan and **Archibald Henry Campbell**. A pair of London modelmakers who unexpectedly come to Tommy's aid in Spain.

Sergeant Cortado. A soldier at the castle prison of Torida.

Ezra and Elvira Blenkinsop van Houten and **Hiram Biggs van Houten**. Fellow guests at the hotel in Santa Brigida who claim to be Americans.

Col. Leonhard Torgius. A prominent Nazi with dreams of a reborn Germany.

Herr Professor Schlagel. A brilliant Nazi chemist with a weakness for brandy.

Lorenz Borian. A Nazi who knows that Tommy is not who people think he is.

Tonio. An enormous yellow Canary dog as big as a calf. He's one of the good guys.

Plus assorted innkeepers, prison guards, Communists, Nazis, and bystanders.

Books by Manning Coles

The Tommy Hambledon Spy Novels
Drink to Yesterday, 1940*
A Toast to Tomorrow (English title: *Pray Silence*), 1940*
They Tell No Tales, 1941*
Without Lawful Authority, 1943*
Green Hazard, 1945*
The Fifth Man, 1946*
With Intent to Deceive (English title: *A Brother for Hugh*), 1947*
Let the Tiger Die, 1947*
Among Those Absent, 1948
Diamonds to Amsterdam, 1949
Not Negotiable, 1949
Dangerous by Nature, 1950
Now or Never, 1951
Alias Uncle Hugo (Reprint: *Operation Manhunt*), 1952
Night Train to Paris, 1952
A Knife for the Juggler (Reprint: *The Vengeance Man*), 1953
All that Glitters (English title: *Not for Export*;
Reprint: *The Mystery of the Stolen Plans*), 1954
The Man in the Green Hat, 1955
Basle Express, 1956
Birdwatcher's Quarry (English title: *The Three Beans*), 1956
Death of an Ambassador, 1957
No Entry, 1958
Concrete Crime (English title: *Crime in Concrete*), 1960
Search for a Sultan, 1961
The House at Pluck's Gutter, 1963

Ghost Books
**Brief Candles,* 1954
**Happy Returns* (English title: *A Family Matter*), 1955
**The Far Traveller* (non-series),1956
**Come and Go,* 1958

Non-Series
This Fortress, 1942
Duty Free, 1959

Short Story Collection
Nothing to Declare, 1960

Young Adult
Great Caesar's Ghost (English title: *The Emperor's Bracelet*), 1943

* Reprinted by Rue Morgue Press as of March 2011

Let the Tiger Die

A Tommy Hambledon
entertainment by

Manning Coles

Rue Morgue Press
Lyons, Colorado

ISBN: 978-1-60187-053-7

Rue Morgue Press
87 Lone Tree Lane
Lyons CO 80540
www.ruemorguepress.com
800-699-6214

Printed by Pioneer Printing
Cheyenne, Wyoming

PRINTED IN THE UNITED STATES OF AMERICA

About Manning Coles

Manning Coles was the pseudonym of two Hampshire neighbors who collaborated on a long series of entertaining spy novels featuring Thomas Elphinstone Hambledon, a modern-language instructor turned British secret agent. Hambledon was based on a teacher of Cyril Henry Coles (1895-1965). This same teacher encouraged the teenage Coles to study modern languages, German and French in particular, having recognized Coles' extraordinary ability to learn languages. When World War I broke out Coles lied about his age and enlisted. His native speaker ability in German prompted him to be pulled off the front lines and he soon became the youngest intelligence agent in British history and spent the rest of the war working behind enemy lines in Cologne.

The books came to be written thanks to a fortuitous meeting in 1938. After Adelaide Frances Oke Manning (1891-1959), rented a flat from Cyril's father in East Meon, Hampshire, she and Cyril became neighbors and friends. Educated at the High School for Girls in Tunbridge Wells, Kent, Adelaide, who was eight years Cyril's senior, worked in a munitions factory and later at the War Office during World War I. She already had published one novel, *Half Valdez*, about a search for buried Spanish treasure. *Drink to Yesterday,* loosely based on Cyril's own adventures, was an immediate hit and the authors were besieged to write a sequel, no mean feat given the ending to that novel. That sequel, *A Toast to Tomorrow*, and its prequel were heralded as the birth of the modern espionage novel with Anthony Boucher terming them "a single long and magnificent novel of drama and intrigue and humor." The Manning Coles collaboration ended when Adelaide died of throat cancer in 1959. During those twenty years the two worked together almost daily, although Cyril's continuing activities with the Foreign Intelligence Branch, now known as the Secret Intelligence Service or, more commonly, MI6, often required that he be out of the country, especially during World War II. Cyril wrote *Concrete Crime* on his own but the final two books in the series were the work of a ghostwriter, Cyril not wanting to go on with the series without Adelaide. While the earliest books had shown flashes of humor, it would not be until *Without Lawful Authority*, published in 1943 but set in 1938, that the collaborators first embraced the almost farcical humor that would come to be their hallmark. For more details on their collaboration and Cyril's activities in British intelligence see Tom & Enid Schantz' introduction to the Rue Morgue Press edition of *Drink to Yesterday.*

To amuse D.O.M.

Chapter One
Overture to Murder

Tommy Hambledon came out from the Grand Hotel on the sixth morning of his holiday in Stockholm, and lit the first cigarette of the day. He crossed the road to the water's edge and looked at the Royal Palace which seemed to float like a lily on the sparkling blue water. Small yachts with white sails slid quietly past him. Tommy thought them very preferable to the motorcycles upon which high-spirited youth enjoyed itself at home in England. A ferry steamer went by with high sides painted white and decks crowded with passengers; they were near enough for him to see that they were of the same type as the people who, at this hour at home, would be filing into tube stations, gliding down alarming escalators and being conveyed with noises and swaying through dark tunnels fed with reconditioned air and synthetic ozone. Stockholm folk went to their business on decent steamers over sparkling water, breathing real air and warmed by the sun. No doubt it would be a good deal more Spartan in the winter, but in August, thought Hambledon, Stockholm was the place to inhabit.

He turned right and strolled along the waterfront, planning another lazy day. He would hire a motor launch and visit some more enchanted islands. He would sit on a bench, sunning himself, in the Stadshustrad gardens. He might even—so warm was his heart towards Stockholm—visit a museum, for Hambledon was not by nature a museum visitor. It would be as it were a graceful acknowledgment of favors received. After which he would go and have a drink somewhere—it was really very odd how the mere thought of a museum suggested a drink to follow—and have lunch at the Rosengrens Källare. But first of all he would stroll along to that little antique shop and have a word with the proprietor about bubble glasses.

He turned up the Kungsträdgårdsgatan. They were very fine bubble glasses, the largest he had ever seen. Perhaps the proprietor would have some views about packing them safely to travel to England, though they looked so fragile as hardly to bear handling. Still, Swedish bubble glasses actually are exported from time to time and do arrive whole, unlikely though it might seem. He turned left into Hamngatan and two men, speaking German, passed him outside the Nordiska Kompaniet stores. There was nothing remarkable in hearing German spoken but it served to remind him of another item of interest in Stockholm, the German-who-was-being-followed.

Tommy told himself firmly that he was on holiday in a foreign country and that it was therefore no business of his if all the Germans in Sweden were severally and habitually followed about by a whole procession of gentry from Mitteleuropa walking two by two, each with a candle in one hand and large knife in the other. But Hambledon's curiosity was too deeply ingrained to be weakened by a mere holiday. The man not only looked like a German, he certainly was one; by his speech he came from Munich or thereabouts. Hambledon had stood next to him in a shop when the man was buying handkerchiefs. The two Middle Europeans were farther down the street on the opposite side, looking in a shop window which displayed delicate lingerie. They did not look the sort of men to take a genuine interest in lingerie, however delicate, but one never knows with Middle Europeans. What language they used between themselves it was difficult to discover since they never spoke when one was near enough to overhear them. There were, apparently, three of them although one never saw more than two at once. Hambledon in his own mind called them Brown, Jones and Robinson.

The German never gave any sign of knowing that he was being followed, though he must have been the most unobservant of men if he did not know it. He did not look unobservant; quite the contrary. Therefore either he did not mind or could not prevent it. They might, of course, be a bodyguard, but guards and guardees usually speak sometimes; these people did not so far as Tommy could see. Besides, they had not the air of a bodyguard, and, what was more definite, they did not keep near enough to the German to be any protection to him. They were not guarding, they were watching.

Hambledon had seen this interesting group on several occasions during the five days he had been in Stockholm. It would seem that the German confined himself entirely to the Norrmalm and Vasastaden district; it is possible that he felt safer in thronged streets. Ill-mannered violence is not tolerated in Stockholm.

Hambledon turned uphill at the end of Hamngatan and walked more slowly. The antique shop for which he was making was down a narrow turning to the left; when he came within sight of the corner he saw that the two he called Brown and Robinson were standing there together, apparently waiting for something or somebody. The German was not in sight; probably he was in one of the nearby shops.

"Buying socks, perhaps," said Tommy to himself. "He can't want any more handkerchiefs."

Brown and Robinson glanced carelessly at Hambledon as he approached; they were, in fact, looking with some eagerness up the street ahead of Tommy as though they expected something or someone to come down the hill towards them. There was a good deal of traffic, for it was a busy street; while Hambledon was still twenty yards away a saloon car drew in to the pavement just short of the turning and the two men hurried towards it. They had a few words with the driver and both got into the car. At the same moment Tommy reached the corner and, glancing down the side turning, saw the German standing outside the antique shop apparently lost in thought.

"They will turn in here," said Tommy, preparing to dodge, for the pavements in the side road were extremely narrow and the long car would have some difficulty in turning into it. It did not turn, however, it went straight on by the way Hambledon had come and passed from sight, giving him just time to recognize the driver as the man he called Jones. It was the first time he had seen all three together. He looked after the car for a moment and then turned down towards the shop. The German had awakened from his reverie and was walking rapidly away in the opposite direction; the next moment he also was lost to view behind a heavy porch built out upon squat round pillars at the edge of the pavement.

"Looks as though the party's breaking up. I shall always wonder what that queer charade was all about. I only hope he hasn't been in and bought my bubble glasses." Tommy strolled along more slowly than ever and spent several minutes looking in at a shop window which displayed knitted garments in gay and varied patterns. Adam Keppel Denton's birthday was imminent and a present would be required. One of those cheery little pullovers—how big is a boy of five?

A saloon car came along the narrow street towards him; it looked like the same car—it was, there was Jones driving it. It passed close by him, and though his eyes were dazzled by the sun he saw that something queer was going on in the back seat. A general impression of the Laocoön in tweeds; a struggle, in short. What had happened was immediately obvious; the Middle European gentry had not given up the chase and gone away. They had driven round a block, met the German farther on and abducted him.

Hambledon was still not far from the main road. He turned and sprinted after the car, confident that the men in the back were too busy to look out of the rear window. The car slowed for the turn and Tommy reached the corner almost simultaneously. He looked round for a taxi; as luck would have it there was one coming slowly up the hill.

Tommy signaled it to stop, dashed at it and jumped in, telling the driver to follow the blue saloon in front and not lose it on any account. The driver said, with typical Swedish courtesy, that the gentleman's wishes were his pleasure but that the car in front was much faster than his own. "While he keeps to the town we may hold him in view; if he drives out into the country he can lose us in five minutes."

"Never mind," said Tommy. "See what you can do. I don't expect miracles. Though why I'm doing this at all," he added to himself, "I cannot imagine. What's it to me if Germans get their throats cut all over Europe? Serve 'em right, they've asked for it. It's just a nice excuse for a pleasant run on a fine morning, that's all," he said, arguing with his wiser self which ignored this casuistry and reminded him that curiosity killed the cat.

However, the cars went on, the blue saloon twisting through the traffic and the taxi hanging on like a bulldog. Presently they left the streets behind, entering upon country roads, and the blue car put on speed.

"This, sir, is where we become like the cow's tail, all behind," said the driver, exacting the last ounce from his machine till it leapt on its springs like an April lamb. "They are, as I said, too fast for us."

"It can't be helped," said Tommy, clinging to his seat in order not to be thrown up and brained against the roof, "it is—good gracious, look at that."

The leading car swerved suddenly. There followed a sort of inaudible explosion at one side of it and glass showered out upon the road.

"He's kicked the window out!" said Tommy.

The driver used a form of words quite new to Hambledon and stood on his brakes in a vain attempt to avoid the broken glass. The off front tire burst with a loud bang and the taxi swerved off the road and slid, bumping heavily, into the ditch, where it canted over on its side against the bank and stopped. The driver almost wept, but Hambledon was so interested in what was happening to the other car ahead that he hardly noticed their own adventure. There was something coming out of the window, a man, headfirst. Tommy scrambled out of the disabled taxi and began to run up the road. Before he had gone a dozen yards the man at the window came farther out, furiously struggling, fell on his head in the road and lay there, moving feebly. The blue car put on speed and disappeared round a bend.

Tommy, who could run when he liked, was bending over the man in the road before he opened his eyes. He was, as Hambledon had expected, the luckless German. He tried to straighten himself and groaned.

"Take it easy, brother," said Tommy in German.

The man looked up. "Are you," he gasped, "one of us?"

"Of course. I'm going to carry you to the taxi and we'll get you to hospital in no time." Hambledon made a rapid examination of the man, who appeared miraculously to have escaped severe bodily injury although his head was much cut about. At least, Tommy could find no broken bones. "Can you put your arms round my neck?" he went on. "That's right, hang on tight. It's lucky you're no bigger." He heaved the man up with a grunt of effort and staggered along the road towards the taxi. The driver saw him and came to help.

"And to think that I supposed the gentleman to be in pursuit of some charming lady," he remarked. They laid the German down on the roadside grass near the car; the driver said something about a cushion for the poor head and went to fetch one.

"Take this," said the German, fumbling inside his coat. He produced a packet sewn up in linen and thrust it into Hambledon's hands. "Hide it—keep it safe—you know what to do. I'm done for, I think. Now get out before they come back, run away and keep clear. It is an order."

"But," began Tommy.

"Listen! They're coming."

Away in the distance they heard the whine of an approaching car.

"Get out," gasped the German, "quick!"

Tommy jumped the ditch and scrambled up the bank. There was woodland here on both sides of the road; not, fortunately, pines with bare ground beneath them, but birches growing in long grass, many clumps of broom and bracken and patches of a bushlike juniper. Hambledon, from his vantage point six feet above the road, saw in the distance a blue car approaching. He dived into the bushes and disappeared from sight.

The sound of the approaching car grew louder. "Probably not the same one," said Tommy to himself. "The world is full of blue cars. I think I'm behaving like a fool." He heard the car slow down and stop. "Of course, any driver would stop when he saw a ditched car and a man lying beside it. Any good Samaritan—" There were voices, not loud; he was too far off to distinguish any words. He rose to his knees preparatory to returning to the road, still obsessed with the idea that this was a different car and that it was merely silly to run away and hide. A trail of bramble engaged his sock and he paused to release it—

Three shots rang out and Hambledon with one convulsive movement dived under the juniper bushes and lay still. Of course they would now come to look for him and they would certainly find him. These bushes were no cover at all, but it was too late to get up and run. "Oh dear, oh dear," said Tommy, "why the hell did I want to mix myself up in this mess? Kind Heaven, if ever I get out of this I'll mind my own business forever and ever. And all over a blasted German, too—" He left off muttering to listen, but there was no sound of approaching steps and no man could move silently through that undergrowth. There were not even voices that he could hear; if Brown, Jones and Robinson were talking they were doing so in whispers. A new idea occurred to him; perhaps it was the German, miraculously reviving beneath the spur of circumstance, who had shot Brown, Jones and Robinson, one shot for each. Pretty, sir, pretty. Tommy began carefully to withdraw from his lair; for one thing it was damp and thorny and there was something sharp digging into his stomach. Then he froze again, for there came to his ears the sound of the car being started. It was put into gear and went off apparently in a hurry, for the fellow bungled the change into second. Third gear, top, and away fast, very fast. Now, was that Brown and supporting company, or the taxi driver going for the police? The car was headed for Stockholm.

Five minutes later Hambledon put his head cautiously over the bank, having crawled the intervening distance and decided en route that he would never, no, never go in for deerstalking. He took a careful survey of the scene before him, rose to his feet and jumped down into the road.

The taxi driver was lying limply, like a discarded rag doll, against the running board of his car; he had a bullet through the head. He was quite dead, but the German, with two bullets in him, was still faintly alive. He twisted feebly when Tommy stooped over him, and murmured: "Santa Brigida." He then died also.

Tommy straightened up and took his hat off, partly out of respect for the company and partly because fresh air to the head might help him to think. He looked round him at the sunlit empty road, the green and flower-starred banks on either side, the delicate birches swaying against the blue sky above, and said in a tone of intense exasperation: "But why shoot the taxi driver? Because he saw them and could recognize them, of course. I also have seen them and can recognize them. How very unfortunate. For me. Probably. Oh dear. Oh, damn. Now, suppose I go for the police, will they believe me? I doubt it. Especially if Brown, Jones and Robinson have already arrived at the police station and are describing with a wealth of picturesque detail how they saw me do the foul deed. The dirty treacherous dogs. It's just what I should do in their place. I think I'd better leave here. If anybody comes along—"

He scrambled up the bank again and departed. He found a narrow path through the wood and followed it at a good five miles an hour. Even so, before he was quite out of earshot of the road he heard a heavy lorry rumbling along; it slowed suddenly and stopped. Tommy broke into a run.

Two hours later he strolled placidly into the yard of a lonely farmhouse high upon a hillside and at least eight miles from the scene of the murder. He said that he had been walking; entranced by the magnificent scenery and the splendid mountain air, he had gone farther than he intended and was tired and hungry. If the excellent housewife could possibly provide him with a lunch of bread and cheese and allow him to rest for an hour, he would be immeasurably grateful.

He was welcomed and comforted, led into a vast kitchen with the date 1567 carved over the fireplace, and urged kindly into a chair. Ham was produced to go on with while the eggs were cooking, also cold goose and several kinds of bread. Spirits in a square bottle and a jug full of icy spring water tasting of damp moss. Hambledon pulled his chair up to the table and proceeded to enjoy himself. The moment the meal was over he sighed contentedly, leaned back in his chair and fell asleep. He had not taken so much violent exercise for years.

He awoke three hours later, feeling stiff but refreshed, and asked the nearest way to Stockholm. Just round the shoulder of the hill, quite a short distance, not two kilometers away, the gentleman would come upon a road along which a country omnibus would pass at sixteen hours, bound for the city. There was plenty of time, the gentleman could take it easily, and it was all downhill. Hambledon expressed very real gratitude in his halting Swedish and set off.

On the way to the city he thought the matter over. The packet must be important since Brown, Jones and Robinson had stalked a man for days on end and finally committed two murders to get it. British Intelligence should at least be given an opportunity to look at it, and quite obviously the sooner Hambledon got rid of it the better. The wisest plan would be to take it to the British Legation and ask them to forward it. If there were to be any trouble about the taxicab murders—if he were connected with them in the minds of the police—he had better get out of the country at the earliest possible moment by the first available means. There are few events which a legation dislikes more fervently than the arrival of one of its nationals upon its doorstep pursued by the justly enraged police of the country concerned. Besides, it would be of no use, a legation is not sanctuary; at least, no respectable legation would lend itself to concealing a wanted criminal, and British legations are nothing if not respectable. In a case of murder they would merely hand him over to stand his trial, and rightly.

Tommy sighed and rearranged his feet in the refreshing draft from the door of the omnibus. Another point was that he did not know where the British Legation was, though no doubt his hotel porter could tell him. Also, there was a bill owing at the Grand Hotel which had better be paid at once in case he had to leave suddenly. Plainly the first thing to do was to return to his hotel at once, tidy up his affairs there, pack his bag, and then take this intriguing little packet to the British Legation. Or, still better, wrap it up and post it to them. There was a letter box in the hall at the hotel, he need not even go outside. Tommy discovered in himself a strange aversion to roaming the streets of Stockholm with the three Middle Europeans presumably looking for him. "I'll leave tomorrow morning," said Hambledon, "whether anything untoward happens or not. There must be a ship or a plane going somewhere tomorrow. I don't mind where it goes to so long as it's out of Sweden. This holiday is spoilt anyway, curse Brown, Jones and especially Robinson."

Hambledon took a taxi from the bus terminus to the Grand Hotel and arrived without having even seen the three undesirables. The junior porter, who was on duty in the afternoons, told him the address of the British Legation; Tommy wrapped and addressed the package in the hotel writing room, bought the appropriate stamps from the porter, and posted it with a covering note asking the legation to forward it to M.I.5, London.

He went up to his room, packed his bag, and returned downstairs to the manager's office to pay his bill. A clerk in the outer office said that the manager was engaged at the moment if the gentleman cared to wait, or to return in ten minutes' time. The manager would not be long. Hambledon's legs were still in that condition where one cannot see a chair without wanting to sit in it; there was a chair beside him, he decided to wait. The clerk went on with his work for a few moments and then left the room. As he opened the door a draught blew in from outside; the inner door to the manager's office opened with a faint click and remained ajar.

Hambledon was not very fluent in Swedish but he understood it well enough and the conversation he overheard from the inner room sharpened his perceptions. He recognized the manager's voice in the act of saying that it was an unheard-of calamity for the hotel to have the police come and arrest one of the guests, and upon such a charge—murder!

"But I have already told you," said another voice, "that we have no intention of arresting the gentleman. We only want him to answer a few civil questions."

"Do you surround a hotel with hordes of constables watching every exit," said the agitated manager, "whenever you wish to ask a foreign guest a few civil questions? Is he, then, a desperado? A gunman? Is this my quiet office or are we, then, enacting a gangster film at the cinema?"

The policeman urged calmness upon the manager, but he refused tranquillity.

"And upon such evidence, if you call it evidence! A mysterious telephone call from some man with a strong foreign accent, who speaks from a public call box and declines to give his name——"

"But the rest of what he said was true," urged the policeman. "There was a taxi in the ditch at the place he specified, the taxi driver was lying against the running board shot through the head as he described, and there was another man not yet identified lying on the grass near by, also dead, with two bullets in him. All quite true. When our informant adds that he saw a man, whom he recognized as a guest at this hotel, running away from the scene with a smoking revolver in his hand, is it reasonable that the police should not enquire into the matter? It is true that we have not his name, and not a very good description either, but your guests—"

Tommy rose silently from the chair and left the room. In the passage outside he paused for thought. Not a very good description, but it would certainly include his well-cut English tweeds. A change of clothing at least—

The passage led to the service quarter and a little way along it there was a door giving to the street. The low rays of the evening sun entered at this door and lay across the passage; as Hambledon looked wistfully at it a figure passing slowly outside threw a shadow within and was visible for a moment. The figure wore the neat uniform of the Stockholm police.

"Coming events," said Tommy to himself, "cast their shadows before them." He sighed.

At that moment a bell rang somewhere; the junior porter emerged in haste from another door along the same passage and went into the front hall to deal with a fresh arrival of visitors. An idea occurred to Hambledon. He hurried down the passage and into the porter's room; as he had hardly dared to hope, the head porter's uniform coat and gold-laced cap hung behind the door. Tommy put them on; they fitted not too badly since the head porter was a square man like himself. He listened for a moment by the door, then crossed the passage and strolled out into the street. The policeman glanced at his retreating back without interest.

Chapter Two
Baltic Cruise

Hambledon proceeded in a dignified manner towards Blasie-holmen and the dock area, praying that he might not meet the real porter returning from his afternoon off. Too embarrassing. He had no particular wish to visit the docks, but to turn up the street meant meeting the policeman face to face, which would be unwise, and to walk past the front of the hotel in that uniform would be idiotic. He bore left and strolled along the waterfront. Dock areas have small shops open at odd hours in which is sold clothing of a utilitarian sort. Some kind of overcoat to cover his suit, and these too resplendent garments could go in the dock. He was particularly conscious of the golden words "Grand Hotel" across the front of his cap; there only needed someone who knew the real porter to come up and accost him and the game would probably be well up. "And I should be well down," thought Tommy disconsolately. "Everybody knows head porters of good hotels and this one looked as though he'd been there for years and years and was a man of unimpeachable respectability. I don't feel respectable at all—oh dear, here's another policeman—I feel like a fugitive from justice which, after all, is what I am, and all over a so-and-so this-and-that German. The policeman is looking at me; oh, why didn't I go to Scotland with Denton—"

But the policeman passed safely by and Hambledon strolled on. He came to a small harbor where private yachts and motorboats were at moorings or tied up alongside. There was a rather large cabin cruiser lying at the foot of an iron ladder; three men standing close together on the quayside were apparently giving last-minute instructions to another man in the boat and handing down suitcases for him to stow away. The language they used was, by courtesy, French; it was very bad French but that was at least the language they thought they were speaking. "It is well that all is ready," one said. "Await us, then, until whenever we come."

Hambledon narrowed his eyes against the glare of the setting sun and recognized them for the three Middle Europeans. "It only wanted this encounter," he said and almost turned to flee. Wiser and bolder counsels prevailed; moreover, a brilliant idea struck him. He lengthened his stride and advanced purposefully upon them.

"Good evening, gentlemen," he said in French, and touched his decorative cap. He spoke in a low tone so that the man in the boat below could not hear. "It is well met, I have a message for you from *M'sieu le Commissaire* of police. He thanks you for your telephone message. He has acted upon it and is even now at the Grand Hotel apprehending the criminal. He—"

"But," broke in the one called Robinson, "what is all this of the most absurd regarding a telephone message to the police? I and my friends—"

"No doubt," said Tommy courteously, "M'sieu has his reasons for being discreet. I should not know. Who am I to know these things? A nobody. Only the porter, as you see." He indicated his cap. "All I know is that *M'sieu le Commissaire* sent me here, saying, 'Go, my good Ragnar, and see if the gentlemen are at their little ship' "—the three men paled visibly and backed away—" 'and ask them to do me the honor to come to me here at once,' that is, to the Grand Hotel, gentlemen. Some matter concerning a murder, I understand."

"But," said Robinson again, "how do they know—the police, I would say—they cannot know who it was who—" Brown nudged him sharply and his voice tailed off.

"Little happens in our dear Stockholm which is not known to the police," said Tommy earnestly. "A very able body, the Stockholm police. Active. Intelligent. Well informed, very. Incorruptible. Conscientious—"

"We will go," said Brown, taking his friends by the arms. "There is some mistake, but it shall be explored. Come, Jean. Come, Michel."

"It is well," said Tommy, wandering after them as they retreated along a street which would take them anywhere except to the Grand Hotel. "Wise, also," he added just before they were out of earshot.

They walked yet faster, leaving him tagging along behind. They went round a corner; fifteen seconds later Hambledon reached it also to see them walking more slowly with their heads turned to look behind them. When they saw him still coming they hurried again and crossed the road to a turning on the other side; as they entered it Tommy saw them break into a run.

He returned to the quay where the cabin cruiser was lying, climbed carefully down the iron ladder and stepped on board. The engineer came out from the cabin in which he had just stowed the last of the suitcases, looked at Tommy with surprise and opened his mouth to speak, but Hambledon forestalled him.

"The orders are changed," he said authoritatively. "You are to set forth at once and I am coming with you. The others are to follow later."

The man looked at him distrustfully. "I don't know you," he began.

"Of course you don't. Why should you?" said Tommy coldly.

"It is not likely that I should take out this boat at a moment's notice on the orders of a porter from the Grand Hotel," said the man with a sneer. Hambledon took off his cap and looked at it with a faint smile.

"I am not a porter from the Grand Hotel or any other," he said, and then addressed the cap. "You have been a good friend to me, it seems ungrateful to drop you overboard. But I fear it will have to be done later on." He moved to the cabin door and threw the cap on the table inside. "Now we will start, if you please."

"But—"

"Listen. I am here because three men killed a German on the Saltsjöbaden road this morning. They fired three shots; one killed the taxi driver and the other two the German. After that, the three men—do you know them?—drove back to Stockholm and telephoned the police from a public call box in order to put the blame on someone else. All this they did in order to get possession of a certain packet. Now, will you take this boat out when I tell you?"

The man nodded sullenly, untied the painter and coiled it upon the deck, returned to the cockpit aft and started up the engine. The boat moved off and Tommy sat down upon the stern cushions with a sigh of relief. This journey would probably not be without incident, but at least he would be able to rest his feet. They went at half speed until they were clear of the water traffic of the city, then the engineer opened the throttle and the boat gathered speed. Her bows lifted in the water, the note of the engine settled down to a steady drone, and the spreading angle of the wake widened across the glassy surface to cast small waves against wooded islets a mile or more away on either hand.

"She is very fast," said Tommy admiringly.

"She needs to be," said the engineer bluntly.

Hambledon made no further comment and the boat roared on while the sun sank behind mountains and dusk gathered and spread across the fiord. Tommy was beginning to think that it would be nice to know where they were going if only he could frame a question which would hide the fact that he did not know, when the engineer broke the silence.

"Did you know my brother?"

"I don't think I ever met him," said Tommy politely. "What is his name?"

"Karl."

Tommy considered for a moment and then said: "No." It seemed best, there are so many Karls.

"Then you've never been in this boat before?"

"Never."

There was another silence. Hambledon broke it this time.

"Was your brother engineer on this boat before you, then?"

"It's our boat. We used to run it together on little trips across from Åbo." Smuggling, thought Tommy. "Then he hired it out to your lot and went with it."

Hambledon did not like the man's tone. It was truculent, and the expression "your lot" definitely uncivil. However, there was no point in quarreling, so he merely said: "I see," in a noncommittal manner, and turned to study the wooded shore which they were passing at the moment. There was an entrancing house among the trees, a garden down to the water's edge and a boat slip with a very rakish speedboat alongside. An extremely pleasant life could be enjoyed by the owners of that house and boat. He imagined them running up to Stockholm for dinner and a show and returning in the cool of the long evening. There would, naturally, be something agreeably feminine in the party. Most Swedish girls were fair-haired; Tommy had always had a weakness for blondes.

They left the islands behind and entered upon a stretch of water which was, for a space, wide enough to give the effect of loneliness. The engineer did not pursue the conversation but he glanced at his passenger from time to time and his manner made Hambledon uneasy. However, a small steamer came up, bound for Stockholm, and passed near enough for them to discern the faces of those on board. The engineer relaxed and presently they were among islands again.

"No change in the arrangements, I suppose?" said the man abruptly.

"None. Just carry on," said Tommy. Perhaps they were bound for Åbo in Finland; he did not particularly want to go there but it would do. At least the Finnish police would not be chasing him for a murder he had not committed. He yawned; it had been a long day full of fresh air and exercise.

"Tired?" said Karl's brother suddenly.

"A little."

"You shall rest soon."

So presumably they were not far from their destination, wherever it was. Not Åbo, apparently. Then something in the man's tone echoed unpleasantly in Hambledon's memory. The words were civil enough, but the tone held menace. Hambledon glanced at his watch; over three hours since they started.

"Plenty of time," said the man and Tommy nodded. He almost dozed off but was aroused by a change in the note of the engine, which had been throttled down and was running much more slowly. When he looked about him the islands were far behind and the sea was empty of shipping. The engineer left the boat to steer itself and came to stand over Hambledon, looking down at him.

"My brother is dead," he said.

"I rather gathered that he was," said Tommy quietly, "by the way you spoke of him."

"You know how he died, don't you?"

"My dear chap, I never heard of him until you spoke of him."

"You did not know I was his brother, no. I did not tell anyone that. He died, so I took his place here, but I did not say I was his brother."

"Dear heavens," thought Tommy, "the man's mad."

"He found out too much about what you and your gang were doing, so do you know what they did?"

"No," said Hambledon firmly. "I do not. I only joined the gang two days ago. What they did before that is no business of mine," but the man was not listening.

"They threw him overboard. Just about here, it was, only it was in winter." The man was quivering all over and Hambledon braced himself against attack. "So I am going to throw all your gang overboard here one by one, and you are the first," he yelled, and sprang at Hambledon. There ensued a struggle which made up in violence for what it lacked in science; Hambledon was nearly defeated at the outset because it took him a moment to realize that the man was not trying to punch his head or strangle him, but simply to heave him overboard. They wrestled furiously in the cramped cockpit. Once the engineer heaved up Tommy and nearly broke his back against the cockpit coaming. Hambledon dug his toes into the cushions and managed to wriggle down again at the expense of an agonizing pain in his ribs. At some moment during the fight somebody's foot, Tommy never knew whether it was his own or his assailant's, kicked the throttle lever to full out and the boat roared on at top speed. The man was as strong as a bullock and seemed untiring; Hambledon was almost at the end of his resources when the engineer's foot slipped, he fell back against the side of the boat, which caught him behind the knees, and went overboard, tearing the sleeve out of Hambledon's coat and nearly taking him with him. Tommy collapsed, gasping, into the bottom of the cockpit, then dragged himself up and looked astern, but there was nothing to be seen, no head bobbing in the wake.

He throttled down and circled round the spot where the man had disappeared, but there was no sign of him. Probably the propeller—

Tommy shuddered and set his course as nearly as he could estimate to the direction in which they had been going, since presumably it led away from Sweden. Also, this particular area of the Baltic seemed unfriendly; one had a sense of things

below the surface, waiting. As time passed he became calmer and the recent trag-
edy just another unpleasant incident in a life which had known many unpleasant
incidents.

After a time he left off thinking about it and began to worry about the boat instead. He had a look at the motor and found it was a Diesel engine, about which
he knew nothing. There were sundry dials upon a sort of dashboard in front of the
wheel; these had needles which quivered excitedly and Tommy eyed them with
distrust. If those agitations meant that something ought to be done and he did not
do it, what would happen? Did Diesel engines blow up?

The Baltic seemed much larger than it looked upon the map. Somewhere ahead
was Finland, but he had no idea how far ahead. He had kept the boat fairly steadily
upon the compass course which they had been holding before the trouble began,
but perhaps he ought to turn off somewhere, as it were. The night was at no time
darker than a clear dusk in that high latitude, but it did not help him since there was
nothing to look at but sea and stars, and Tommy was no navigator. He hummed
tunelessly to himself.

> "We joined the Navy
> To see the world,
> And what did we see?
> We saw the sea."

Presently one of the quivering needles went back, flickered violently once or twice,
and came to rest at zero.

"I suppose you know what you mean," said Tommy, addressing it, "but I'm
hanged if I do. If you're important, no doubt I shall presently find out."

He did. In a matter of minutes the steady roar of the engine faltered, became
a stutter, and lapsed into a series of horrible noises which reminded him of the
Pilgrims' Chorus from something or other by Wagner, which he had unwillingly
heard when he was last in Berlin.

"I wish I were there now," he said plaintively, when finally silence spread her
balm. "I should at least know where I was, yes, even in the Russian sector."

He examined the engine respectfully, but recoiled before the cracking sounds of
cooling metal contracting upon itself. In point of fact the motor had run out of oil
and seized up. When he pressed a series of buttons one by one and produced (a) a
searchlight beam which rivaled the stars, (b) a raucous blast from a siren, and (c)
a strangled grunt from the self-starter, he gave it up. The night was calm but chilly
and Hambledon had no overcoat; even the coat he wore had one sleeve missing
and other damage. He retired to the cabin and saw there the several suitcases which
had been passed down from the quay at Stockholm.

"Confiscated as reparations, I think," said Tommy aloud. "Also I want a new
suit, preferably not of English tweed. Now, the one I called Brown was something

of my build." He examined the contents of the luggage with practiced ease. They were easy to identify because the so-called Jones was short, fat in front, and round-shouldered, while the alleged Robinson was tall and thin. Hambledon selected from Brown's change of clothing a suit which was reasonably hushed in pattern and put it on; it fitted well on the whole if a little distantly in places. He emptied his own pockets and transferred the contents to the pockets of Brown's suit; they were dusty and gritty at the bottom, he turned them inside out to shake out the debris. Among the rubbish was a grubby creased fragment of paper, Hambledon flattened it out, it had an address written in pencil. "Street of the Seven Candles 4, Rotterdam."

"I wonder who lives there," said Tommy thoughtfully, "and whether I'd better take a chaperon with me if I ever go there. Probably. Still, let's keep it just in case."

He put it carefully away in his wallet and went on tidying up. The mangled tweed suit went overboard followed by the hall porter's uniform. Further search among Brown's effects uncovered a wallet containing letters addressed to Isidore Skutnas and a photograph undeniably of Brown himself. It had a background taste-fully composed of a pillar, a lace curtain and a statue of Aphrodite; it had been taken in Paris.

"So now we know," said Hambledon. "Brown is Isidore Skutnas. *Nom d'un chien!* Now then, who are the other blighters?"

He repacked Isidore's suitcase and turned to the others. The fat Jones's pos-sessions were grubby and inadequately aired. Tommy wrinkled his nose and persevered until he found a particularly repulsive picture post card addressed to Lukas Olgar.

"Lukas Olgar, alias Jones, the one who drove the car. I don't like you or your smell, I think this lot is going overboard. It would have to, in any case, of course, or whoever picks me up will think I have thrown the owner into the Baltic. The third man's must go, too. Now, who is the long thin Robinson?"

Robinson's only treasure was a letter written in French on mauve paper in green ink; the writing was thin and spidery. It began: "Moritz, *cher adore,*" and went on to describe, in terms which made Tommy blush, the joys that would be theirs when the writer was Mme. Wenezky, but not before. Definitely, not. The writer was a woman of heart, etc., etc., but also of pure and lofty principles which her *cher* Moritz, a man of perceptions of the most delicate, would be obliged by his sense of honor to respect, and so on. It was signed Gabrielle-Victorine, forever his own.

"Gabrielle-Victorine knows her way about, evidently," commented Tommy. He dropped the letter and wiped his fingers on his handkerchief. "So Robinson is Moritz Wenezky, and since nothing of his is worth keeping, the Baltic can have these two suitcases." He put them over the side and watched them sink. "Skutnas, Olgar and Wenezky, I hope I never see any of you again."

The sky was growing light in the east when he had finished tidying himself and made a cup of coffee from some stores in a cupboard. There was no milk so he added a dash of Schnapps for luck and drank it off.

He took a rug from the cabin and went out to sit on the edge of the cockpit to wait for a rescue of some kind; it would not be safe to go to sleep for fear some ship passed by and did not see him. He sat there, nodding and jerking himself awake again while the light grew, sea and sky turned from gray to blue and the sun rose behind Finland. Just when he was admitting to himself that he could not possibly keep awake for another ten minutes, he was startled into activity by the sight of a ship which, by the favor of heaven, was heading towards him. She was a small cargo boat, heavily laden with timber which was even piled upon the deck. Still, a ship at last.

Hambledon waited till she was reasonably near, put his thumb on the button of the siren and blew a long blast.

Chapter Three
Retired Schoolmaster

Hambledon looked anxiously at the ship's national flag; if it was the blue with yellow cross of Sweden he would have to be careful what he said. He was happy to see that it was the horizontal red-white-blue of the Netherlands; not only would the men aboard her be completely uninterested in his doings in Sweden but they would never even have heard of Skutnas, Olgar and Wenezky. They couldn't care less, how lovely. His spirits rose.

The ship hove to and a line was flung to him from the bows, he caught it and a loud voice told him to haul it in. It was followed up by a rope and the same voice instructed him to make it fast. He managed this also with an effort, then the rope became taut and he found himself moving through the water. The cabin cruiser came alongside the cargo boat with a bump and the loud voice from the deck above said something rude. A rope ladder tumbled down the side of the ship, unrolling as it came, and a sailor came down it almost as quickly.

"What's your trouble?"

"Engine seized up," said Tommy briefly.

"You're to go aboard. This your suitcase?"

"Yes. Just that one," said Hambledon, and climbed lightly up the rope ladder. As he stepped upon the deck of the ship he was met by an authoritative man who was, in shape, exactly like a pillar box with feet, since his oilskin reached within six inches of the deck. He had a round red face, a short red beard and a cap rather too small for him.

"Who are you and what nationality?"

Tommy told him, and added, "And I have the honor of addressing—?"

"Captain Gielink of Rotterdam, and this is my ship. What is your trouble?"

"I ran out of lubricating oil and the engine seized up."

"Oh. Very well. I am on passage to Rotterdam and I will take you there. I am not putting in anywhere before Rotterdam."

"Thank you," said Tommy politely, "that will suit me very well indeed. I am much obliged to you."

"Your boat we will tow," said the skipper.

"Oh, please don't bother. I don't want her."

The skipper stared. "Not want her? But she is a good boat. Valuable."

"I still don't want her enough to pay for her tow all the way to Rotterdam," persisted Tommy, who had taken a violent dislike to the cabin cruiser. "Just leave her, or still better, sink her."

Captain Gielink stared harder than ever. "You must be very rich," he said slowly.

"Oh no. Not really. But I have no further use for her."

"In that case I will have her myself. It is wicked to abandon a good boat. We will tow, as I said." He turned away and gave a string of orders which resulted in the *Melicent Myrdal* resuming her labored progress down the Baltic with the disabled motorboat jibbing and ducking at the end of a towrope astern. Hambledon, having discussed terms with the skipper, found himself installed in a stuffy but surprisingly clean cabin from which the second engineer had been unwillingly evicted. Tommy told himself that he had been lucky again; he unpacked Isidore Skutnas's simple but adequate kit and prepared to enjoy a few days' peace. The only gnat in his garden looked like being the skipper, who continued not to understand how anyone could wish to abandon a good boat. He resumed the subject over lunch.

"You must, as I said, be unusually rich," he remarked suspiciously. "No ordinary man would do such a thing."

"But I am not," protested Tommy. "You don't have to be rich in order not to want a motorboat. Plenty of quite ordinary people don't."

Captain Gielink shook his head and relapsed into silence which he broke five minutes later by asking suddenly: "Are you a company promoter?"

"Heavens no," said Hambledon. "Why? Do I look like one?"

"I do not know," said Gielink, justifiably, "what all the company promoters in the world look like. I asked you if you were one."

"And I told you I was not," said Tommy, a little annoyed. "I am a retired schoolmaster," he added, with a certain amount of truth.

"I always heard," said Gielink, "that schoolmasters, as a class, are not well paid."

"Quite right. They're not."

"And yet you wish to cast away a boat worth many thousand guilders. It does not make sense."

"I do think I am extremely fortunate," said Tommy firmly, "in being blessed with such really delightful weather on this trip. The sea so calm, the sun so bright, the sky so blue—it is delicious, and just what one wants for a holiday. Do you think, Captain, that the weather will hold until we reach Rotterdam? Or do you expect a shift in the wind?" The skipper did not answer and Tommy babbled on. "Just what is wanted for the hay, too. Also for the corn, though I really am not sure when these agricultural occupations are performed in Scandinavia. The apples, too—"

The skipper swung his chair round and left the saloon.

Hambledon, sitting on a balk of timber and sleepily enjoying an after-lunch cigarette, was mildly surprised when the chief engineer approached him with some appearance of cordiality and offered to show him round the engine room. Grateful for this piece of kindly courtesy, Tommy said that he would very much like to see the engines though he was, in fact, no engineer. The chief smiled and said he would try to make it interesting, and led the way below. Tommy spent the next half hour in an atmosphere of oily heat skating about on slippery steel gratings, climbing up and down vertical iron ladders and staring awestruck into a deep pit from which dark shining cranks rose up, looked at him and sank again. The engineer officer talked in loud and cheerful tones about oil pressure, steam pressure, condensers, thrust blocks, expansion chambers and other mysteries while Tommy nodded his head brightly and made appreciative noises. He was finally released with his head singing and his hands covered with oil; he drew long breaths of fresh sea air at the head of the companion and then went down to his cabin to wash. Here came the steward to him, saying that the captain wanted to see him.

"Very well," said Tommy cheerfully, "tell him I'll be there as soon as I've got my hands clean." Then something in the steward's expression attracted his notice, a look between pity and amusement. Hambledon looked straight at him and asked bluntly: "What's the matter?"

"He doesn't like company promoters," said the man with a sheepish grin.

"Why not?"

"He put some money into a match syndicate and lost it."

"Very annoying. I sympathize with him, but it's nothing to do with me. I'm not a company promoter."

The steward said no more and Hambledon pulled out a drawer to find a clean handkerchief. He was a tidy man by nature and he had only just unpacked; the drawer was neatness itself when he left it. Now the contents were all jumbled together, socks and handkerchiefs in an untidy roll. Tommy looked at it for a moment and hastily examined the other drawers, which were similarly topsy-turvy. The photograph of Isidore Skutnas was still there but the letters had gone.

Plainly, he had been invited to tour the engine room in order to get him out of the way while somebody went through his things. Tommy's jaw came forward and his temper began to rise. Discretion, however, would be necessary. He was not very conversant with the law at sea, but he had an idea that a captain within his own ship is a complete autocracy. He could certainly lock up a passenger who offended against the laws or disobeyed orders, though Hambledon's conscience was, for once, unspotted. But his possessions had been searched as though he were a suspected criminal.

He put the clean handkerchief in his pocket and told the steward to lead the way.

The captain was sitting at the table in his cabin with Skutnas's letters spread out before him. He looked up when Hambledon came in and his faded blue eyes were alight with anger.

"You tell me a lie," he began. "I thought you did. You, an English schoolmaster! You are Isidore Skutnas and you were escaping from justice when I was fool enough to pick you up."

"I am not Isid—"

"Do not lie. Here are your letters. The police are after you in all countries, swindler, and when we get to Rotterdam they shall have you. Then you will find what happens to people who deceive poor folk into putting their well-earned money into your rotten companies."

"When we get to Rotterdam I shall appeal to the British consul," said Tommy. "I am an Englishman."

"Then where is your British passport?"

It was, in point of fact, locked up in an attaché case in his bedroom at the Grand Hotel, Stockholm.

"I have not got it with me at the moment, but the British consul—"

The captain made the noise which is usually written "Bah!" It sounded like an elderly sheep at the end of its patience.

"The British consul at Rotterdam," persisted Hambledon, "knows me personally. He—"

"I suppose you were at Etonanarrow together," said Gielink with heavy sarcasm.

"Well, not at both of them."

"Both of what? You have Isidore Skutnas' letters, I see in the paper he is believed to be in Sweden, you are escaping from Sweden, you say you are not rich but you desert a motorboat worth many thousand guilders. You are an absconding company promoter and you have stolen my money—"

"I tell you," said Tommy impatiently, "that I never sold a box of matches in my life, let alone—"

"Matches! How do you know I put my money in matches if you are not Isidore Skutnas?"

"This is absurd. A company promoter doesn't know by heart the name of every investor who puts money into his companies."

"Then how did you know I put my money in matches?"

Tommy paused momentarily. It was no use saying: "The steward told me," because if the man got into trouble for doing so he would certainly deny it and bear a grudge against Hambledon into the bargain. Tommy felt he might have a use for that steward.

"You told me yourself," he said calmly.

"That is a lie. You will be kept in your cabin till we reach Rotterdam and I send for the police. The cabin is too good for you but I have nowhere else so convenient to keep you." Gielink rang a bell for the steward, who must have been just outside the door, for he entered immediately. "Take this man back to his cabin, lock the door and bring me the key. And if you give any trouble," added the captain, addressing Hambledon, "I'll put you in irons. Get out."

Hambledon was not very seriously perturbed. It was exasperating to be locked in his cabin in mistake for an absconding match merchant, but what he most wanted at the moment was rest and peace, and he looked like getting both. He followed the steward to the cabin and was duly locked in. It would be tiresome to be handed over to the Dutch police at Rotterdam, but perhaps something would occur to prevent that when the time came, or there was always the British consul, who really had been to school with him, though not at Eton or Harrow. St. John's, Leatherhead, in point of fact. Tommy promised himself to avoid appealing to the consul if possible; he had one of those laughs which rattle windows and Hambledon did not wish to awaken it on his account. Arrested by the Dutch police—everybody would laugh, including Denton.

Tommy took his boots off, threw himself on the bunk and immediately fell asleep.

He was awakened some four hours later by the entry of the steward bearing a large tray with his supper upon it. Herrings soused in vinegar, a plate of bully beef and a jug of coffee. Evidently the captain did not intend to starve his prisoner. Tommy greeted the steward cheerfully and attacked his meal with good appetite. When he had finished he lit a cigarette and the cabin became even stuffier than before. There was a porthole; he struggled with the stiff fastening and got it open. Fresh air poured in, accompanied by a smell of the sea and the cry of circling gulls. Hambledon said "Ah," in a satisfied tone, arranged himself comfortably on the bunk and stuck his head out through the porthole. It was a lovely evening, the sun was setting on the other side of the ship and throwing long shadows across the water, dove-gray shading into blue. The *Melicent Myrdal*, heavily laden, wallowed steadily on; there was no land in sight and nothing to hear but the thud of the ship's engines, an occasional footstep overhead, the swish of water against the side and the cheerful scream of sea gulls hoping for the best. Tommy threw out some crusts, the gulls chattered and splashed and returned to ask for more.

"Idyllic," said Hambledon sleepily, "quite idyllic. Sell your little farm and go to sea." He arranged his pillow against the porthole so that the air should blow on his face and drowsed again till he was disturbed by a heavy tread above him and voices, the captain's voice and others. "She's coming very close," one said.

Hambledon put his head out again. There was another ship coming up, over-hauling them, a small vessel, fast without being showy. Tommy put her down as an ocean-going tug. She was drawing in towards the *Melicent Myrdal* and soon he could distinguish faces looking over the rail towards him, a group of men with binoculars apparently interested in something towards the stern. "Trying to make out our name, I suppose," said Hambledon. "I do hope they're not the Swedish police. How could they know I'm here?" He drew back modestly.

A man on the other ship lifted a megaphone and his voice came clearly across the water.

"Ship ahoy! Who are you?"

A short pause while presumably Captain Gielink found his megaphone for a reply.

"*Melicent Myrdal* of Rotterdam."

"Where are you bound for?"

"Rotterdam."

There was visibly a short consultation between the group of men coming momentarily nearer across the water, and then another question.

"Where did you get that boat you are towing astern?"

Hambledon shot backwards from the porthole like a shy tortoise into its shell. He had thought for some moments that three of the figures on the other ship were familiar, but had told himself firmly that he'd got Skutnas, Wenezky and Olgar on the brain. He put one eye round the rim of the port and knew he had told himself a lie. Captain Gielink's voice, resonant with fury, replied at once.

"What the"—several thousand unpleasant objects of dubious ancestry—"is that to do with you? Go to—" a destination precisely specified.

A laugh came across the water and a less audible remark which sounded like "See you later." The sound of the other ship's engine-room telegraph followed, she increased speed and drew slowly ahead out of Hambledon's sight. Peace supervened, marred only by Gielink's comments which floated down from above. The sea gulls chuckled loudly and turned away.

The idyll, however, was spoilt. Hambledon sat up on his bunk, drummed with his heels against the long drawers below and comprehensively cursed the cabin cruiser, the skipper for keeping her, her engineer for going overboard and himself for getting mixed up in all this. "What should I have said," he asked himself, "if one of my young cubs had got himself into a mess like this?" He answered himself with fluency but no satisfaction. "They think I still have that blasted packet, whatever it is," he added. "They will get to Rotterdam before us and be sitting on the quayside waiting for me to arrive. When the skipper tells them that I was alone in the boat when he picked me up, they will go to the authorities and accuse me of murdering the engineer. And the German who gave me the packet on the Saltsjöbaden road. And, of course, the taxi driver. It will be much simpler than murdering me themselves and save them the trouble of disposing of the body. Wouldn't one think," said Tommy, in tones of unbearable exasperation, "that a quiet decent man might have a fortnight's holiday without being accused of three murders?"

He brooded over the problem for some time without finding an answer. Even the British Consulate would be no sanctuary now; the consul could prove that

Hambledon was not Isidore Skutnas, but not that he was innocent of murder. He did not sleep well that night.

On the second morning following, the sun appeared to have turned round; it was rising on the same side of the ship as that upon which it had set the night before. The *Melicent Myrdal* had turned the southern point of Sweden in the night and was proceeding northward up the Öre Sund between Sweden and Denmark. Hambledon was allowed to come up on deck for an hour while his cabin was cleaned out by the steward. He looked with interest at the green shores on either hand, for The Sound is very narrow in places. He asked one of the crew what was the land on the port side, the man answered shortly that it was Zealand, Denmark. "Just passed Copenhagen," he added, jerking his head astern. Then the captain bellowed at him from the bridge and he went quickly away.

When the steward brought Hambledon's supper to the cabin that night he shut the door carefully behind him, fussed noisily with the things on the tray and spoke rapidly in a low voice.

"Are you a friend of Isidore Skutnas?"

"Why do you ask?"

"He has a friend on board," said the steward in a whisper.

"Really! Who?"

The man indicated himself with a grin, but at that moment the captain's voice was heard outside the door. The grin disappeared at once and the man went out without another word, locking the door behind him.

"Dear me," said Tommy thoughtfully, and waited impatiently for the morning. When the steward came in with the breakfast tray Hambledon leaned forward and began urgently: "If I were a friend of Isidore Skut—"

But the man hushed him at once with a gesture of the hand and backed out of the cabin, saying loudly that that was all the sugar Hambledon would get and it was no use asking for more. There was plenty there, anyway. The door slammed and the key turned in the lock.

Hambledon had to wait all day until suppertime before the man spoke again.

"Where is Skutnas now?" he asked.

"On his way to Rotterdam," said Tommy confidently.

"And you wish to meet him there, is it not so?" Tommy nodded. "And not be handed over to the police? Who would? Have no anxiety, the thing will be arranged."

"I will tell him," said Hambledon gravely, "that he had a good friend in you."

"Er—there will be expenses," said the steward.

"There always are," said Tommy, and gave him a couple of English pound notes.

Chapter Four
Unmistakable Identity

On the evening when the *Melicent Myrdal* came into the port of Rotterdam Hambledon was as restless as a canary in a cage. He was not allowed on deck and when he stuck his head out at the open porthole the skipper saw him and sent the steward down to shut it, screw it up tight and tell the prisoner not to do it again.

"Look here," said Tommy in an urgent whisper, "what are you going to—"

"Quiet," murmured the steward. "Get ready to do what I tell you on the jump. I've got it all weighed up." He made a really frightful grimace apparently intended to inspire confidence, instill caution and evoke courage, and withdrew whistling. Tommy flattened his nose against the glass but little can be seen from a closed porthole. Objects slid past, tugs of various sizes, a string of barges, a ferryboat crowded with people, a ship at anchor so close that he only saw sections of her at a time; at the break of her poop a man with a cat on his shoulder waved a hand to someone on the *Melicent Myrdal's* deck. The engine-room telegraph rang continually and the engine revolutions varied in response. Houses came into view, wharves with ships tied up alongside and cranes working busily, and a large red brick building with a square tower having a clock face upon it.

Hambledon's cabin door opened suddenly, the steward threw in a bundle and told him to put those things on, "all of 'em, and be quick about it. Captain says I'm to take this door key up to him on the bridge, but it don't matter, I've got another as fits. Be ready when I come." He vanished again; Hambledon snatched up the bundle and unrolled it. It contained a complete suit of dark blue cloth of a vaguely nautical cut, a white scarf of fine woolen material, a navy-blue raincoat and a peaked cap. Tommy tore off the suit he was wearing, threw it in a drawer and dressed hastily. The trousers could be made long enough for him by letting out his braces considerably, and the raincoat covered up the resultant surplus in the back areas. "It really does feel most peculiar," said Tommy. "As though I were coming undone." He tried on the peaked cap at various angles and it settled comfortably into a rakish tilt over the right eye. "Rather becoming, actually," he commented. "Now I know why so many people with funny faces wear yachting caps." He looked out at the porthole; they were moving very slowly now. A wall built of huge blocks of stone came by so close that he started back, the engine-room telegraph rang twice with a note of urgency and there followed a noise of rushing water as the engines were put into reverse. The cabin darkened as the ship closed the dock wall, a moment later there was a gentle bump, an outbreak of creaking noises and shouted orders. The sounds died down, the telegraph rang three times for "Finished with engines," and all motion ceased.

"We're alongside," whispered Tommy, and rising excitement tingled in his fingertips.

He waited after that for what seemed immeasurable time but was probably twenty minutes, then the steward came in hastily and locked the door after him.

"Listen," he said. "The port officials have just come aboard to go through the ship's papers and that. Then they'll have a drink with the skipper and go ashore again. There's six of 'em. They'll pass this door when they leave. The moment they've gone by I'll open the door, you slip out and just walk ashore close behind them. Nobody'll notice one more. You just keep on walking and don't speak to nobody. You'll be all right."

"Sounds simple enough, certainly," said Hambledon.

"Oh, and if you want to see Skutnas at once, he's at the Bells of Haarlem Café in Veenenbos Street. Wenezky came along and told me so just now. I'm to go there but I shan't get ashore not for another two hours yet."

"Oh, right," said Tommy casually. "Is Wenezky still on the quay?"

"I expect so, but I shouldn't hang about looking for him if I was you. You get clear away and talk to your pals later. I must go now, you be waiting to come out the minute I open the door. 'Bout half an hour or so I reckon."

The half hour was barely up when Hambledon heard men's voices in the passage outside his door and someone laughed. The key turned in the lock but the door did not open, only the handle moved slightly as though someone were holding it on the outside. More conversation, footsteps moving away, and the door opened suddenly. Hambledon was just inside and came out with the door, which the steward immediately shut and locked behind him.

"Get away, quick," said the man hastily. "Captain's going ashore any minute to phone the police he's got a prisoner for them. Get cracking."

Tommy obeyed at once and strolled casually ashore in the wake of the six men; no one looked twice at him. He turned right and walked steadily but unhurriedly up the quay avoiding porters, moving cranes, lorries, and railway lines, with an air of automatic habit as of one who walked there every day with his mind upon other matters. Even the dockyard police at the gate took no notice of him. Tommy drew a long breath of relief when once he was out in the streets. Rather dreadful streets; though cleared and filled with traffic they were bordered by acres of brickbats roughly levelled with weeds growing over them. Hambledon remembered an assistant he had once had, a chemist from Rotterdam, and the things he had said about the infamous bombing attack. The place was a vast graveyard.

He quickened his pace and kept going until he was out of that haunted area and among houses once again, wholesome upright houses inhabited by ordinary living people. He knew where to go since there are those in Rotterdam who are of assistance to British Intelligence and he knew the city of old, but he drifted almost unconsciously towards Veenenbos Street and the Café of the Bells of Haarlem, for an idea had come into his mind. By the time he came within sight of the place the plan was formed except for details which could safely be left to the inspiration of the moment. Captain Gielink must have telephoned to the police by this time.

The Bells of Haarlem had a restaurant on the ground floor with wide windows upon the pavement. Inside, the lamps were lit, for by now dusk was falling, and passersby could look in between the orange curtains and past the palms in green tubs at the diners sitting round small tables. Hambledon took a cigarette from his case and stopped outside the window apparently having trouble with his lighter. His eyes passed quickly from table to table; surely, at that one near the hatstand, that was Olgar, but the dark-haired man with him had his face away from the window, for he was watching the orchestra on a small dais at the back of the room. He turned to speak to Olgar and Hambledon saw him laugh; it was undoubtedly Skutnas.

The flame leaped in Hambledon's lighter, he applied it to his cigarette and walked away.

When the port authorities had finished their business aboard the *Melicent Myrdal* and gone ashore—followed by Hambledon—Captain Gielink spent a few minutes tidying up. He put the ship's papers away in the safe, locked up the Schnapps in a cupboard, collected the seven used glasses on a tray for the steward to remove and glanced round the saloon with a satisfied expression. Another trip success-fully completed and a further pleasure in store, dealing with that swindler Isidore Skutnas. He picked up his cap and went ashore to the nearest telephone call box to ring up the police.

He announced his identity to the superintendent at the other end of the line and then said he had a prisoner for whom the police were looking.

"A prisoner?" said the superintendent in a surprised tone. "I thought the *Melicent Myrdal* was a small cargo boat."

"No reason why she shouldn't have a prisoner aboard," said Gielink stiffly.

"Well, no. It is a little unusual. Who is he?"

"Isidore Skutnas. He is a dirty foreign crook."

"And how did you come to have him aboard your ship?"

"I picked him up in the Baltic. Off Ornö. He was in a motorboat which had broken down."

"How do you know this man is Skutnas? Did you recognize him?"

"No, of course not," said Gielink crossly, for he had expected excited thanks, not a barrage of questions. "I've got his papers."

"Just a moment," said the superintendent. "Hold on just a moment." He covered the mouthpiece of the telephone with his hand, but not so effectively that Gielink could not hear a murmur of voices and a few scattered phrases. "Last heard of in Czechoslovakia," was one, and "practical joke" another. "Have a look at him," someone advised, and Gielink simmered with wrath. "Are you there? Listen, Cap-tain Gielink. Is your prisoner safely confined?"

"Of course he is," snapped Gielink. "What do you take me for?"

"Then would you be so good as to come here and tell me your story in person, bringing with you the papers of which you spoke?"

"I've a good mind not to bother," said Gielink angrily. "Why don't you just send a man down to arrest him?"

"I'm very sorry to give you trouble, Captain, but I think it would be as well to have a few particulars first. How soon can you be here? In a quarter of an hour?"

"Longer than that. I've got to change into shore rig first. Say half an hour, no, three quarters."

"As you wish. Thank you, Captain."

Gielink stumped back along the quay to his ship. If it wasn't for letting that scoundrel go free he'd kick him off the ship and let those stiff-necked muttonheaded boobies of police do their own dirty work. But the thought of releasing Skutnas was more than he could bear. Very well, he'd change his suit and stroll up to the police station in his own time. It would be pleasant to make them apologize when they saw how wrong they were to doubt him.

He entered his cabin where his best shore-going suit should have been laid out on the bunk by the head steward, who waited on him personally, not the same man who had been Hambledon's jailor. But there was no neat blue suit there, no fine white wool scarf, no dark blue raincoat. Gielink flung the door open and shouted for his man, who came, running.

"Where are my clothes? Why aren't they put out ready for me?"

"I did put them out, sir. I know I did."

"You started to, you mean. There's a clean shirt there, then I suppose you thought of something else and mooned off."

"But," said the man, staring.

"Get them out!" bellowed the skipper, and the steward dived at the drawer where they were kept and pulled it out.

"They're not here, sir. I did put 'em out. There's something funny going on aboard this ship."

"I suppose," began the skipper slowly, and stopped. He took a key out of his pocket and walked across the saloon and down the passage to the cabin in which Hambledon had been confined. When he threw open the door, the place was empty. The head steward, nervously following behind, saw with astonishment Captain Gielink rush back into the saloon and aim a terrific kick at a swivel chair fixed to the floor at the end of the table. The chair spun violently round and the captain ran up the companion ladder to the deck above and out of sight. He returned to the telephone box, rang up the police station again and told them his prisoner had escaped.

"He has also stolen my best suit," he added indignantly.

"Then you can, no doubt, describe how the man is dressed," said the superintendent. "Since, presumably, he took your clothes to wear as a disguise."

"I don't know that he's still wearing them, do I?" said Gielink. "He may have changed again since then. Half a dozen times, perhaps."

"In half an hour?" said the superintendent thoughtfully. "Well, he may have changed."

"I am not conversant with the habits of criminals. I shall be with you shortly as soon as I have made sure that he has not stolen anything else."

"I shall expect you," said the superintendent, and was accordingly not surprised when Hambledon walked in to report that Skutnas was at the Bells of Haarlem. The arrest was effected without conflict and the sergeant returned with his prisoner and escort in a cab. They did not arrest Olgar. The superintendent looked Skutnas up and down, comparing him with photographs and a description which had been officially supplied and then nodded.

"Take him away and get his fingerprints. Looks like the man," he added to the sergeant as Skutnas, protesting copiously, was led away. "But where's our informant the sea captain?"

"Isn't he here, sir? We left him outside the café and when I didn't see him as we came out I supposed he'd come back here."

"He'll turn up," said the superintendent. "Perhaps he's gone home first to reassure his family."

The fingerprints were compared and found to be identical, and the police were naturally delighted, since it is not every day that one captures a man for whom the authorities of five countries are looking. Still Hambledon did not return and the sergeant was just saying that it was a bit odd when there was a commotion in the outer office. The door opened and a constable entered.

"There's a man here, sir, who says he's the captain of the *Melicent Myrdal.*"

"Show him in, then," said the superintendent impatiently. "I am expecting him."

"But," said the constable, and stopped. "Very good, sir."

He ushered in a short red man with a short red beard and a temper to match. The superintendent stared at him and asked him who he was.

"Captain Gielink, master of the *Melicent Myrdal.* I rang you up on the telephone about the swindler Skutnas who escaped from my ship."

The superintendent and his sergeant exchanged glances. Hambledon had warned them that an attempt at rescue would probably be made, and the warning was in the minds of both. Although the opening gambit was a little unexpected no doubt this was it. A darker suspicion followed naturally; what had become of their previous caller, who should have returned before this? If this man here did not know that his predecessor had visited the police it might have appeared safe to remove him. These international crooks . . . Besides, this man was dressed in shabby gray flannel trousers, a striped shirt and a pullover with large darns in the elbows, and did not look like the master of anything more important than a canal barge, if that. Captain Gielink was not a dressy man when at sea.

"You have your identity papers with you, of course?" asked the superintendent.

Gielink patted his pockets distractedly. *"Damfer,* I've left them on the ship," he said. "It doesn't matter, it's Skutnas you're after, not me. If you'd get on with your job of arresting criminals instead of pestering me over trifles you'd—"

"Oh, we've got him," said the superintendent calmly.

"Got him! How? Where?"

"You will, no doubt, be prepared to identify him?"

"With all the pleasure in the world! But how did you—"

"Sergeant! Bring in the prisoner."

"Yessir," said the sergeant smartly, and left the room while Gielink continued to ask questions which did not receive answers. Presently the door opened again and Skutnas was pushed into the room. Gielink glanced at him without interest and went on talking.

"Captain Gielink," said the superintendent formally, "will you look at this man and tell me, if you know him, who he is?"

Gielink looked at Skutnas with attention but without the faintest sign of recognition, and the prisoner looked equally blank.

"Never seen him in my life before," said the captain.

"I thought you'd say that," said the superintendent ominously.

Skutnas demanded the attendance of a lawyer at once and was told that he should have one in the morning. He was then removed and the superintendent gave his whole attention to his latest visitor.

"You still maintain you don't recognize that man who has just gone out?"

"Certainly I do," said Gielink stoutly. "Why should I know who he is?"

"That," said the superintendent, watching him closely, "is Isidore Skutnas, who is wanted on a charge of false dealing in connec—"

"Oh no it isn't. Nothing like him."

"Believe me, it is."

"No. I had the man on my ship for nearly a week. I ought to know. Skutnas is fair with gray eyes, for a start."

"Listen, here is his official description," said the superintendent, and read from a paper on his desk. "Hair dark brown, receding from forehead. Eyes, brown. Nose long, drooping tip," and so on.

"The description's wrong," said Gielink.

"No. It is official and accurate. What is more, we have Skutnas' fingerprints and they are the prints of the man you have just seen."

Gielink shook his head impatiently. "There has been a mistake, you have got the fingerprints of the wrong man."

"There has indeed been a mistake," said the superintendent with alarming energy, "and you are going to explain it. Where is the captain of the *Melicent Myrdal?*"

Gielink gaped at him and asked what the devil he meant. "I am the captain of the *Melicent Myrdal* and have been this last fifteen years, I, Dirk Gielink. You can look me up in the port registration list."

"I shall find that name, no doubt. The captain rang us up twice; once to say he held Skutnas a prisoner and again to say the prisoner had escaped."

"Ja, ja, that was me. I did," said Gielink, nodding violently.

"A little later the captain walked in here—oh yes, he did—and told us he had seen the missing man in a café in the town. I sent some men and arrested the man whom the captain pointed out to them; the prisoner was brought here and proved to be Isidore Skutnas. Now you walk in with this absurd story, I ask for your papers and you say you have left them behind. I ask you again, where is the captain? I tell you frankly I suspect foul play."

Gielink tugged at his beard. "This is madness. I live in Rotterdam—"

"Then you can produce reputable witnesses to prove your identity."

"Of course I can. There is my wife, for one. There is the minister of my church. There are the owners of the *Melicent Myrdal*. There are the port authorities—"

The superintendent blinked. If this were a bluff it was the toughest he had ever heard; besides which, the man sounded as though he were speaking the truth. A short list of names and addresses was collected and a constable was sent out to bring back somebody reliable and credible.

"While we are waiting," said the superintendent in a slightly less ferocious voice, "perhaps you will tell me the whole story of how you came to encounter this man you thought was Skutnas."

Captain Gielink did so, in full detail, and a shorthand writer took the statement down.

"What name did this man give?"

"I can't remember," said Gielink. "An English name. He said he was an English schoolmaster."

"But, according to your statement, he carried Skutnas' papers."

"Yes. I asked him for his own—I didn't believe he had any others but I did ask him—and he said he hadn't got them with him, or some such tale."

"And how did he account for being out in a cabin cruiser off Ornö?"

"He didn't. He just said the engine had run out of oil and had seized up."

"And you thought it suspicious that he wished to abandon the boat?"

"Certainly. I still do. A valuable boat, worth many thousand—"

"Yes, yes, you said that before. And you say he gave it to you? Any document to prove that?"

"Any docu—no. My crew can witness to the gift."

"No doubt they can," said the superintendent with emphasis. "They will certainly be asked. I suppose there was such a man?"

"What—"

"Or did you just find the boat adrift, take her in tow and hatch up this story to evade any attempt to find the real owners?"

This was too much and Gielink exploded. He gave the superintendent a series of sparkling sketches of his past, present and future, his ancestry, his habits and his moral character. Just as the sergeant was reluctantly deciding he would have to leave the room before his self-control broke down, Gielink ran out of breath, there came a knock on the door and a constable put his head in. One of the port lading clerks and a minister of the Lutheran Church were in the waiting room prepared to identify Captain Gielink.

They came in and did so without any hesitation, were heartily thanked and departed. The superintendent apologized to Gielink, who was still bristling. The captain told all the police within earshot to be more careful in future, stalked out and slammed the door behind him. The superintendent and the sergeant looked at each other.

"Queer case, sir," said the sergeant.

"Very odd. Wrong skipper, wrong prisoner, fishy story which will no doubt be fully substantiated, and Skutnas arrested after all. What I want to know is, who is the other man and why did he say he was the captain of the *Melicent Myrdal?* And why had he got Skutnas' papers?"

"Does it matter, sir? We've got Skutnas," said the sergeant tactfully.

"Yes. But what I want to know is, how much of this farrago am I to put in my report?"

Chapter Five
At the Place of the Fountain

Hambledon stood for a few minutes on the pavement outside the Bells of Haarlem to watch through the windows the arrest of Skutnas. It was like a scene in a play and he, he told himself, was the author, the actor-manager and the producer all in one. The diners looked up from their plates as the police threaded their way between the tables, men and women laid down their knives and forks and turned in their chairs to watch. As realization spread through the room those farthest from the center rose from their seats and even stood upon them to see the better. Olgar first noticed the police advancing upon them; his look of horror warned Skutnas, who turned round, saw what was about to happen and rose to escape. He was too late, the police surrounded the table; the sergeant leaned towards Skutnas and apparently addressed him in words which obviously alarmed him. He shook his head energetically and made gestures of disavowal.

At this point Tommy tore himself unwillingly away. It was cruelly hard, but it would never do to stay until the police came out again and demanded his attendance as a witness. He slipped through the crowd which was beginning to gather and made his way, chuckling, along the dark streets to the house of a friend. This house was in the old town, in a district of small twisted streets; a man who knew his way less perfectly than Hambledon would have lost himself a dozen times. Tommy came at last to a narrow entrance, an arched tunnel with the houses continuing uninterruptedly above and a stout post in the middle of the way to check the passage of anything wider than a small boy on a bicycle. Hambledon sidled past, wondering again as he had so often wondered before how in the world the inmates of this retreat ever moved their furniture in or out of this, the only entrance. At the further end of the tunnel he came into a tiny hidden square of tall old houses with steep gables leaning forward against the stars; the square was paved with flagstones and had in the center a fountain of ancient stone so weathered that no man could say what the design had originally been nor what the lumpy irregular shape was meant to represent.

The huddled houses showed lights behind curtains in their windows, squares of amber, rose or blue. Hambledon walked across to a house at the far end with windows open upon the night; there came from them the sound of one who played upon a piano with infinite delicacy Ravel's *Pavane for a Dead Infanta*. The un-musical Hambledon did not recognize it but he paid it the compliment of waiting till the music resolved into silence before he pulled at the iron handle of an ancient creaking bell.

The door opened almost at once to show a dark hall within and the dim figure of a man who leaned forward asking who was there.

"It is I, Johannis," said Hambledon, "after all these years."

"I know your voice," said the man, "come in and let me look at you."

"Your hall light," said Tommy with a laugh, "is still out of order, I notice."

"I have a lot of trouble with that hall light," said the man gravely. "Every time my neighbors peep from behind their curtains to see who comes to my house after dark the wretched thing blows its fuse. Come into my—good gracious alive, it is Mr. Hambledon."

"How are you, Johannis? It is very pleasant to come here again."

"Come and sit here," said Johannis, fussing round him. "Let me switch on the fire, it is chilly tonight. You will take a small glass of something with me—how are you and what fair wind blows you here? For myself, I am well and fortunate, for this house escaped damage though those which backed onto mine were destroyed."

"I came to Rotterdam because I couldn't help it, I'll tell you about that in a minute. I have come to see you because I wanted to, and you can, perhaps, tell me something I want to know."

"Tell me what it is and let us get business over, then we can talk like civilized men. You will stay here tonight, will you not?"

"Thank you, I should like to. First of all, then, do you know this address and perhaps something of the people who live there?"

Hambledon took from his wallet the crumpled scrap of paper which he had found at the bottom of Skutnas's pocket, and passed it to his friend. Johannis felt it with his long fingers, held it up to the light and touched it with the tip of his tongue.

"Cigarette paper," he said thoughtfully. "Rice paper."

"Where from?"

"Impossible to say with certainty, but probably Turkish. This address, now, the Street of the Seven Candles, number 4."

"Do you know the house?"

"Oh yes. And the people who live there. Where did you find this paper, my friend, or is that asking too much?"

"It was in the pocket of a man named Skutnas, Isidore Skutnas."

"Who is wanted by the police, I think," said Johannis, nodding his head like a mandarin doll, "for extensive defalcations in connection with shares in a match company."

"They don't want him now," said Tommy, with simple pride. "They've got him." He broke into a laugh and Johannis beamed appreciatively upon him.

"You have been up to your mischiefs again, I see. Why? Had you, then, bought some of his shares?"

"No, he murdered a German in the outskirts of Stockholm and tried to pin it on me. He nearly succeeded, too, I had to leave in a hurry."

"A German, you say? That is odd. The inhabitants of that house of which this is the address are Germans."

"Know anything about them?

"One, I do. Not the other two—there are three of them."

"Tell me," said Hambledon, clasping his hands round one knee and rocking himself in his chair.

"One Horaz Kenrade from Frankfurt am Rhein. An SS man of some notoriety."

"One of the 'wanted' ones?"

"He will be when they get to know about him. He calls himself Kalvag and comes from Finland—at least, that's the name on his passport."

"How do you know all this?"

"You could guess, could you not? I myself composed that passport. A particularly nice one," said Johannis simply. "I was very pleased with it."

Hambledon broke into a laugh, for he had guessed what was coming. Johannis was one of the most expert passport forgers on the continent and his "compositions" were worth every penny of the large prices he charged for them.

"But—an SS blighter?"

"Why not? He would have got away in any case, he had so much money. If he had gone anywhere else he would have been lost indeed. Here he sits down comfortably in his house and thinks himself safe; when he is wanted we know where to find him. In the meantime he is paying for his own keep, is he not, instead of becoming chargeable to the Allies in a prisoner-of-war camp?"

"There's something in that," said Tommy "One hundred and twenty-five millions a year of my country's money—"

"And he has contributed substantially to my upkeep, too," said Johannis frankly. "Why not? There is not much money, my friend, in being a teacher of the piano to little snubnosed boys and girls with hands so small they cannot strike an octave. 'Not B natural, Gottlieb, B flat there, I have told you that twenty-seven times already.' What a life! And then they only pay you for your time and nothing for the torments you endure."

"It's a good cover, though," said Hambledon.

"I remind myself of that when I have had to listen to *Für Elise* more than six times in one day. However, to return to Kenrade. He was so anxious for one of my passports that he sent all the way from Frankfurt am Rhein for it. It must have cost him a fortune one way and another."

"What about the other two?"

"Nilsen and Peycke. Probably not their real names but I don't know what they are or anything about the men except that they are living there with Kenrade."

"I think I will go and call at the house tomorrow evening," said Tommy thoughtfully.

"In the name of heaven! Why?"

"There is some devilment afoot and I want to know what it is." Hambledon gave Johannis an outline of his doings in Stockholm and about the kidnapping and murder of the lonely German on the Saltsjöbaden road. "He gave me a packet and told me I knew what to do with it. He was mistaken, but I put it in my inside breast pocket and bolted, and to this day I don't know why Skutnas, Olgar and Wenezky didn't chase me over the mountains for it."

"I expect they thought you'd got clean away. Please go on."

Hambledon told him the rest of the story and added: "You see, I don't know what was in the packet though doubtless M.I.5 do, by now. I thought I'd better get rid of it at once. I had enough troubles without that."

"I don't see where the match swindler and his friends come into it," said Johannis.

"After money, of course. There's money in it somewhere, so they killed the Stockholm German. They carried the address of Kenrade's house. Is there a connection between Kenrade and the German in Stockholm? Sounds like it, don't you think?"

"Was the Stockholm German on his way here, do you suppose?"

"I haven't got so far as supposing, I'm just wondering."

"Did he not mention any name at all—man or place?"

"Just before he died," said Hambledon, "he said 'Santa Brigida.' Does that convey anything to you?"

"He pronounced it like that, did he?" asked Johannis, for Hambledon had said "Briheeda." "That is Spanish, surely. More likely to be a place name than his patron saint. He might have been a Roman Catholic, but he would have said it in German if he were appealing to the lady, surely. *Heilige Brigitte* it would be."

"Unless he was speaking Church Latin," suggested Tommy. "Would the Roman Church call her 'Briheeda'? I don't know."

"I should guess that it's a place name somewhere in Spanish territory, but I expect there are dozens of Santa Brigidas. A very pious race, the Spaniards."

"A gazetteer of the world might help."

"I'm sorry, I do not own one," said Johannis.

"Never mind. Your suggestion is extremely valuable, and I'll bear it in mind. Now, about my visit to Kenrade and company. I shall tell them I want a passport; I should think they would send for you, wouldn't you?"

"Almost certainly. There is another—er—composer of passports in Rotterdam, but I doubt if they know him. They have dealt with me before, as I said."

Tommy nodded. "I should think that's a safe bet. I will tell them to send for you to come and photograph me. Now, this is what I want you to do."

The two friends talked far into the night, first about immediate plans and afterwards about the past, remembering old friends and exchanging news. When Hambledon at last retired to an enormous feather bed in Johannis's attic he was rested and refreshed; he fell asleep still chuckling over Skutnas's face as the police walked into the Bells of Haarlem.

Early next morning a message was sent to London with a detailed list of things Hambledon desired to be flown to Rotterdam at once for his immediate use. He spent the day in Johannis's house, not wishing to be observed by the neighbors or recognized in the streets. Skutnas had been eliminated but there remained Olgar, Wenezky, Captain Gielink and all the crew of the *Melicent Myrdal*, besides such members of the police as Hambledon had met the evening before. A discreet seclusion was indicated and Hambledon observed it.

Towards nightfall, when the dusk was already gathering but the lamps were not yet alight in the streets, Hambledon shook hands with Johannis and set out to walk to the house in the Street of the Seven Candles. He found it without difficulty although he had to make a sudden detour to avoid a man who looked like the *Melicent Myrdal's* second steward. The house, small and detached, stood in a garden in a suburban road of similar houses and was in no way remarkable among its neighbors. There was a brick path leading between prim flowerbeds to the front door. Hambledon walked up with an assured step and tried the handle; the door was locked so he put his finger on the electric bell and kept it there. Hurried footsteps approached from inside; the door opened enough for a man to look round it and no more.

"Be quick," said Hambledon impatiently, "you kept me waiting and I do not like to wait." He pushed past the man into the narrow hall, shut the door after himself and locked and bolted it.

"Who the devil are you?"

"I may perhaps tell you when I know who you are." There were sounds of movement in one of the rooms and Hambledon assumed that Kenrade would not answer a door himself if he had a subordinate to do it for him. "Are you the fellow calling himself Nilsen or the other fellow calling himself Peycke?"

"I am Nilsen," said the man, "but what I want—"

"What I want," interrupted Hambledon, "is the Herr Kalvag. Is he within?"

Nilsen gave it up and opened a sitting-room door for Hambledon, who strode in without hesitation, shutting the door behind him and leaving Nilsen in the hall. Inside the room a man sat at a deal-topped table reading a paper, a broad-shouldered man with the look of an athlete run to seed. He looked up as Hambledon came in and Tommy recognized at once the cold impersonal stare in the colorless eyes and the thin mouth which tried to be grim but was only cruel. This was the type which had looked on horror and enjoyed it.

"You are expecting me," said Hambledon before the other could speak, "or you ought to be if you have received your instructions."

"I have received no instructions which, so far as I know, apply to you. Who are you?"

"I come from Sweden," said Hambledon, dropping his voice.

"Oh, do you? And where is Goertz?"

Presumably Goertz was the name of the Stockholm German, it was worth gambling upon anyway.

"In his honored grave," said Tommy solemnly. "He was murdered by a man named Skutnas. Isidore Skutnas."

"I will remember that name—"

"No need. I have taken the necessary steps and he is in the hands of the police."

The remark had the unmistakable ring of truth and produced the desired effect. The man rose from his seat and offered Hambledon a chair with sufficient courtesy if no more.

"I have not the honor of your name—"

"For that matter, you have not told me yours," said Hambledon bluntly. "My name is not one to be told to every chance acquaintance."

"I am Stefan Kalvag from Finland."

"Oh, are you?" said Tommy slowly. "That's a long way from Frankfurt am Rhein, is it not, Herr Kenrade?"

"Who the devil are you?"

"An old friend. Don't you remember me? No? How forgetful you are. Think back and perhaps it will come to you."

The man was taken aback and looked it. "It is, perhaps, the dress which misleads me," he said, for Tommy was still wearing Captain Gielink's decent if uninspired suit and his peaked cap.

"It is possible," said Hambledon carelessly. "It does not matter, you will remember sometime. I think you will remember sometime," he repeated, and looked hard at Kenrade with a slow smile which gradually broadened. The German appeared to find it alarming, for he drew back in his chair and busied himself filling his pipe with fingers that were not too steady. Tommy reverted at once to the incisive tone he had used when he first entered.

"Delightful as it is to chatter about the dear old days," he said sarcastically, "we are wasting time and I am in a hurry. I am on a journey, you know, or don't you? Of course not, you said you had no instructions—"

"That was when I did not know who you were."

"It is not important. I am going on a journey and I want an English passport and a suit of English clothes. You will get them for me, by tomorrow or the day after at latest."

"English—but English—"

"Of course. I speak English like a native, you should remember that even if you've forgotten the rest. I wonder if you have," said Hambledon reminiscently, and became incisive again. "It must be obvious even to you, my good Kenrade, that I can't travel south across Europe in the Sunday-go-to-meeting suit of a Dutch skipper. Even the clothes are not so important as the passport. Surely the energetic and intelligent Horaz Kenrade can obtain a simple thing like an English passport? Are there, then, no pickpockets in Rotterdam in these degenerate days?"

"I know a man who can produce passports—"

"Then produce the man."

"Tomorrow he shall be sent for."

"Tonight he shall be sent for," mimicked Hambledon. "I am in a hurry, I thought I had told you that already. How long will it take this fellow to produce a passport?"

"He will answer that himself," said Kenrade. He went to the door, opened it and shouted: "Nilsen! Peycke!" into the dark hall. Nilsen appeared promptly, stood at attention in the doorway and said that Peycke was out at the moment.

"You will do. You know where that fellow Johannis lives, the passport faker? In the Place of the Fountain, yes, can you find it? Go and fetch him. When I say 'fetch' I mean it, bring him back with you and do not return without him."

"Tell him to bring his camera," said Hambledon in a bored voice.

"See that he brings his camera. Go."

"Jawohl, meinherr," said Nilsen, and disappeared behind the closing door. The next moment the hall door also was heard to shut and the sound of footsteps receded down the path outside.

"When I give an order," said Kenrade fatuously, "it is obeyed."

"Why not?" said Hambledon with a yawn he made no attempt to conceal. He picked up a newspaper which was lying on the table and read it attentively, interrupting himself only to light a cigarette and throw the match into the empty fireplace. Kenrade fidgeted about the room for a few moments and then sat down again in his chair at the table.

"Will Your Excellency excuse me," he said with more than a hint of sarcasm, "if I continue with some necessary correspondence?"

"You have my leave," said Hambledon absently, and went on reading. The German shuffled papers, made a few notes and studied in covert glances the calm resolute face of his guest, the unruffled composure of his manner and the grim lines round his mouth. Not a man to be trifled with, obviously, and if it were true that Goertz was dead it was to be expected that some stranger would take his place. Kenrade tried to remember whether he had ever seen this man before and, if so, where; as always happens when one tries to do this the idea immediately became possible though no corroborative detail would present itself.

Hambledon interrupted his reading to throw away his cigarette end and Kenrade asked in a voice from which all sarcasm had disappeared whether it was in Berlin that he had had the honor of meeting the Herr.

"No," said Hambledon calmly. "How long is your servant likely to be in fetching this man?"

Kenrade glanced at his watch. "Another twenty minutes, if the man is at home. It is some distance from here, the Place of the Fountain."

"And is he likely to be out? What does he do for a living besides faking passports? Anything?"

"I understand he is a teacher of the piano to children."

"Not at this hour of the night, surely. All well-brought-up children should be in bed."

"That is so. It is a for-their-health-imperative rule. Is the Herr a family man himself?"

Hambledon favored him with a look in which contempt dominated amusement, turned a page of the paper and went on reading without any other reply.

Some time later Kenrade broke the silence by asking whether Hambledon proposed to honor his house by remaining in it until he resumed his journey. "If so, a few simple preparations will be necessary."

Hambledon put down his paper and allowed his eyes to wander round the room. It was clean and tidy like a room in a barracks and carried no suggestion of a home. Four hard chairs stood about the deal table, which was covered with a blanket, soldier fashion. There was a cupboard against one wall, roller blinds masked the uncurtained windows, and the only attempt at decoration was a calendar with a picture of a windmill upon it which hung squarely dead center over the mantelpiece.

"It all depends," said Tommy finally, "upon how long it takes to produce this passport. If it is only a day or two, it might suit me to remain. If it is any longer, I think I should prefer someplace with a few more civilized amenities."

After which the silence was naturally unbroken until two sets of footsteps were heard coming up the garden and Kenrade, with a word of apology, went himself to admit them. A moment later Johannis was shown into the room. Tommy turned in his chair and looked the visitor up and down.

"This the merchant? Have you brought your camera?"

"I have," said Johannis calmly, "since I was particularly asked to do so. Is this gentleman the subject of my art?"

Chapter Six
English Passport

Johannis took several photographs of Hambledon posing, with a completely blank expression, against an equally blank wall.

"Surely one is enough," protested Tommy. "Passport photographs are so frightful that no one could want more than one of them."

"It is in case the film is faulty," explained Johannis. "As for being frightful, not at all. Quite the contrary. The Herr is definitely photogenic. But definitely. I am sure Herr Kalvag will corroborate me."

But Kenrade appeared not to hear, so busy was he with his papers. Hambledon frowned down this frivolity.

"An English passport, Herr Johannis—I understand that is your name. A suit of English tweeds and a tailor capable of making any necessary adjustments. A small hide suitcase such as the English use, not too new. I am a tourist, you understand."

"Are there, then, already English tourists abroad?" asked Johannis. "If Your Excellency would deign to be a traveler in some line of business in universal demand, such as lavatory fittings—"

"Oh, go to blazes," said Tommy in English, and translated it into Dutch. "How long do you think it will take you to produce these things?"

"Heaven has ordained that tomorrow should be a day upon which an English boat comes in," said Johannis piously. "If it is only a question of substituting this photograph for the one already there—"

"You could hardly substitute it for one that wasn't there," said Tommy justly.

"Your Excellency is a purist. I will come tomorrow evening and at least relate whether I have had good fortune or bad."

"In that case we need not detain you now," said Hambledon. "Good evening, Herr Johannis."

Johannis scrambled his photographic kit together and left in haste.

"That type of fellow," said Tommy coldly, "will become familiar if not checked. Since my stay may well be short, Kenrade, it seems futile to look for other accommodation if you can oblige me with a room and a few simple meals. I suppose your fellows know how to wait upon an officer?"

The following evening soon after dark Johannis came again to the house. Hambledon, who by this time was bored to sobs with having nothing to do but exhibit hauteur for hours on end, was very pleased to see him. Johannis, with an air of childlike pride, brought in a suitcase of good brown leather and produced a passport from his pocket.

"I am happy to announce," he said, "that I have been successful beyond anticipation. I am an artist, gentlemen, a musician, accustomed to aim at perfection in whatever I undertake. How seldom, alas, do one's efforts meet with that collaboration from Providence which one does one's poor best to deserve! Today, however, was marked with a white stone in the road of my destiny. I rose early and burned a wax candle to St. Christopher. I then went down to the docks and met the English boat, waiting outside the customs sheds until all the formalities had been completed by the passengers. That is psychology, gentlemen, for people fidget with their passports when an examination is about to be made and forget about them directly thereafter until they are upon the point of being required to show them again. I then—"

"Herr Johannis," said Hambledon, "you are being paid for deeds, not words."

"Your Excellency is more than right. I remembered in what great haste the Herr wished to depart, and there are personal physical particulars on these passports which take time if alteration is required. Did I, therefore, abstract the first passport which offered itself? I speak metaphorically, passports do not literally leap from the—"

"Cut the cackle," said Tommy, and translated it for their benefit.

Johannis bowed. "I selected an Englishman who superficially resembled Your Excellency in height, coloring and general appearance, and unostentatiously abstracted his passport while he was engaged in controversy with a porter. There remained the problem of the tweed suit the Herr desired."

"I suppose you unostentatiously removed his suit while he was engaged in controversy with a fishwife," said Tommy.

"No, Excellency, I removed his suitcase. Here it is."

"Let's look at the passport first," said Hambledon, and Kenrade also leaned across the table to see it. There was Hambledon's unflattered likeness duly indented with the Foreign Office stamp; he grunted approval and read out the particulars on the preceding pages.

"Name of Bearer: Thomas Elphinstone Hambledon. National Status: British Subject by birth. Profession:—"

He was interrupted by a savage roar from Kenrade at the unhappy Johannis.

"Idiot! Donkey! Half-witted baboon! Miserable louse! Diseased camel!"

"Heavens above, Herr Kalvag! What have I done?"

"What have you not done! Do you know what you have done, senseless blockhead—"

"Control yourself, Kalvag," said Tommy firmly. "It is obvious that this poor wretch does not know what he has done. Nor, in effect, do I, so that your inordinate strictures might almost be taken to apply to me also. Be careful, Kalvag."

Kenrade controlled himself with an effort which brought out the veins upon his temples.

"This passport is that of a notorious British intelligence agent, a most dangerous man. If this fool's action should bring that man down upon us—"

"But—but he has gone, Highborn," protested Johannis, wringing his hands. "He was but in transit to the British Occupied Zone of Germany, he did not propose remaining in the Netherlands. I myself saw him go away in the train and he had not even missed his little suitcase."

Tommy burst out laughing. "I think this is a beyond-all-measure-profitable happening," he said. "I will travel on this passport and with this luggage, and travel safely, for who questions the journeys of such a man as you describe? If he says he is going to Germany and turns up elsewhere, the authorities will think it only natural and under the circumstances to be expected. Well done, Herr Johannis," added Tommy, and patted him kindly upon the shoulder. "It could not by any means better have been done."

Johannis cheered up at once.

"And his little suitcase," he said, dumping it upon the table. "It even has this dangerous man's initials upon it, look."

It had, indeed, T.E.H. stamped upon the lid, which was not remarkable when one realizes that it was one of Tommy's own flown out from London to Rotterdam together with a new passport. Hambledon had said that he was tired to death of being Herr This and Monsieur That and would give his memory a rest by being himself for once, quite safely since nobody would believe it.

Kenrade protested but was imperiously overborne; Tommy Hambledon tried on the suit, found a few faults in the fit which were unjust since it had been made for him in Savile Row, and Johannis, magnificently rewarded, went away happily beaming upon everyone.

"Now that that difficulty has been triumphantly surmounted," said Hambledon, "let me first of all congratulate you, my good Kenrade, upon your perspicacity in being in touch with this man, Johannis. Your staff work must be beyond praise, and I will so report it."

Kenrade would have blushed if he had not forgotten the art during the past ten years.

"I am gratified—" he began.

"Naturally," said Tommy kindly. "Next, tell me what arrangements you have made for me to meet our friends. I know the general outline, of course, but I have every confidence in your management of the details."

"Thank you," said Kenrade in a slightly choked voice. He cleared his throat and continued: "I have made full arrangements for the meeting except as regards the date; this could not be finally settled before your arrival as we did not know exactly when to expect you. Today is Thursday, will next Monday suit you?"

"Perfectly."

"That is good. The place is the restaurant known as Le Petit Enfer in Montmartre in Paris, you know it, perhaps?"

"That place, yes. Where the tourists go to get a thrill," said Tommy reminiscently.

"That is it, yes. If you will enter exactly at a quarter past twenty hours wearing a black felt hat and with a white camellia in your buttonhole, and pause in the doorway, looking round as though expecting to see a friend, one man will rise from a box where three are sitting and say, in French of course: 'You are welcome, Michel.

We were at the point of fearing that you were not coming.' You will say: 'Forgive me, I have been at a wedding,' and you will find that all will be well."

"Excellent," said Tommy gravely, and repeated the two phrases. "On Monday next at a quarter past twenty hours."

"It cannot well be arranged before Monday in spite of the need for haste," said Kenrade. "As you are aware, Kurt Rougetel has to come from London."

Tommy nodded carelessly. "Are you sure that will give him time enough?"

"But plenty. He enjoys a first-class priority, naturally." Kenrade laughed. "These English!"

"Quite, quite," said Tommy, and laughed also. "We should be thankful for it, Kenrade."

"We are," said the German simply.

"It is now just upon nineteen hours," said Hambledon, looking at his watch. "There is ample time." He picked up the suitcase and took it up to his room to pack away the few necessaries he had brought in his pockets from the *Melicent Myrdal*. He rewarded Nilsen by giving him Captain Gielink's decent suit; Peycke received the peaked cap and the raincoat.

"Your Excellency is leaving?" said Peycke. "I regret."

"I also," said Nilsen. "This is a beautiful suit. Such good cloth."

"One of you," said Tommy genially, "can carry my case to the railway station for me. Now. At once."

He returned to the sitting room and said abruptly: "I am now going to Paris. *Auf Wiedersehen*, Kenrade. I thank you for your hospitality."

"But," said Kenrade. "A moment—you cannot go to Paris tonight—"

"Why not? There is a train which goes. If I sit in it I shall go also, *nicht wahr?*"

"But I have not told you about your hotel. Accommodation has been reserved—"

"In Paris, my good Kenrade, I accommodate myself," said Tommy. He grinned broadly, winked at Kenrade and dodged out of the room, slamming the door behind him. Nilsen was waiting for him, with the suitcase, outside the front door; Tommy set off at a pace which soon evoked symptoms of distress from the ex-sergeant of fortress artillery.

"His Excellency," panted Nilsen, "covers the ground like a stag of the mountains."

"I am a mountain stag," said Tommy, "didn't you know? Especially when I've got a train to catch."

"The honored gentleman is going far?"

"To Paris," said Hambledon, and broke into a trot.

"Ah, Paris," said Nilsen. "It is understood," and he lumbered along behind. When they reached the devastated area round the railway station Tommy fairly ran and consequently had to wait at the station entrance for Nilsen, who arrived gasping and leaned against the doorpost.

"Thank you," said Tommy, taking the suitcase from his yielding hand. "You know, you don't take enough exercise. You must, or you won't get into that suit much longer. A ten-mile walk every day, and resist the temptation to drink. Here is a spot of temptation to practice on," he added, and gave the man twenty guilders.

Nilsen detached himself from the doorpost and said that His Excellency was not only a man of heart and understanding, but without doubt a nobleman of the highest rank, and, if he received his just dues, would prosper wherever he went. Hambledon missed the closing phrases because, in the middle of the speech, two men strolled out of the station behind him and glanced back as they passed. One was short, fat in front, and round-shouldered, the other was tall and thin; there was a light at the station entrance and Tommy saw their faces distinctly. They were Olgar and Wenezky.

They also recognized him, there was no doubt of it. He saw their eyes widen, though they looked away again at once. They walked a few paces forward and then Olgar—the fat one—gave an extremely good impersonation of a man who has just remembered that he has forgotten something. He stopped abruptly, smote his hands together, and said something with a gesture towards the station. Wenezky nodded, signified agreement, and stepped aside as one who is prepared to wait. Olgar turned back and reentered the station, passing Hambledon without a glance.

Nilsen, having completed his remarks, saluted smartly and walked away; Wenezky lit a cigarette and lounged after him.

"Only one for me to deal with," thought Hambledon. "Now, if I could push him under a train—"

He swung his suitcase and walked energetically towards the fat man, who was standing near the inner door reading a timetable. Perhaps Hambledon looked dangerous, or possibly Olgar was a thought reader, for he made up his mind suddenly and moved on, with Tommy striding after. He pursued the fat one past the "local" booking office and dived into it himself; there was a queue at the ticket office and Tommy slid through them, out by another door and took to his heels. He was in the act of buying his ticket at the mainline office before Olgar found him again and he could not have heard Hambledon's destination.

Tommy went straight onto the platform. He glanced over his shoulder during the moment when the ticket inspector at the door delayed him; Olgar was conducting a frantic search through his pockets and the intending passenger next behind him was exhibiting exasperation.

"The poor boob's come out without any money," said Hambledon contemptuously, and found himself a corner seat in a first-class compartment from which he could watch the booking-office door. Passengers emerged, running, but no Olgar. Porters shouted, doors banged and a whistle blew. The train clanked into motion and the last sight Tommy had of Olgar was a fat unhappy face pressed against the glass of the booking-office window.

Nilsen walked on until he reached a district of habitable houses and found a bras-serie in which to spend his guilders. It was all against orders, of course; Kenrade, who was rightly anxious about the effect of alcohol upon discretion, had absolutely forbidden his men to drink in public houses. But Nilsen had a thirst that would not wait and it was months since he had had a drink in cheerful company. He would have just one and then buy a bottle and take it home. Just one, or maybe two at most. He pushed the door open and walked in. The place was not so cheerful as he could have wished; there were only four men there beside the landlord and it was very quiet and rather dull. No music, either. He'd have just one and then perhaps try somewhere else.

He was finishing his first drink when a tall thin man walked in and came to stand beside him at the bar, a friendly soul who grinned at him and got into conversa-tion at once. He told a couple of funny stories, new to Nilsen, who cheered up and ordered another glass. Nilsen's Dutch was not particularly good and the landlord took him for a Flamand, but he could follow what was said perfectly well and make himself understood. The thin man went to the door once or twice; he said he was expecting a friend of his to come along and celebrate a stroke of luck they'd had. He was not sure whether the friend would come to the right place at once or whether he would go to another house in the next street, in the meantime would Nilsen oblige by having one with him, and so on. He went to the door again, ut-tered a cry of joy and returned with a little fat man whom he introduced as "my pal Lukas. Have another."

Nilsen's conscience, or his fear of Kenrade, was making him uneasy; he said he would have just one more if they would let him stand treat and then really he must go home. His friends said they quite understood but he must just try this stuff, and passed him another glass. He found it pleasant; the room seemed suddenly to be-come warmer and much larger, also he wanted to sing. Nice fellows, good friends, devil take Kenrade. A jolly evening.

When Olgar and Wenezky wanted to give him another the landlord demurred. He said his was a respectable house and the gentleman had plainly had enough already. But Wenezky said that that was quite all right, he knew this man, who was a sort of general factotum to a friend of his, and he would see him safe home. it was on his way, anyway. They had just one more after which Nilsen could not be withheld from song, so they all three left together, arm in arm, with the carolling Nilsen in the midst. *"Berlin bleibt Berlin,"* he sang, as he always did whenever he was in the least drunk, "Berlin remains Berlin." It is a statement of doubtful accuracy at best, and anyway one doesn't bellow songs in praise of Berlin in Rotterdam today, nor will for some years to come. Nilsen's companions tried to hush him but he was beyond hushing, so they did the next best thing, they sang something else louder than he did, though even that did not stop him. Cheerful but discordant they rolled through the streets, coming at last to one in which the houses still stood indeed, but roofless and empty, having been ravaged by fire.

They turned in at the vestiges of a gateway and came to a place where steps led down into the ground, being in fact the stairs down to the basement kitchen of a once decent house. Here Nilsen jibbed.

"This isn't where I live," he said.

"Where do you live?" asked Wenezky.

"I'm not supposed to say. But I know where it is. At least, I knew where it was when I knew where I was, but now I don't know where I am. Do I? Nev' been here. Nev' mind. *Berlin bleibt*—"

"Listen," said Wenezky. "This is where we live. You come and have some coffee with us, then you'll feel better when you get home."

"Coffee," said Nilsen. "Good idea, coffee. Mustn't let the major see me like this, he'd be 'noyed. Very 'noyed. Very savage man, *unser Obersatz."*

He proceeded down the steps with the help of Wenezky's arm and Olgar's electric torch; at the bottom was a door which would still open and shut and within it a large subterranean room insulated from the outer world by a cascade of brickbats which had blocked up the basement window. Olgar lit a couple of candles and shut the door while Wenezky led Nilsen to a chair.

"Now then. Where do you live?"

"Eh? I want some coffee."

Wenezky nodded to Olgar, who picked up a bucket of water and emptied it over Nilsen's head.

"Ach! Ouch!"

"That'll sober you quicker than coffee. Now, where do you live?"

"I mustn't say."

"Where do you live—where do you live—where do you live—"

"Ach! Don't do that, it hurts. Why are you hurting me—"

"Where do you live—"

When they eventually got an answer to that, other questions followed.

"Who was that man whose bag you carried to the station tonight?"

"A highborn baron. I do not know his name."

Wenezky did not believe this for some time filled with discomfort for Nilsen; when finally he whimpered that he only knew the gentleman was expected but had never heard his name, they gave it up and turned to another point.

"Where was he going?"

Nilsen had liked Hambledon and it took more persuasion to elicit "Paris."

"Paris, eh? Oh. Now then. This major of yours, who is he? What's his name?"

"Who else is there in the house? . . .

"How many people are there in your house? . . .

"How many people—ah, I thought you would. Only one other, what's his name?"

When at last they had received all the information which the unhappy Nilsen had to give they stood back in silence while he doubled himself up, moaning, with his head on his knees. Wenezky swung up the hand which held the coal hammer, there was a dull thud, and Nilsen rolled from the chair.

"Dead rats don't squeak," said Wenezky.

Chapter Seven
Little Hell

Kenrade was well pleased to see Hambledon go and did not even grudge him the services of Nilsen to carry his bag to the station, but when the man did not return long after he might reasonably have been expected to do so, the German major was both anxious and angry.

"Peycke!"

"Sir?"

"Where d'you suppose that damned fool Nilsen has got to all this time?"

Peycke said that, with respect, he had not the faintest idea. It was not quite true, he guessed the tip and the drink and only wished he had gone also.

"You do know. He has gone on the booze."

Peycke did not argue the point. Kenrade took a turn across the room and back.

"I suppose he babbles when he's drunk just like all the rest of you half-witted apes."

"Well, no, sir. I can't say as I've ever 'eard Nilsen talk much. 'E sings, mostly."

"Sings!"

"Yes, sir. *'Berlin bleibt Berlin'* as a rule. Besides, sir," added Peycke hopefully, "'e can't talk much Dutch anyway, so 'e couldn't—"

"So you think that if he only staggers round Rotterdam bellowing songs about Berlin nobody will notice anything?"

Peycke wisely held his tongue.

"Let us hope he is only arrested by the police and thrown into a concentration camp. Get out."

Nevertheless, neither Kenrade nor Peycke was easy enough in his mind to go to bed, though it was nearly two in the morning before they heard unsteady steps coming up the brick path and a thick voice chanting about Berlin between hiccups. Kenrade and his servant met in the hall but the major reached the door first.

"Get back, Peycke, I'll deal with this myself." Somebody bumped clumsily against the door outside, Kenrade turned the handle and flung it open.

"Nilsen, what the hell is the meaning—who the devil are you?"

For there were two men on the doorstep and both were very obviously armed. The short fat one pressed a revolver against Kenrade's midriff and the German noticed with horror that it had a silencer upon it. These people meant business and had come prepared for it.

Peycke, further down the hall, realized that something was very wrong and leapt for the kitchen, but the tall man outside put his hand over the short one's shoulder and shot Peycke neatly through the head.

"Now we talk," said Wenezky. "Back into that room behind you."

Kenrade could only obey. He soon discovered that his visitors were only interested in Hambledon, and though the German disliked Hambledon personally, he desired to remain loyal to him as part of an organization to which they both belonged. He was much more stubborn than Nilsen and also more enduring, but there are limits to endurance and Olgar and Wenezky were experienced in finding them. There was a clock in a church tower near by which struck two soon after the visitors arrived; by the time it struck three Kenrade was trying to convince them that he did not know Hambledon's name. "He did not tell me. I asked, but he did not tell me. He came in place of Goertz who—"

"We know what happened to Goertz. Do you mean to tell us you harbored a total stranger without credentials? Nonsense."

Kenrade admitted that Hambledon had said he was an old friend, but protested that he personally could not remember him. "I asked if we met in Berlin but he would not answer." The admission was a mistake because Wenezky did his best to stimulate his memory and Kenrade fainted. When he came round the inquisition proceeded and Kenrade told them about Hambledon's departure for Paris with a new outfit and a passport. It was an English passport, stolen that morning, and the name on it was Thomas Elphinstone Hambledon.

"Nonsense," said Olgar at once. "That man—I have never seen him but we have all heard of him—he is—"

"That's what I told him," said Kenrade. "I said it was dangerous but he wouldn't listen."

"I don't believe it," said Wenezky, but Olgar said the point was of no importance. "He will change his name and passport in Paris, of course. We know him by sight. It is only necessary to know where he is going in Paris and we can pick him up there. Where is he going to stay in Paris?"

Kenrade said with perfect truth that he didn't know.

"The things you don't know," snarled Wenezky. "We have wasted over an hour on you already and learned no more than we had already from your muttonheaded servant. Do you want me to become really annoyed?"

Kenrade said with tears that he certainly did not. "This man—he is undoubtedly a leader. How does one remain safe? By not talking of one's plans, what is not told can't be repeated. He knows this, he does not talk."

"It is possible," said Olgar slowly. "Nevertheless, I think you must know something of your organization in Paris. He would meet them. Where would he meet them?"

Kenrade did not wish to answer, but his objections were gradually overborne and he gasped out the name of the Petit Enfer.

"Date and time?"

Kenrade tried to lie but had not enough resolution to do it convincingly and Olgar was not deceived. Finally he told them. "Monday next at a quarter past twenty hours."

"Who will be there to meet him?"

Kenrade said that the only one whom he knew would be there was Kurt Rouge-tel, who was coming from London. He did not know who else would be there, if anyone, Rougetel might be alone.

"Where will they go to from Paris?"

But this was the final secret and Wenezky could not uncover it however industri-ously he searched. At last Kenrade, stretched across the table, arched his back and died; Wenezky wiped his hands on a corner of the blanket and shook his head.

"No stamina, these Germans," he said.

"I suppose," said Olgar, "the packet is not in this house all the time?"

"We can look."

"It is a pity he is already dead; he could have told us and that would have saved the trouble of looking."

"You should have asked him sooner," said Wenezky cheerfully. "We may find something else worth having to repay us for the extra trouble. In any case we will find some food; I am hungry. These exertions give a man an appetite."

"You are well called Wenezky the Wolf," said Olgar gracefully, and led the way to the kitchen.

Hambledon, having told everybody that he was going to Paris, very naturally went to London instead. He felt he would like a little more information about all these embroilments and especially he wanted to know what was in the packet received from the late Herr Goertz in Stockholm and posted to the British Legation there. He returned, accordingly, to his own room at the Foreign Office and proceeded to give and receive information.

The packet contained two samples of a dirty gray substance, differing slightly in specific gravity and in other important respects, and several pages of remarkably cryptic notes.

"I saw them myself," said Denton in a tired voice. "To be accurate, I took a hasty glance and averted my eyes. They were then passed on to someone stronger. They are scientific notes of some kind, but to make them more exciting the symbols used are not the usual ones but an entirely fresh set which nobody has ever seen before. I even gather no one particularly yearns to see 'em again. The wallah who did his best to explain it to me said it was something like being set an algebraical problem where the usual x's and y's had been replaced by letters from the Chinese alphabet and the signs of the zodiac had been used instead of plus, minus, and so forth. He said that that was not an exact parallel because in algebra one could, with care, deduce the substitutions, but in the case of these formulae it was not so simple. The gray powder was like cigar ash only heavier. Our chemists have got to work on it, their first preliminary report came in this morning. Exhausting, very. I had one look at that and sent out for some beer. What passes for beer these days. It was no help at all."

Denton had worked for Hambledon for so many years that Tommy was used to his ways. The more serious matters were the more languid Denton appeared until the moment came, when he would interrupt a yawn and go into action with the startling efficiency of a rocket-gun battery.

"What did they think it was?"

"They thought somebody'd been trying to produce synthetic thorium."

"Thorium," said Tommy thoughtfully. "Uranium. Atomic material, so to speak. Had they succeeded, whoever they are?"

"Don't know yet. They've sent the stuff on to Didcot," said Denton, referring to the British Atomic Research station.

"You know, there's one good thing about all this atomic bomb business."

"Tell me," urged Charles Denton.

"Think how popular work down the coal mines will become. People will be queueing up in thousands offering to pay large sums for the privilege of hewing at the coal face."

"Reminds me of Epstein," yawned Denton. "Can't think why. What else did you do on your holiday?"

Tommy told him in considerable detail.

"Isidore Skutnas, how do you spell him? Moritz Wenezky," said Denton, writing the names on a slip of paper. "Lukas Olgar. What nationality, do you know?"

"No. Some sort of Middle Europeans. Nasty ones." Hambledon added a detailed description of them. "I don't think we need bother about Skutnas, he looks like getting about fifteen years anyway."

"Somebody might want to hang him," said Denton hopefully. "Horaz Kenrade from Frankfurt am Rhein, SS man, now calling himself what? Kalvag from Finland, yes. Address so-and-so in Rotterdam. Probably a quite simple enquiry will settle his hash. Also the servants—Peycke, thank you, and Nilsen."

"Very small fry," said Hambledon.

"And the man said to be in London, Kurt Rougetel. No description and probably doesn't call himself that here. Still, we have some German technicians here, more or less trusties, if one of 'em wants to go to Paris for the weekend—"

"I think he's a bit more than that," said Hambledon, and quoted Kenrade's remark that Rougetel could always get priority for journeys to the continent.

"Oh. Very superior. A VIP, in fact. Wonder who the devil he is. Never mind, we shall know on Monday night in Paris, when he is observed in your company. Mr. T. E. Hambledon and friend at Le Petit Enfer. Anything else we can do for you?"

"Yes. I want another packet made up to look like the one poor dear Goertz so trustingly confided to me. It should resemble it inside as well as outside, Denton.

Do you think someone could write some of that fancy stuff you described in approximately the same handwriting? All those zodiacal signs or whatever they were? As though scientific formulae aren't quite bad enough to start with without putting them into code. What a people, what a race, what a mess. Epitaph for Germany."

"I'll see if someone can be bribed to do it," said Denton. "When are you crossing?"

"Sunday night."

"You want some samples put in too, of course."

"Of course. I suggest Gregory powder. Then, if they want to know how it is loaded I shall recommend raspberry jam."

"Humane variant of castor oil," said Denton. "Perhaps you can persuade one of your heroes to swallow it and then park himself on a British warship and await events. Anything else?"

"Where is Santa Brigida?" asked Tommy.

"What is Santa Brigida?"

"I don't know. I am assuming it's a place."

"Or a ship. Or a convent or church. Or a password. Or the name of a street. Or the holy lady herself. She's in heaven, doubtless," said Denton helpfully. "Why?"

"Goertz mentioned her—or it—when he died."

"Perhaps he was just rambling in his mind."

"It looks," said Hambledon, "as though we shall have to await a little more illumination on the subject. But it does sound like a place name and, if it is, it's in Spain or Spanish territory. And Spanish territory is now about the only place in the world where the gentle Nazi can still buzz unswotted."

"So you think you might be going to Spain."

"I might. Whom have we got who is useful in Spain?"

"There's Gibson," said Denton, "but he's in a nursing home parting with his appendix at the moment. There's a man named Callaghan—"

"I don't know him. I'd rather have someone I know. There are those two fellows I ran across in connection with the Gatello gang, James Hyde and Adam Selkirk. Selkirk's lived in Spain for years, and Hyde is a useful man to have about. He does look so very respectable. I suppose they're out in the Argentine now."

"Selkirk's in the Argentine but Hyde's in London, I ran into him in Piccadilly yesterday," said Denton. "He asked after you."

"I think I'll go and see him. Some scheme will doubtless present itself," said Hambledon.

The Montmartre restaurant called Little Hell is well known to tourists; there is nothing in the least damnable about it except the general idea, which is the product of a macabre imagination. The waiters are dressed as undertakers, the dance hostesses are angels in every respect doubtless but particularly in appearance, the style of decoration is that of a high-class mausoleum and the tables are coffins. One eats off the lid.

Hambledon had known it of old; on the appointed Monday evening on the stroke of eight-fifteen he strolled in and looked about him with the air of one expecting to meet a friend. He wore a white camellia in his buttonhole and carried a black felt hat in his hand. Immediately a young man, who had two companions with him, rose from beside one of the coffins—hence Kenrade's reference to "a box at which three are sitting"—and came towards him saying, in the appointed formula, "You are welcome, Michel. We were at the point of fearing that you were not coming."

"Forgive me," said Hambledon, shaking hands with him. "I have been at a wedding."

"I want you to meet my friends," said the young man, leading Hambledon towards them. "This is M'sieu Rougetel, a distinguished friend of my family these many years, he is an authority upon antique glass. The walking skeleton on your left is Antoine Marillier, who is an authority upon oysters and racing automobiles. Do sit down. *Garçon!"*

Hambledon greeted his new friends politely. Kurt Rougetel was a middle-aged man with a thin face, anxious eyes behind gold-rimmed glasses and a neat beard turning gray. Antoine Marillier, the "walking skeleton," was one of the most obese young men Tommy had ever met, with beady black eyes peering between rolls of fat and smooth black hair that shone, reflecting the lights like a ball of polished bakelite. "Queer-shaped head," thought Tommy while his drink was being served. "Flat in front and round at the back. Just like a tomcat." Hambledon lifted his glass and drank their healths. "Also to our better acquaintance, messieurs. My friend here can always be relied upon to introduce me to interesting and charming people."

"Frolich has a large and miscellaneous assortment of friends," said Marillier. "Last time we had an evening out together he introduced me to a second violinist at the Folies and a verger from Notre Dame."

"You seem to have had an assorted evening," said Hambledon with a laugh. Frolich, evidently, was the name of the sandy-haired weasel-faced young man who was his host. They talked easily throughout the excellent dinner until the liqueurs came and went; Rougetel, who had gradually become absentminded and a little fidgety, leaned across the table and said in a low tone: "Excuse me—I don't think I caught your name when we were introduced?"

"I don't think Frolich mentioned it," said Tommy frankly, "but no doubt Kenrade told you. For official purposes it is still Hambledon."

"Is that safe?"

"Is anything safe?" said Hambledon, and Marillier laughed. "I don't know much about me," Tommy went on, "but I gather I am not the sort of man of whom one asks questions. If anyone attempts to interrogate me I shall glare at them and refer them to the British Embassy, who certainly won't answer silly questions. But how convenient."

"That was the name which Kenrade gave us," said Frolich, "but we thought you might perhaps give us another."

As Hambledon had no idea what name they expected he had no intention of complying.

"Tomás for happy gatherings like the present," he said, "Tomás for our lighter moments, yes?"

"And for our more serious interludes?" urged the anxious Rougetel.

Hambledon leaned back in his chair and surveyed the company with an air of contempt.

"You ask me who I am," he began slowly. "That is childish, as you know perfectly well. I will tell you this much, my name is one which is better forgotten though I think that is not very likely. I will not tell any of you what it is lest someday one of you might talk in his sleep or babble in fever. It is well known that I am dead and I prefer to remain so. We meet in a good place among the coffins and the mourners, do we not? At least, I am here instead of being with those who sat in the dock at Nuremberg."

Kurt Rougetel made a little helpless gesture with his hands, Frolich nodded slowly and Marillier crushed out the end of his cigar in the ashtray, continuing to grind it down long after it was out. There was a short silence after which Tommy took the lead again.

"Do not think," he said gently, "that I do not appreciate your point of view. You want credentials, naturally. I am in the same boat, gentlemen. None of us have ever met before and, except for Rougetel, I did not even know the names of those whom I was to meet tonight. How do I know that the real Rougetel, Frolich and Marillier are not bound and gagged in some cellar or dead in some pit, and that you three are not members of British or American Intelligence? Can you prove it?"

"No," said Frolich. "At least, not conveniently."

"It would seem then," continued Hambledon, "that we must trust each other or call the whole scheme off and lurk impotently in corners until we die."

"It is all quite true," said Rougetel, "and I apologize for my indiscretion, the more so as, if you are indeed he who was to come, we have a little business to transact, have we not? Shall we, then, retire for a moment to the cloakroom?"

"By all means," said Tommy, and followed him into seclusion where Rougetel, peering earnestly through gold-rimmed glasses, came close to Hambledon and said: "You have something for me, I think?"

"Certainly," said Tommy, and gave him Denton's packet.

"Ah," said Rougetel, and stowed it away with care. "You know what is inside this?"

"In general terms only. I am not a scientist—"

"No, no—"

"I am a follower, a messenger, a dreamer, that is all. I look forward and I hope."

"Give me your hand," said Rougetel, and they clasped hands emotionally in an environment of white tiles and chromium plating.

"Thank heaven he's German, not French," said Tommy to himself. "At least he doesn't want to kiss me."

"May I say," added Rougetel confidentially, "how right you were not to give your distinguished name to those two out there? Marillier particularly, he takes drugs."

"I thought perhaps he did," said Tommy, "his eyes are too bright. Yet," he added with gentle reproach, "it was you who asked me."

"I am a stupid old man," said Rougetel humbly. "I had not then guessed—"

"Hush!" said Hambledon sharply.

"Again you are right. See, I put it out of my mind and we speak of something else. You will travel with me, will you not?"

"Travel with you," said Tommy, stressing the preposition. "I had not fully considered the matter."

"We have the way prepared through Spain and beyond, we shall be able to make things easy for you once we are over the frontier. It is only to get out of France—"

"I myself have one or two simple ideas about that," said Hambledon truthfully, since he had discussed it in London. "Once over the frontier, though, I should be glad of your help."

"You shall have it," said Rougetel in a voice which was almost cheerful. "Besides, the plan is simplicity itself; once across the frontier all you have to do is to get yourself arrested."

"Arrested? By whom?"

"Either a policeman or a frontier guard. You will then be put in prison and your name will be forwarded to a central office in Madrid for instructions. There is a man there who is looking out for it, as soon as he sees it he will order you to be sent to Madrid at once. Then all will be well."

"I hope so," said Hambledon in a doubtful tone. "What's the catering like in these Spanish prisons?"

Rougetel actually laughed. "I understand that that depends on how generously you fee the warders. Take plenty of Spanish currency with you. It is a pity," he added, preparing to return to the others, "that Santa Brigida is quite so remote and I admit with shame that I am a bad sailor. The sea affects my liver."

"It has that effect upon many otherwise healthy people," said Tommy solemnly, but within him his heart was dancing, for he had guessed whereabouts Santa Brigida might be. "I should also like to know," he added to himself, "who the devil you think I am."

He followed Rougetel back to the restaurant where Frolich and Marillier placidly awaited them. Tommy glanced casually across the room, not expecting to see anyone he knew, but there near the door were two men whose appearance sent a little quiver of excitement down his spine. The fat Olgar, white-faced and flabby, was reading the menu with an expression of alarm probably occasioned by the scale of prices, and Wenezky was lounging forward with his long arms before him as though he were clasping the end of his coffin in a familiar embrace. With a wolfish grin on his thin face he was watching one of the angel hostesses as she walked gracefully across the room; Olgar, Tommy told himself, was just an unpleasing object, but Wenezky—Wenezky was at home here. He poisoned the atmosphere; the illusion of death ceased to be a joke and became a menace. Tommy sat down quickly.

"It is well," said Rougetel to the others. "Our friend is all he should be, and more."

"It is good," said Frolich. "In that case, if you have no further use for Marillier and myself for the moment—we have an unimportant engagement and doubtless you have arrangements to discuss. . . ."

They took their leave and went out. The little stir drew Wenezky's eyes from the lady to Hambledon's party; he stared for a moment and nudged Olgar, who also looked. Tommy asked Rougetel for his address, promised to tell him at once as soon as plans were perfected, and generally prolonged the conversation till the two by the door were well into the hors d'œuvres. Now there would be delay while they paid, they could not simply put down their forks and rush out after him.

"If you will excuse me," began Tommy, "a delightful evening, I have enjoyed it immensely, besides the pleasure of making your acquaintance—"

"The pleasure and the privilege are entirely mine," said Rougetel, beaming through his glasses. "I shall hear from you, then—"

"Tomorrow, or at latest, the day after," said Tommy. He rose from his seat, picked up his hat in the same movement, and walked rapidly out into the street. By the favor of heaven a taxi had just set down a party of people at the door and was being paid. Hambledon leapt into the taxi, gave the driver an address, and was whirled away.

Chapter Eight
Black Marketeer

It is no indiscretion to say that there is a thriving black market in Paris; all the world knows it and the Parisians best of all. It is well organized, soundly financed, and works with the precision of a public utilities company. There are the meat purveyors; the wine sellers; the chicken, egg and butter merchants; the providers of fruit and vegetables, of coal and coke, of silk stockings and velvet gowns; of everything, in short, which a civilized city requires in order to live. Most of the operators have a regular beat, a source of supply in the country somewhere and a fleet of lorries running in convoy to carry the goods. When Hambledon in London had discussed with Denton and James Hyde the quickest and most inconspicuous way to travel from Paris to the Spanish frontier or wherever else his fortunes should lead him, Denton explained the black market system and suggested that an empty lorry leaving Paris to obtain further supplies would be happy to earn a little extra dividend by conveying a passenger or two. "You could rest the driver by taking a turn at the wheel sometimes," he added. "That would make you at once more popular and less conspicuous. Besides, most of these blokes have a regular route; if you want to meet Hyde somewhere it should be easily arranged."

Tommy said that, so far as he knew, he had no black marketers upon his visiting lists, and Hyde said that surely this sort of people must be difficult to find. "Otherwise they would be locked up, wouldn't they?"

"Not inevitably," said Denton. "You see, the French black marketeers are not all scabs and scoundrels like the English ones. They started as part of the Resistance Movement and were officially encouraged because they annoyed the Hun. But it was a paying game and now the war's over they are regrettably difficult to stop. There's a man I know who can put you in touch with the right people to take you wherever you want to go," added Denton, and gave Hambledon a name and an address. "When you've fixed it all up, ring me up and I'll arrange with Hyde if you think you'll want him."

"I still can't speak much French," said Hyde humbly. "Nobody would ever take me for anything but an Englishman, I'm sure."

"I shouldn't want you to be anything but an Englishman," said Tommy. "They still have their uses, believe it or not."

Accordingly, on the morning after the little dinner at Le Petit Enfer, Hambledon emerged early from his hotel and went to a pleasant small house in a residential district to call upon a slim young man in sports clothes and a beret, who sent him on to a stout elderly man in a striped suit who lived in a flat over a shop. From there Tommy was directed to a lean man in overalls who owned a garage and lived in lodgings, who introduced him to a square man miscellaneously dressed who spoke a variety of French which Tommy had never met before. He came, it appeared, from Morbihan originally, but was not at the moment living anywhere in particular unless his lorry could be described as home. It had, indeed, a few attributes of permanent residence, personal possessions in the cubbyholes and in one or two small lockers screwed to the floor, and a photograph on the dashboard of a dark-haired boy with a snub nose. The photograph was mounted in a heavy black frame above which was fastened a knot of the tricolor and a tiny metal badge of the Cross of Lorraine. When the driver showed Hambledon round the lorry, exactly as any suburban dweller will show a visitor round his garden, Tommy glanced at the photograph and the driver followed his look.

"My son. The Boche. April 19, 1943. God curse them." He spat ceremonially.

"God rest his soul," said Tommy, and changed the subject. The driver's name was Anatole Brihou and he would certainly drive Hambledon and his friend down towards the Spanish frontier. There were four lorries in the convoy and they all belonged to him. He did not go right down to the frontier, his destination was just short of Auch in the Department of Gers, but from there it would be easy to reach the frontier, easy. Simple. Quick. But two skips of a flea and M'sieu would be in the mountains.

"But, splendid," said Hambledon. "How soon can you start?"

That depended upon Jean le Mari; tomorrow or possibly the next day. He drove the third lorry always.

Hambledon supposed that John the Husband had to obtain leave from his wife, and said so. But no, it was the tooth of Jean le Mari which tormented him though it was true that Madame did so also. There was a little matter of a visit to the dentist today, after which he might require to repose himself for a day before starting to drive. M'sieu would understand, the cold draft upon the tender jaw.

"Oh, perfectly," said Tommy. "If I come and see you this evening, will you know by then? Splendid, then I'll come along tonight and make the final arrangements."

On his way home he rang up Rougetel from a telephone kiosk to tell him about Brihou and his convoy, partly as an act of courtesy which would, he hoped, be appreciated, and partly to make sure that Rougetel was still extant. Hambledon was sure that Olgar and Wenezky had not managed to follow him from Le Petit Enfer; it was all the more likely that they had frozen onto Rougetel and even followed him home. However, Rougetel was quite well and, for him, happy. Tommy returned to his own hotel and had a telephone conversation with Denton.

"So you were right after all," said Denton. "Santa Brigida is a place, and it's over the sea from Spain. It—"

"It's either in Spanish Morocco or the Canary Isles," said Tommy. "I guess the latter."

"It's in the Province of Ontario."

"What," said Tommy feebly.

"Ontario. Canada. I looked it up."

"Good heart alive. Surely not."

"Well, there is one there," said Denton. "And Canada is very interested in atomic energy. What's the fuss about? Grand country. Wonderful climate—at this time of the year. Marvelous scenery. What more d'you want?"

"Well, it sounds like a damn long walk to me," said Hambledon. "And why take synthetic thorium to Canada, anyway? And why go through Spain?"

"You'll find out. In time. Where do you want Hyde lurking? At Auch? Right. Ring me late tonight and I'll give you a telephone number there where you can ring him."

"There's just one more item for your agenda," said Tommy. "Rougetel's comates and brothers in exile, Frolich and Marillier. Something should be done about them."

"You mean 'done to them,' don't you? All right, I'll see to them."

"After I've had enough time to get clear away. I don't want their deaths laid to my account by their vindictive friends while I am still in their midst," urged Tommy.

"Of course not. We will wait till after your visit to Santa Brigida, wherever it is."

"I still don't believe I'm going to Canada," said Hambledon, but Denton had rung off.

Brihou, interviewed later that night, said that Jean le Mari was sore but relieved and considered himself well enough to start the following morning. The convoy would, accordingly, move off at half past six, if that was not too early for M'sieu and his friend. It would take three days to do the trip, "We are not of the grand rapidity, you understand," and every day wasted meant money wasted.

"That cannot be contemplated," said Hambledon. "I will let my friend know at once and we will be here in good time."

"He is anxious, your friend," said Brihou.

"He always is," said Hambledon.

"He sent a messenger here this afternoon to ask when we should be starting. I told him I did not yet know whether it would be tomorrow or the day after."

Hambledon was mildly annoyed. It had been left to him to make the arrangements and there was no need for Rougetel to have stuck his little oar in. However, it might not have been Rougetel but Frolich or Marillier being officious. It didn't really matter.

"He is of the anxious type, that one," remarked Tommy. "I will let him know the time and he will be here early."

At half past six on the following morning Hambledon arrived at the meeting place to find Rougetel already there and fussing.

"I shall travel in the third lorry," he said, "I have already put my luggage, such as it is, therein. You will travel with the *patron* in the front one, will you not? Thus, if any not-to-be-foreseen misfortune should occur, it is unlikely that we shall both be involved."

"You think of everything," said Hambledon, who was rather pleased than otherwise. Rougetel was a dear good soul—for a German—but definitely a wet blanket. A little of his depressing company went a long way.

Brihou strolled up to apologize for a short delay; it was Jean le Mari, or rather, his wife. She always withheld him at partings though she never seemed to want him when he was at home. "These women," said Brihou, and wandered away. Rougetel beguiled the time of waiting by describing a funny scene which took place at Le Petit Enfer directly after Tommy had left. There were two men near the door who had only just begun dinner when they suddenly threw down their napkins, snatched up their hats and rushed out. The commissionaire at the door did his best to stop them, the waiter rushed after them and the manager sprang forward, all to no effect. The two men escaped, as it appeared from what Rougetel heard the waiter telling the manager, in a taxi.

"They did, did they?" said Tommy thoughtfully. "I suppose they suddenly remembered another engagement."

"It is to be supposed so. They left, however, enough money upon the table—the coffin, I would say—to pay for what they'd had and even a *pourboire* for the waiter. He said they were real gentlemen."

"And waiters always know," said Hambledon sarcastically. "What did they look like, these gentlemen?"

Rougetel said he only caught a passing glimpse of them but he gave a recognizable description of Olgar and Wenezky.

"Really," said Tommy. "It must have been most amusing. Excuse me, I think I'd better put my traps in the other lorry, I should think we should be starting soon." He went away, thinking it over. He had been had for a mug, the two men had followed him. True, a taxi had passed his hotel at the moment when he was going in, it had slowed down as though someone within were trying to identify a house, but he had thought nothing of it. Mug. He looked round him; it was a cheap and malodorous district and there were a few small shops already open for the convenience of early customers. Tommy went into one of the shops and bought a brown drill dust coat and a peaked hat such as French drivers wear, adding a pair of sunglasses as an afterthought. He had them rolled up just in case somebody was watching him and returned to Rougetel on the third lorry.

"I forgot to ask you," he said. "Did you come here yesterday afternoon to ask what time we should be starting?"

"Me? No. Why should I? You undertook the negotiations, I did not interfere. Why?"

"Only wondered," said Hambledon and strolled away again. So he had been followed here also; the two Middle Europeans must have improved their methods considerably since they used to dog the wretched Goertz round Stockholm, or more probably they employed some other man he would not recognize. If so, the man might be here now, looking at him. One of that group at the corner, for instance.

Tommy hopped into the first lorry, got inside and sat down upon the floor just as the belated Jean arrived, running. The convoy moved off.

It was an uneventful trip for the first two days. The lorries rolled on, unresting—except at night—and unhasting southward across France. Brihou unfolded his philosophy and talked about his boy. Hambledon, barely recognizable in his peaked hat and dust coat, sunglasses and a two-day beard, took turns in driving the leading lorry or dozed and smoked in the cabin beside the driver. All too often they had tire trouble and all hands—except Rougetel—got out and helped. Hambledon became rapidly grubbier and still less recognizable, also his French was acquiring a strong Breton accent. Tommy collected accents as lesser men collect birds' eggs or corporation enamelled-iron notices.

Early on the third day they topped a rise and looked across an immense plain, admirably decked with trees, rivers, towns and other accessories of rural France. The plain extended far into the distance where a faint blue cloud lay upon the southern horizon.

"Les Landes," said Brihou, indicating the plain. "Down there, that river, that's the Garonne. Far away, as far as M'sieu can see, the mountains. *Les Pyrénées*, m'sieu."

As they went forward the blue cloud became more solid and also higher, it rose before them into a jagged wall even when still very far off. Hambledon, who had not previously visited that part of France, was very impressed.

"To surmount that, one would say that it was necessary to fly," he remarked.

"No, no," said Brihou. "There are passes. One drives over in comfort—providing one's papers are in order."

"And suppose they are not?"

"Then one exercises more energy and walks, but not along the roads, m'sieu. It is very pleasant, to walk in the mountains. So they say, I have never done it, me. I have neither the leisure nor the figure, as M'sieu sees. One ruins one's health with the sedentary existence, but what would you? A man must live and there must be lorry drivers."

Hambledon was about to reply when a large open Lancia car, with two men in it, overtook them; the man sitting next the driver turned in his seat and looked back at the lorry without the faintest sign of recognition in his face. Hambledon sat like a statue and watched them go on ahead and disappear round a bend in the road. Wenezky was driving; the man who was scanning the lorries was Olgar.

"Caught us up at last," said Tommy to himself. "Now what happens?"

A couple of miles farther along the road he saw the Lancia again; it was pulled up at the side of the road while the driver and his passenger were ostensibly looking inside the bonnet. They both glanced up as the first lorry went by, but without interest; Wenezky looked back along the road they had come for the next lorry to come into view. Brihou's convoy did not keep station with the precision of military vehicles, it straggled over a distance of a mile or more, and one of Hambledon's duties was to look back at frequent intervals to see if vehicles were all present and correct. Rougetel, who was still wearing the same clothes in which he had left Paris, and upon whose beard the exigencies of travel had little effect, was sitting beside the driver of number three, in full view of any onlooker.

Presently the Lancia overtook them again and a little later still, on a particularly lonely stretch, they passed it once more, stopped, with driver and passenger standing by it.

"Those gentlemen have a little trouble, it would seem," said Brihou.

"A little trouble is certainly suggested by their demeanor," said Tommy smoothly.

The lorry came over the crest of a hill and entered upon a long downward slope.

"This is where we save petrol," said Brihou. He put his gear lever into neutral and switched off the engine; they rolled forward in a sudden silence occupied only by the swish of the tires on the road. Tommy glanced back; the second lorry was just coming into view.

"Another twenty miles," said Brihou, "and we are— Blessed Virgin! What was that?"

The noise he had heard was a loud metallic crash accompanied by sounds of sliding and splintering.

"That's a car crash," said Brihou anxiously, and he brought his lorry to a standstill. "Though whether it is some other car or one of my lorries—"

The second van in the convoy slid to a stop behind them, the driver leapt out and came running to Brihou's side.

"It will be one of ours," he gasped, "there was no other car within sight when I topped the rise bar the Lancia on the roadside—"

"I will turn and go back," said Brihou, and his front wheels were turning into the middle of the road when there came a long blast from a horn behind and a shout of warning from the second driver. Brihou stopped and the big touring car, which they had seen four times already, came roaring down the road gathering speed on the gradient and flashed past within inches of their radiator.

"I have his number," said Tommy quietly and the second driver shook his fist and called them murderers and brigands. Brihou turned in the road and went back over the crest of the rise.

The third lorry had run off the road down a steep bank and overturned; it was blazing furiously and a thick column of black smoke rose heavily in the air and drifted away towards Bordeaux. The fourth vehicle in the convoy was pulled up near by and its driver was leaping agonizedly about the wreckage with a small fire extinguisher. Tommy reached another from its bracket just behind him as Brihou reached the spot; they both jumped out and ran towards the blaze.

"Careful," gasped Brihou, "he was carrying the spare petrol."

Tommy directed the jet from his extinguisher upon the cabin of the wrecked lorry and kept the flames back while Brihou and his driver dragged out the body of Jean le Mari. Rougetel they could see but not reach; he was obviously dead, it was plain that he had fallen out and the lorry had rolled on him. Another petrol can inside burst with the heat, the flames roared up again and their efforts were clearly useless. The three men retired, dragging the body of Jean with them.

"What happened, in the name of God?" said Brihou. "Did you see the accident?"

"I was some way behind," said the driver of the fourth lorry. "I came round that bend just in time to see Jean turn off the road, crash down the bank and roll over. Then the car which was standing just here started up and drove quickly away. I think Jean must have had a burst tire, *patron.*"

"Strange that I didn't hear it," said Brihou, "did you, m'sieu?"

"No," said Tommy, who was bending over Jean's body. "Come here a moment. See that? That's a bullet wound. He was shot through the head."

Brihou straightened up, threw down his cap and shook his fists in the air.

"This was no accident, my friends. This is murder." He paused for a moment and added: "And those scoundrels in the Lancia did it."

"I agree," said Hambledon.

"The police," urged the other driver. "And who will tell his wife?"

"You will remain here and guard the wreckage," said Brihou. "Chicot in the other van will drive on to Auch and tell our friends that we are delayed, and M'sieu and I will go at once and inform the police about"—he drew a long sobbing breath—"this abominable outrage, this devil-inspired brutality." He became so increasingly Breton that his later comments were lost upon Hambledon.

"Calmness," urged Tommy. "Calmness and dignity. Speed also, lest the foul perpetrators make good their escape."

"M'sieu is right, as always," said Brihou, ceasing to wave his arms in the air and leading the way back to his lorry.

"Is your vehicle insured?" asked Hambledon.

"No, m'sieu. And if it were, would they pay out on a murder?"

They drove to the next village, Ste-Marie-en-Marais, and informed the police that a murder had been committed and valuable property destroyed—to wit, one lorry—by two men, whose description was supplied by Hambledon, in a Lancia open touring car number so-and-so, last seen heading south from the scene of the crime at approximately twenty minutes past sixteen hours. They probably passed through this village.

"They did," said the policeman gloomily. "I saw the car myself. It was being driven with a recklessness to terrify. I myself had to leap for the hedge accompanied by the female goat of *M'sieu le Curé.*" He took up the telephone and spoke earnestly with his nearest superiors.

When the conversation was finished, he said that the superintendent was coming at once and would be obliged if the gentlemen would wait in the station for the few minutes until he should arrive.

"But, certainly," said Brihou. "It is inevitable." He leaned back in his chair and stared gloomily out of the window.

"These murders," said Tommy in an exasperated voice, "are they really necessary?"

Chapter Nine
Duck Gun

The superintendent of police visited the scene of the accident, where the lorry was still burning steadily, having collapsed into a heap of unrecognizable debris. The body of Rougetel was somewhere underneath it and could no longer be seen. Any papers which he was carrying would certainly be completely destroyed including, to Hambledon's relief, the dummy packet. It had served its turn but it would not have survived for ten minutes in the hands of any man who knew what it was all about and the code in which it was supposed to be written. Those samples, too—Hambledon had, in point of fact, thought out several hopeful schemes for depriving Rougetel of his packet before it could be put to the proof. The fire had saved him the trouble.

The superintendent, who was a man of decision, looked at the blaze for a moment and then sent for the nearest fire brigade.

"Even when it is extinguished," he said, "the debris will be too hot to touch for some time. Let us, therefore, utilize the period of waiting for the accumulation of evidence. To the police station, messieurs, if you please!"

Hambledon did not like police investigations unless he was on the side of the police, but there was no help for it. The evidence was all perfectly straightforward until it came to the question of Rougetel's identity. Brihou told the police that he himself knew nothing about the poor gentleman except that he was a friend of this gentleman here, who would doubtless provide all the information required.

The superintendent then turned to Tommy, who gave his own name and showed his own passport. Happily the Department of Gers had never heard of Thomas Elphinstone Hambledon, and since his papers were all in order no interest was aroused. Tommy said that he was a retired schoolmaster on holiday, and since expense was a matter he had to consider carefully, he had been advised to take this method of touring France. *"Ah, la belle France, m'sieu!* It has always been my dream—"

The superintendent, as representing France at the moment, bowed his acknowledgments.

"You speak our language," he said, "with, for an Englishman, a fluency and purity of the most impeccable."

"My life's study," said Tommy, with touching simplicity.

"My felicitations, m'sieu—"

"My good fortune in my teachers—"

"Now, as regards your friend. His name?"

Hambledon did not want Rougetel's death announced in the papers. One never knew. His face assumed an expression of mournful resignation.

"A very dear old friend of mine," he said. "A colleague. Charles Denton by name. He lived at a place called Blackheath, near London. He taught history."

After that it was easy, and Hambledon gave every detail about his friend which the most conscientious policeman could desire. If the French police ever took the trouble to check the information in London Charles could just deny it with every circumstance of authority, Hambledon would be far away by that time, and all would be well.

By the time the enquiry was finished it was night, and the superintendent said that they would return in the morning to examine the wreckage by daylight.

"The poor M'sieu Denton," he said, "is beyond human aid. More respect can be exhibited in the removal of his remains when we can see what we are doing. The body of the driver, Jean le Mari as you call him, will remain in the mortuary for the night. Rest assured, m'sieu, that every effort will be made for the apprehension of the miscreants. Accept, m'sieu, the renewed assurances of my most profound sympathy. The enquiry will be reopened at an early date and the attendance of all the witnesses will be required. Until tomorrow, messieurs."

"So we remain here," grumbled Brihou when he was out of earshot, "while the police run round on their misshapen feet looking for two brigands who are over the Spanish frontier by this time. As though one could not pay honor to the dead without wasting the valuable time of the living. Every day my lorries are not earning—"

Hambledon led him away to the village inn and stood him a drink.

The inn was roomy and reasonably comfortable; Hambledon, Brihou and the driver who saw the crash could all be accommodated there for the night. They had a meal which was rough but sufficient, after which the driver went into the public bar for a drink while Brihou sat with Tommy in the inn parlor over a bottle of the local wine. Hambledon grew sleepy and yawned, an example which infected Brihou.

"It is our jaws which tell us it is bedtime," said the black marketeer. "The day also has been exhausting and tragic. Nevertheless I shall lie awake wondering how to write the sad tidings to the wife of Jean le Mari."

"She is, perhaps, religious?" suggested Tommy.

"No doubt that will afford her consolation," agreed Brihou.

"No doubt. The thought, however, which occurred to me was that her parish priest was the man to—"

"To go and tell her! But M'sieu in inspired! He has the *métier diplomatique!* The old Father Ambrose, it is for him. I thank M'sieu, I shall now retire to my couch and sleep like the innocent baby without a care for ten hours and as much longer as the blue-nosed police—"

There was a yell from the bar next door, and it was the voice of Brihou's driver. "The assassins! Apprehend them! Police! Police!"

Brihou and Hambledon made a rush at the connecting door; Brihou, being nearest, reached it first. He lifted the latch, but at that moment there came the crack of a revolver and a bullet came through the door just above his hand and missed Hambledon's head by inches. Brihou, with great presence of mind, dropped the latch again and bolted the door instead of opening it.

When Olgar and Wenezky had finished with Kenrade in Rotterdam, they went carefully through the house looking for the packet though not really expecting to find it. They assumed that Hambledon had taken it with him, but anything in the way of loot would be acceptable. After all, Kenrade had no further use for worldly possessions. They found quite a lot of money, which pleased them, and a few papers of no particular importance. They divided the money between them, tossed for Kenrade's wristwatch—Wenezky won—and started for Paris. After Hambledon left Le Petit Enfer they followed him to his hotel, watched him go in, and held a conference.

"Let us enter the hotel," urged Wenezky. "Hotels are easy. We will cut his throat and take the packet."

"Not so," said the cautious Olgar. "He may not, now, have the packet with him. He may have handed it to the bearded man who is probably Rougetel."

"Or one of the other two."

"No. They are only strong-arm men. Alexis told me about them. They are well known in Paris. No, if the so-called Hambledon has not got it, Rougetel has. We made a mistake there in both following Hambledon, one of us should have followed Rougetel."

"What do you, then, suggest?"

"We will put Alexis on to follow Hambledon, he will not be recognized. Then we shall see."

Hambledon had guessed right, it was a man whom he didn't know who had followed him round Paris until he found Brihou. Alexis went back to Olgar and reported.

"He has arranged passage for himself and friend in a lorry convoy going to the South of France."

"And friend," repeated Olgar thoughtfully. "That should be Rougetel. They will go together to this place of meeting, wherever it is."

"Let us now find Rougetel," said Wenezky, "and deal with both of them before they leave Paris."

"One of these days," said Olgar angrily, "you will do something so excessively silly that you will be arrested and hanged by a newborn constable on his very first beat. Will you never learn to respect the French police? No. We will buy a fast car and follow them to some unfrequented spot. There, we can act. Not in Paris. When do they start, Alexis?"

Alexis went to Brihou that afternoon and tried to find out; he failed, as will be remembered, because Brihou did not then know himself.

"You will go back and watch until they do start, then you will come back and tell us. We can easily pick them up on the road, we know the numbers of those lorries."

When Alexis reported the convoy under way, he added that Hambledon's friend was a nervous little man with gold-rimmed spectacles and a short brown beard turning gray.

"Rougetel," said Olgar. "What did I tell you?"

They had a good deal more trouble in tailing the convoy than they had anticipated. For one thing, the friends of black marketeers do not babble to total strangers who do not look like customers. The proprietor of a filling station near Tours told his wife about it.

"They asked me," he said indignantly, "whether I had seen such-and-such lorries pass by. Brihou's lorries, in effect. Two men, strangers, in a Lancia Lambda long-chassis model, how do I know who they were? They were not even French, their manner of speech was of the most barbarous. Did I reply? I said I had never seen the convoy they described. We of the Resistance—"

However, Olgar and Wenezky picked up their quarry at last and chose an unfrequented stretch of road to overhaul it. Hambledon they did not recognize, they took him for a spare driver, but Rougetel was unmistakable.

"They are together, of course. Probably Hambledon is inside the lorry, asleep," said Wenezky. "The fourth lorry is lagging behind, if we are quick we can do our business and be gone before he comes up. You are the better shot, you shoot Rougetel when they approach. The lorry will stop and we will attend to them."

But Olgar shot the driver by mistake and the lorry, instead of stopping, went off the road and burst into flames. Moreover, the driver of the fourth lorry had a spasm of conscience and put on speed to catch up; he appeared before they expected him. Wenezky wanted to stay and fight it out, but Olgar leaped for the Lancia and drove off, Wenezky just scrambling in as she started.

"The trouble with you," said Wenezky with justice, "is that you lose your head in moments of crisis. You plan, you think ahead, you consider all possibilities, I grant you that. I could not do it. But when the moment arrives, where are you? In flight."

"That is why we are still alive," said Olgar, and they argued the point so hotly that they never saw the constable of Ste-Marie-en-Marais leap for the hedge in company with the female goat of *Monsieur le Curé.*

"But the finality of the day's work," said Wenezky, "is that we do not now know who is dead and who is alive, nor where the packet is."

"Then we will go back to the nearest village to the scene of the accident," said Olgar, "and find out. The simple peasantry in the inn will be full of the story. We have but to drink a glass and listen and we shall know it all."

"But they will be looking out for us," objected Wenezky.

"Who will? One country policeman?"

"All the police. They know our number."

"Change it, then," said Olgar. "We will wait until it is dark. Also the police do not know us by sight. We will leave the car outside the village and walk in. What is its name? Give me the map."

"But the men on the convoy," said Wenezky, handing him the map.

"They are in Auch. They end the run there, Alexis said so. They will make their depositions to the police and then go home, it is only twenty miles. They can return for the enquiry. Why should they stay in a one-shop village—where is it—ah, I have it. Ste.-Marie-en-Marais. Besides, if we see them we do not go in."

"Very well," said Wenezky, but he was only half convinced.

When it grew dark they drove the Lancia back through winding lanes to the outskirts of Ste.-Marie-en-Marais and left it in the entrance to an orchard. They strolled through the village, keeping in the shadows, and found the inn without difficulty. The window of the parlor in which Hambledon and Brihou had spent the evening looked out on a yard at the back, but the public bar had two uncurtained windows and an open door upon the village street, and lights shone cheerfully from them all. No song floated out on the night air, only the sound of voices in discussion. The two outside listened for a few minutes, encountering their first difficulty.

"What language are they talking?" asked Wenezky. "It does not make sense to me."

"It is, no doubt, a country dialect," said Olgar patronizingly. "Our peasants at home speak among themselves a language no gentleman would think of understanding."

"But it is necessary that we should understand this."

"When we go in and speak with them they will take pains to express themselves more correctly. Let us look in at the window and see if any of the convoy are present."

It so happened that the driver of the fourth lorry was sitting on a bench against the wall between the two windows, and all that Wenezky or Olgar could see of him was his legs from the knees downwards, one hand holding a wineglass, and the back of his head when he stooped forward to knock out his pipe against his boot. Otherwise the company present were all local men with the stamp of agricultural laborers the world over, and one ancient by the fireplace in the clothes his father had worn for Sunday best in the time of the Second Empire and an extraordinary top hat which he never removed except in church.

"There, you see," said Olgar. "What did I tell you? None but the local country bumpkins. Let us go in."

They strolled in through the open door and immediately the conversation ceased in the bar while everybody stared at the strangers. They wore expressions of surprised delight, like tourists who have come upon the unexpectedly quaint. They smiled widely, like little Red Riding Hood's grandmother's wolf. They did not, at first, look at the faces of those present—having already seen them through the window—they looked about them at the ancient room; the cavernous fireplace where a great pot hung upon a gallows within the chimney breast; the age-blackened rafters from which hung strings of onions and bunches of garlic and herbs; the uneven walls, grimy with the rubbing of many shoulders; the shelves of bottles behind the bar and the casks of wine upon it.

"I say, friend, what a charming pub," said Olgar in his atrocious French.

"Look," said Wenezky, "oak beams," and his French was worse than Olgar's. "I say, is not all this truly Old World?"

"Behold you the pot over the fire," said Olgar. "What have you in it, landlord? Soup of hares and pheasants and ducks, yes?"

"Water," said the landlord nervously, for he was quite sure that they were mad. "Only water."

"Water," said Olgar, with a cackle of laughter. "We are not interested in water. Wine, landlord, a glass of your best wine, and we wish you to partake also. All these gentlemen in the room, too. Let us all be comrades together. Do not keep silent because we come in. Let talk and laughter ring, do not be shy. We are not haughty, we are men who like good company. Come, old ances—" he stumbled over the word and substituted *dudushka*—"in the corner, wine warms old bones."

Still the landlord stared open-mouthed and the company sat as though paralyzed.

"They want money," said Wenezky in his own tongue. "To pay for the drinks."

"Ha!" cried Olgar. "You want to see the color of my coinage, as we say? Quite right, here it is." He slapped a handful of loose change down on the bar counter. "Now, landlord—"

Then at last, suddenly, someone moved. There was a crash behind them as the man who had been sitting between the windows dropped his glass, leapt to his feet and yelled: *"Les assassins! Les assassins! Police! Police!"*

He sprang towards them and stopped abruptly as revolvers appeared, like a conjuring trick, in their hands. Hambledon and Brihou, in the next room, rushed towards the door, the landlord disappeared behind his bar, one or two of the more agile customers bolted out and cries of "Police! One makes a murder! Police!" awoke the drowsy street. The landlord came up again and hurled his bung mallet at Olgar, it hit him on the shoulder. He turned like a flash and fired a round at the landlord; it went through the door behind and changed Brihou's mind for him. The lorry driver profited by the diversion to jump at what looked like a cupboard door and dive inside; it was not a cupboard, for his feet clattered up a wooden staircase and a door slammed overhead. There followed a piercing feminine scream.

"My daughter!" said the landlord, knocked the neck off a bottle and jumped over the counter with his horrible weapon in his hand; Wenezky shot him through the shoulder and he fell. Hambledon and Brihou in the next room opened the window and dropped out into the yard. But it was dark and the gate, when they found it, was locked, they had to scramble over it.

"Now then, dogs, back against that wall," said Olgar, herding the remaining customers against the partition farthest from the door. But the ancient in the top hat, mumbling furiously, tottered out at the door and broke into a palsied trot past the windows. Wenezky laughed.

"The old one has gone to take the air," he said.

"Listen, dogs," said Olgar, "you stand there and do not dare to move. Moritz, to the door." Wenezky obeyed as a fresh pandemonium broke out overhead when two voices in duet bayed from the bedroom window above. Apparently the driver had made friends with the landlord's daughter, for she was helping him to scream.

Hambledon and Brihou dropped over the gate somehow and immediately became entangled in what felt like an iron trellis with spikes but was actually a harrow. Brihou's remarks were such that Hambledon missed his footing and fell into something soft that splashed. When they did eventually turn the corner of the house they saw, in the light from the windows, a figure from a drawing by George

Du Maurier. It held in its arms something like a long tube which it poked through a windowpane, aimed, and fired. This time there was a really resounding bang and the landlord's daughter's shrieks were duplicated all down the street.

"Oh, cat of my sacred aunt," said Tommy, "he's brought the duck gun."

Wenezky, clearly visible in the lights from the bar parlor, leaped out of the doorway and passed them, running furiously down the road until his footsteps died away in the distance.

"Funny," said Tommy to himself, "where's Brother Olgar?"

"I got him," squeaked the ancient, waving his gun, "I got him, I got him, I got him—"

Hambledon looked in at the window to see the three or four men still in the bar supporting the landlord, who had struggled to his feet. They were all looking down at an object on the floor of which they were no longer afraid, for Olgar had received the whole charge of the duck gun full in the chest. The stairs door opened and the lorry driver appeared, behind him a girl with black hair streaming down her back and a shawl thrown inadequately over her nightdress. They also stood and stared, and no one spoke.

"Quite a tableau, is it not?" said Tommy cheerfully.

Chapter Ten
Hero of Waaterloo

The police came to the inn of Ste.-Marie-en-Marais and made enquiry into the death of Olgar. He was identified as being one of the two men concerned in the wrecking of Brihou's lorry, but no evidence as to personal identity was offered, not even by Hambledon. There was also an official enquiry into the deaths of Jean le Mari and Rougetel. There was the grisly business of recovering the remnants of Rougetel from under the wrecked lorry and the question of their disposal.

"M'sieu would no doubt wish to take back the body of his friend for interment in the family tomb?"

M'sieu definitely didn't. Hambledon got out of it by saying that his poor friend had had a French grandmother and had always expressed a wish to be interred in the sacred soil of France and now, if ever, was his chance.

"Without doubt, m'sieu, but—"

"And it will be my melancholy privilege to pay what is needful. I am not a rich man, but the claims of a friendship almost fraternal—"

"It is understood. Dignified, but simple. Absolutely."

Hambledon paid and hoped the department would refund him. He then rang up Hyde at Auch.

"All these enquiries," said Tommy, after giving a brief outline of events, "all these questions and depositions and examination of witnesses look like going on for weeks. I can't have that, you know."

"No," said Hyde, "of course not. Besides, it's such a bore for you. Can't I bring the car and meet you somewhere and we can talk things over?"

"You can bring the car and take me away," said Hambledon, "we can talk afterwards. Listen. Do you know this place? The village, I mean, not specially the pub."

"I don't, but there's no reason why I shouldn't drive out and look at it. There's nothing remarkable in wanting to see a place where such exciting events have occurred. I expect there'll be lots of sightseers there soon, they've done you proud in the local paper."

"They have, have they? I haven't seen one yet," said Hambledon. "What do they say?"

"Oh, what you'd expect. Shocking deed of brigandage, cruel and inexplicable act of murder, and so on."

"Yes, but did they mention our names?"

"Oh, rather," said Hyde. "One of the victims was a certain Mr. Charles Denton—I say, that gave me a turn, as they say—"

"Sorry, that was only me being discreet. Did they mention me by name?"

"Oh yes. A certain Mr. Hambledon, a retired schoolmaster, who was touring France with his friend Mr. Denton, was fortunate in that he happened to be travelling in one of the other lorries at the time or he might otherwise have shared the lamentable fate of his unfortunate companion. I made it all out quite well, French is pretty easy to read, it's the pronunciation that—"

"That's torn it," said Tommy slowly.

"My pronunciation?"

"No. Putting my name in the paper. I don't doubt that Wenezky can read French though he talks it so badly. He now knows that I am still alive. A pity. That he knows it, I mean. Where is a place where they don't have local papers?"

"Eh?"

"Because that's where Olgar and Wenezky come from. You see, there's no doubt they came back to Ste.-Marie-en-Marais to find out what, exactly, had happened and who was killed in the crash, and the result was that Olgar got himself bumped off by Great-grandpapa with a fowling piece. If they'd had the sense to sit tight in Auch or wherever they went, and just buy themselves a newspaper in the morning, Olgar would be alive now."

"Well, we don't want him, do we?" said Hyde cheerfully.

"How more than right. Well, to return to your getting me away. Come straight up the road from Auch, and about a mile before you get here there's a turning to your left—turning west, that is—it isn't signposted but there are two splendid sweet chestnut trees on either side of the turning. You can't mistake it. Have a good look at it and make sure you can find it in the dark. Then you can come on here, indulge your morbid taste for horrors, and go away again. At 3 A.M. tomorrow morning I will meet you by the chestnut trees and we will drive in the general direction of

Spain. Better turn the car into the lane and put the lights out in case you have to
wait, you don't want to be seen. Got that?"

"Yes, thank you," said Hyde rather doubtfully.

"What's the matter?"

"I take it you are going to slip out in the middle of the night and walk along, all
alone, to meet me."

"Quite right," said Tommy. "I say, I like that phrase of yours, 'walk along, all
alone,' it sounds like a song."

"Yes, but suppose Wenezky is hanging about looking for you?"

"Not so like a song. Well, I shall have to look out for him, shan't I? Thanks for
the tip. Well, I'll see you at 3 A.M. by the chestnut trees. If I'm not there by four,
go back, I'm not coming."

Wenezky did indeed read French and the contents of the local paper interested
him extremely. Hambledon, then, had escaped, and might or might not have the
packet with him. It was possible it had been destroyed with Rougetel; if so, it
was even more necessary than before to keep in touch with Hambledon, who was
known to be traveling to attend a conference, as it were, upon the subject of that
packet. If Wenezky could not get the packet itself, as instructed, he might at least
get some information about it. The local paper did not say where Hambledon was
staying, whether he was still at Ste.-Marie-en-Marais or had come on to Auch
where Wenezky himself was living in studied obscurity. Plainly, the only thing to
do was to go to Ste.-Marie-en-Marais and see if he could pick up any information.
A disguise would be necessary, too many people at the inn had seen his face that
night when Olgar died. He would have to hire a taxi also, the too recognizable
Lancia had been left in the depths of a wood.

Ste.-Marie-en-Marais had more visitors that afternoon than even the ancient in
the top hat could remember; their annual Fête Marie itself never brought so many
strangers. Cars drove through the village on their way to the wreck of the lorry
and returned to draw up outside the inn while their occupants inspected a nasty red
stain on the floor and demanded authoritative details from eyewitnesses. Great-
grandpapa's story began by being terse, grew rapidly more picturesque and ended
in incoherent burbles, after which he was removed by a middle-aged granddaughter
and put to bed. The landlord's stock of wine was sold out, hastily replenished from
Auch and sold out again. There was a box under the landlord's bed upstairs in which
the meager contents of the till were nightly stored; on this great day the takings
poured in so fast that the box itself grew heavy and the landlord's wife gave up
serving to go and sit upon it like a broody hen guarding her chicks.

Among the cars which came that day was a taxi from Auch, a good taxi, Jules
Arcache's pride and joy. He had bought it with the proceeds of a lucky ticket in
a state lottery, and it was to be the foundation of his fortunes. He was lucky in
his passenger too, a foreigner as could be told by the exceedingly bad French he
spoke. The poor gentleman had been ill, some malady of the lungs; it was necessary

for him to be wrapped in scarves to the ears and over his mouth and to keep his hat drawn down over his eyes. He coughed most alarmingly at intervals and one would have thought him old by his careful uncertain walk though his dark eyes, what one could see of them, were bright and clear enough and his voice strong and resonant as a young man's. Rather a mysterious person, in fact, but Arcache could put up with a lot of mystery from a man who cheerfully paid double the normal fare. Actually, Wenezky was very well off for money, thanks largely to Kenrade's thrifty ways, and he could not argue about the price because he had to go to Ste-Marie-en-Marais whatever it cost.

Wenezky was not very interested in the wreck of the lorry, he said he had seen wrecked cars before and one burnt-out lorry looked very like another. He said that this account of the fracas at the inn was much more amusing and he would like to see the place where "your veteran of Waterloo" fired the gun through the window.

"But, Waterloo, m'sieu!"

"Sedan, then. Is he on view, the old hero?"

Arcache said that they would stop at the inn and find out. Unfortunately they did not get there until after the ancient had sunk beneath the many tributes offered him, in glasses, by his admirers. Arcache returned to the car and reported this to his invalid passenger. "The gun, however, is on view. But a veritable cannon, m'sieu! No wonder that the miserable assassin was blown, in effect, in two."

Wenezky coughed violently and croaked that a glass of wine would do him good and that Arcache also might be thirsty. Arcache concurred and went in to fetch Wenezky's drink. When he came back with it Wenezky asked whether any members of the convoy party were still there, the *patron* Brihou, for example, or even the Englishman who had lost his friend. Arcache said he would find out, and disappeared once more within the hospitable door.

Wenezky sipped his wine and looked about him. Most of the cars parked near him were of French or Italian make with a few German Opels; since British cars had not been exported for six years they were not yet common on the roads of France. There was one, however, only a few yards from his taxi, a decorous gray Austin saloon with a driver who was unmistakably English in appearance, a respectable middle-aged man with fair hair turning gray and a kindly humorous face. He was talking to a chance acquaintance in his halting French about the advantages of mobile police on motorcycles to check brigandage on the King's highway, a phrase which, literally translated, puzzled the other man. *"Chemin du Roi?* Who, then, is King of the road?"

"In England," began Hyde, and corrected himself. *"En Angleterre nous disons—"*

"Ah! But M'sieu is English! The roads in England, then, are they the perquisite of the King?"

Hyde did his best to explain, but Wenezky did not listen, he was busy thinking. This Englishman was simply too English for words; queer as those islanders were, nobody could really be so Britannic as that. Neat gray suit inconspicuously striped, neat gray Austin car, laborious school French, strange idioms literally translated—*"chemin du Roi"* indeed!—GB plate beside the English number on his car, the fellow was larger than life size. His appearance shouted "Look at me, I'm English!" What a good disguise for anyone wishing to travel through France who otherwise would not be allowed to travel through France—a German, for instance. Wenezky had by nature a violent but simple mind and had relied upon Olgar for the subtler finesses of life. Now that he was deprived of Olgar and had to think for himself he went to the other extreme and became more tortuous than any corkscrew. This Englishman was a sham, and he had come to the place where there was another sham Englishman calling himself Hambledon. Coincidence my onion, there must be a connection. Wenezky was perfectly right, even a corkscrew comes to the point at last.

"Moreover," he said to himself, "the convoy does not go beyond Auch. Is it reasonable to suppose that these German technicians, some of them probably quite well known, are going to hold a conference at Auch? No. Therefore 'Hambledon' will have arranged for transport beyond Auch. Is not this, then, the transport?"

He glowed with the happy consciousness of being even cleverer than he had thought; the only thing that pained him was that there was no one to whom he could display his mental brilliance. However, that would keep. He lit a cigarette and went on thinking.

It was fairly obvious by now where his quarry was going, in fact Olgar had pointed it out as soon as it was clear that Hambledon and Rougetel were not going to Bordeaux. They were going to Spain; the only country, as Tommy had remarked, where the gentle Nazi can still gambol. Wenezky would have agreed with the remark. He memorized the Austin's number, took careful note of Hyde's appearance, and waited.

Presently Arcache returned, saying that he was sorry that none of the convoy party were available. M. Brihou, the owner, had gone to spend the day with friends in Auch, the Englishman had gone out for a walk with *M'sieu le Curé*, and nobody knew where the driver was. They would all be in Ste-Marie-en-Marais on the following morning as *M'sieu le Juge d'Instruction* was coming out from Auch to resume the enquiry.

Wenezky nodded carelessly and said it didn't matter. He added, as one who changes a boring subject, that that was a nice little Austin over there, wasn't it?

Arcache said it was, he had driven one himself at one time. Good cars of the utmost reliability, but himself, he preferred something with a little more of the devil. A Hispano-Suiza, for example.

"It is time that we returned," said Wenezky, adjusting the wraps round his throat, "the evening draws on."

"At once, m'sieu," said Arcache, and drove him carefully home. He knew a good fare when he saw one.

On the following afternoon the local paper came out with a special edition, for there was a piece of startling news for its readers besides the account of the official enquiry. There were headlines. "The Outrage at Ste.-Marie-en-Marais. Further Startling Development. The Englishman, where is he? Kidnapped or Murdered?

"When the eminent *Juge d'Instruction* opened the enquiry this morning into the recent outrages at and near the charming and picturesque village of Ste-Marie-en-Marais, the Englishman, M. Hambledon, whose friend was killed in the lorry disaster, was called as a witness. He was, however, not to be found, and enquiry established the fact that his bed had not been occupied, though no one at the inn where he was staying had heard any disturbance during the night. Several credible witnesses testified that M. Hambledon had said that he would certainly give the police every aid in his power that would assist in the capture of the surviving brigand; *M. le Curé,* in particular, stating that M. Hambledon had spent a large part of the previous day in his company, and had announced his intention of giving evidence on the following day; that he regarded the Englishman as being a man of the highest honor, probity and decorum and that it was inconceivable to him that the gentleman should have avoided his public duty in such a manner except under the pressure of some irresistible and, he must add, sinister circumstance. The gravest anxiety is consequently entertained for the safety of the Englishman whose good sense, friendly manner and recent bereavement have aroused the sympathy and respect of all who met him.

"The first witness to be called . . ." etc.

Wenezky read this in the privacy of his bedroom, smote the paper with his fist and uttered several Middle European curses.

"He has escaped," he concluded correctly. "Now, where is the gray Austin?"

He had remained in such discreet seclusion since his arrival in Auch that he had made only two acquaintances, the widow woman his landlady, who was almost totally deaf, and the taxi driver Arcache. Wenezky rolled off the bed, put on his eclipsing scarves, and went to see Arcache.

"Let M'sieu be welcome! And how is his health?"

"Better, thanks, much better. Arcache, I wish a little enquiry made and I think you are the man to make it."

"Speak, m'sieu."

"You remember the gray Austin at Ste-Marie last night? I admired it, if you remember. Well, I have been thinking about it and I should like to buy it."

"But—"

"You said it was steady and reliable but had not enough devil in it for your taste. But I am no longer so young as I was," said Wenezky, wilting artistically, "and in my opinion a car is no place for devils. I should like to complete my convalescence by driving myself quietly from place to place as the fancy takes me, in a sober quiet car like this Austin. Now, if you can suggest any means by which this car could be traced and the name of the owner ascertained—"

"But," broke in Arcache, "if M'sieu wishes a quiet car of the utmost reliability, I have a friend who—"

"I want the Austin," said Wenezky peevishly. "Listen, Arcache. I am a sick man, and sick men have fancies. I am also a rich man and can indulge them. If you can put me in touch with the owner of this car I will see that you are not the loser."

Arcache gave in at once. Let the gentleman leave it to him and the utmost should be done. Already he had several ideas which would no doubt prove fruitful. Let the gentleman have no care, the Austin would be traced if it were still upon this earth. He, Jules Arcache, charged himself with that.

"It is well," said Wenezky, and gave him five hundred francs. "For the expenses, merely," he explained.

Arcache said that the gentleman was doubtless a prince in his own land and Wenezky went away. The taxi driver stood himself a drink for luck, provided himself with plenty of small change and went to the telephone. He rang up the owners of garages he knew personally or by name in a circle round Auch and told each of them the same story.

"Jules Arcache of Auch speaking. Is that the So-and-So garage? Yes, well, listen. I've got a mug here who wants to buy an Austin—no, I don't suppose you have. He doesn't want just any Austin, he wants one we saw on the road yesterday, a gray saloon—" Arcache added technical details including the number. "Carrying a GB plate and driven by a man who looks like an Englishman. If you could help me to find it there'd be a bit in it for you. You haven't seen it? Oh. Well, can you suggest anyone else I can ring up?"

The fourth call struck oil. Hyde had stopped for petrol at Mirande, south of Auch, early that morning, and the gray car had been seen standing outside a hotel for some little time after that. For breakfast, presumably. No, they didn't know the owner's name, why should they? And which of the two gentlemen was the owner? How were they to know?

"Two gentlemen?" said Arcache. "I only saw one and he looked like an Englishman."

"They were both English. Sorry, I don't know which way they went. Try Moteurs Modernes at Tarbes."

Handed on from one to another, at the end of nearly two hours' solid telephoning Arcache had traced the Austin to the village of Haut Vannes on the slopes of the Pyrenees and only five miles from the Spanish frontier. The car was there, the speaker had seen it drive into the yard of the Green Monkey, the best inn the place possessed, yes, a good inn, distinguished for its wines of Navarre. The baggage had been carried in with the two gentlemen following. Without doubt they were staying there.

"You shall hear from me again," said the triumphant Arcache. "It will be well for you."

He put down the telephone, rubbed his aching ear and dashed off to tell Wenezky.

"They are at Haut Vannes, staying at an inn, and the car is there also."

"They? Who is 'they'?"

"Two Englishmen."

Wenezky drew a long breath.

Chapter Eleven
At the Green Monkey

The hotel of the Singe Vert at Haut Vannes was a survival from an age when war along the frontier was a living menace. Its walls were of stone several feet thick and one or two windows which had not been modernized were still mere slits, but clematis masked the grim walls and reached up to the swinging sign where the Green Monkey, a paintpot in one hand and a brush in the other, admired himself in a gilt-framed mirror. The parlor was a long low room with wide windows looking up to the mountains and admitting the sun, the bedroom above it which Hyde and Hambledon shared looked north across the immense plain; both apartments were spotlessly clean and sparsely provided with oaken furniture black with age. Hyde stood in the bedroom and looked eagerly about him.

"There's no doubt about it," he said. "Travel does broaden your mind."

"Are you referring to the sanitary arrangements?" asked Tommy.

"No," said Hyde seriously. "To the eiderdowns, if that's what they call them. Those huge pouf things. How does one keep them on?"

"One doesn't. After two hours' sleep one wakes up gasping and kicks them off. Let's go down and see if the landlord can give us something to eat."

There was soup and an omelette, mutton faintly suggestive of goat but deliciously tender, pears in syrup, a local cheese, and red wine not unpleasantly resinous. The landlord recommended it.

"It is my cousin in Navarre who makes it, he is a good man for a Spaniard," he remarked.

"It must be a little awkward," said Tommy sympathetically, "to have relations the other side of a frontier."

"With many relatives a frontier is an advantage," said the landlord frankly. "Is it not so? Yes. But Benito makes good wine and I do business with him, for our blessed mothers were sisters. A little more mutton, m'sieu, our mountain air makes the appetite."

"Thank you. Isn't it rather a nuisance having to conduct business through two sets of customs barriers?"

"There are, of course, the customs," said the landlord, "and they are, naturally, a barrier. Nevertheless, as the good God made this country and Spain joined in one piece together and not parted by seas, it is difficult to believe that the customs officials have the support of divine authority. The birds fly over and do not pay; are we, then, of less account than the sparrows?"

"You are a philosopher," said Hambledon gravely.

"M'sieu is mistaken, asking pardon. I am an innkeeper."

"You think," said Hambledon earnestly, "you observe, you draw conclusions. This it is to be a philosopher."

"To an inn come many men of all kinds, some good, some bad; so long as they behave themselves and pay their bills, what is that to me? But they all talk and set out their opinions; one learns by what one hears. Some cheese, m'sieu, I can recommend it, my wife makes it. Then perhaps coffee in the garden? There is an arbor where it is pleasant to sit."

He went away, and Hyde asked what Tommy proposed to do that afternoon.

"Sleep," said Hambledon, "just sleep. In the arbor if the chairs are comfortable and there aren't too many earwigs; otherwise upon my bed. What would you propose, mountain climbing?"

"Heaven forbid. I didn't go to bed at all last night, did you? No, I only wondered whether you wanted to talk to the landlord about getting into Spain. That wine of his doesn't come along the main roads, does it? Though I don't see how they'd ever get a wheeled vehicle over those heights."

"They wouldn't try; it comes on muleback of course."

"Can you ride a mule?" asked Hyde.

"Now don't anticipate horrors, you'll spoil my afternoon's rest. Tonight or tomorrow will do to talk to the landlord, there's no immediate hurry so far as I know."

At that moment Wenezky was hurrying through the streets of Auch to tell Jules Arcache, the taxi driver, to trace a gray Austin saloon. Two hours later Hambledon sat up and rubbed his eyes; Arcache, in Auch, was telling Wenezky that two Englishmen in the gray Austin had arrived at the Green Monkey at Haut Vannes.

"How far is that from here?" asked Wenezky.

"A hundred and fifty kilometers—a little less—"

"You shall drive me there."

"But certainly. When does M'sieu wish to go? Tomorrow, when the sun is warm?"

"A four hours' run," said Wenezky thoughtfully.

"Less, m'sieu, in my car," said Arcache firmly. "Three hours and a half only."

"And the time is now half past seventeen hours. Eighteen—at half past twenty-one hours we should be there."

"Tonight? But the delicate throat of M'sieu—"

"Tonight," said Wenezky. "We start in half an hour's time."

"It is as M'sieu pleases, but it will be both dark and cold when we arrive—"

"It will do me less harm than to lie and fret all night while the car of my desires disappears beyond recall. Come to my lodging in half an hour's time, Arcache."

It was soon after five when the sun sank behind a spur of the mountains; Hambledon, asleep in the arbor, shivered and awoke. Hyde's chair was empty. Tommy stretched himself, rubbed his eyes, and went to look for his friend and an antidote to evening chill. He found both in the bar where James Hyde, glass in hand, was deep in converse with the landlord. "There are great blocks of flats built down by the river now," he was saying in his schoolboy French, "towards Roehampton."

"Izzat so," said the landlord.

"Just fancy," said Hyde, looking round as Hambledon came in, "our friend here knows Putney, isn't it strange? When he was a young man he was valet to an old gentleman who lived there."

"Zat is so," said the landlord. "But," he added in French, "I have forgotten all my English but a few words. I cannot even understand it, muttonhead that I am. What will M'sieu take?"

"A glass of your good wine, thank you. You will be able to practice English with my friend here, it will soon come back."

"Alas no, she is gone beyond recall; I was not at any time clever at languages. That doubtless seems strange to you, m'sieu, who speak our tongue like a native of Paris, and doubtless many other languages also."

"I had a French mother," said Tommy untruthfully, "she taught me. I can get along in Spanish too."

"Ah, Spanish," said the landlord noncommittally, and he refilled their glasses. Hambledon leaned across the bar and spoke in a confidential voice.

"Tell me, while yet we have this place to ourselves, is it possible to slip across the frontier without formality?"

"It has been done, indeed," said the innkeeper, "and doubtless will be done many times again. But it is a rough road and they are rough men who take it. It would be better for a gentleman like M'sieu to get his papers duly authorized and enter by one of the official routes."

Hambledon looked down with some appearance of embarrassment. "I cannot very well do that."

"These politics," said the landlord with a lift of the shoulders.

"No politics at all. Listen," said Tommy. "There is a lady."

The innkeeper grinned suddenly. *"Ah, la belle señorita.* M'sieu is to be envied."

"Señora," said Tommy.

"A very gracious lady, no doubt," said the innkeeper gravely, but the corners of his mouth twitched.

"She is a widow, naturally," added Tommy hastily.

"But, of course."

"Of noble birth."

"Seeing that M'sieu is what he is—"

"With powerful family connections who do not wish her to remarry."

"Ah," said the innkeeper darkly. "There are financial considerations, no doubt."

"Pouf," said Hambledon, waving the financial considerations out of the window. "I am not interested."

Hyde, who had been looking from one to the other with his mouth hanging open, drank up the rest of his wine and choked over it.

"Her brothers, however," said Tommy, thumping Hyde kindly on the back, "think differently. They are influential. They take steps. I am, in short, looked for on all the frontiers. Such things are possible in Spain."

"It is heaven's truth," said the landlord. "In Spain such things are done daily."

"So I also take steps, over the mountains. My lady looks for my coming. Yes. So I go. You will, at least, advise me, will you not?"

"It is well seen that you are English," said the landlord. "There was also Nelson whose tomb I have seen in Trafalgar Square in London. Emilie, was she not? It is understood. Tonight my brother comes and I will bring him to M'sieu. It is he who manages these affairs, I am a quiet married man, I stay at home."

"But when you were courting Madame, did you stay at home then?"

"M'sieu, I would have defied also Napoleon. Tonight it shall be arranged."

Arcache drove into Haut Vannes on the stroke of half past nine, and turned in his seat to say that doubtless his passenger would desire accommodation at the Green Monkey, where the Englishmen were staying. By this means he would be able to open negotiations for the gray Austin in an entirely natural manner, not betraying the fact that he was so eager to buy it that he had driven a hundred miles in order to do so. "Such eagerness makes prices rise," said Arcache wisely. But Wenezky did not at all want to encounter Hambledon, only to follow him wherever he might be going.

"No," said Wenezky. "Some other hostelry. It will be better still if you negotiate for the car and I do not appear in the matter."

Arcache agreed. In fact he thought the idea almost too good to be true, but naturally did not say so.

"It is to be seen that M'sieu is a man of experience in business. We will go, therefore, to the Horn of Roland."

It was, by this time, completely dark and Haut Vannes economized in street lighting. Wenezky, who had never been in the South of France before, peered from the windows of the car and saw nothing but dark stone houses presenting curious angles to the car headlamps and an occasional passerby hurrying home, for nine-thirty is a late hour in Haut Vannes and prudent folk go early to bed to save the cost of artificial light. One man he saw but did not particularly notice, a tall lean man going up the steep street with a mountaineer's long stride, the innkeeper's brother on his way to see Tommy Hambledon.

The inn of the Horn of Roland did not live up to its name, for it was neither mediaeval nor romantic. It was neither new nor old, it was dark, shabby and a little furtive. The patrons of the public bar did not associate as one company, enjoying as one the rude but cheerful jest; they split up into small groups, talked in low tone, and looked up sharply if anyone approached them. When Arcache, followed by Wenezky, entered the room there was a sudden silence and all eyes turned upon the newcomers with a look less of curiosity than of plain mistrust. Wenezky recognized the atmosphere at once and with pleasure, as one who comes home. This was the atmosphere in which he had spent most of his life, among men who were called by nicknames and were against the government and the rich and the Church, against law and order and the police—especially the police. It is not etiquette in such places to look keenly at anyone, only detectives do that and it is wise to establish at the outset that one is not a detective. Wenezky glanced carelessly round, murmured an apology and followed Arcache across the room through a door upon the further side.

"M'sieu must excuse," said the taxi driver. "This place is not such as he is accustomed to use but it is better than it seems at first sight and the cooking is excellent. I can vouch for the cooking."

"Do not trouble yourself, my good Arcache," said Wenezky loftily. "I am a habitual traveler and have stayed in many worse places than this. Where is the landlord?"

A voice at his elbow startled him. "Here, sir, at your service." Wenezky looked down at a man who had appeared from nowhere and stood peering sideways at him as though it were an effort to look so high, as in fact it was, for the man was a hunchback.

"My patron," said Arcache, "desires your best room for the night and possibly for two nights if you satisfy his wishes. A private sitting room also, and supper at once. My patron is a gentleman of culture and refinement who knows how things should be done."

"We shall do our best to satisfy the gentleman. Be pleased to follow me," said the hunchback, and led the way upstairs to a small sitting room, clean indeed, but overcharged with furniture and disquieted with ornaments. Also the window had not recently been opened, but Wenezky was no devotee of fresh air.

"The gentleman will be comfortable here," said the landlord.

"It is a nice room," said Wenezky sincerely.

"Such lovely things you have, too," said Arcache. "See the little ivory tower beneath the glass cover."

"It appears to be crooked," said Wenezky critically.

"It is the Leaning Tower of Pisa," said the landlord. "Here is your bedroom, conveniently near, it opens from this room."

Wenezky inspected that also and said it would serve well enough. "There is a blind at the window, is there? I dislike to be overlooked."

The landlord said there was, it should be lowered, and in any case the window looked only upon gardens. "I will send up the supper," he added, and retreated to the door. "I will leave M'sieu to refreshment and rest," said Arcache, and went out. The landlord paused momentarily in the doorway, looked searchingly at Wenezky and lifted his hand as though to scratch his head, but the fingers were closed with the thumb over them. Wenezky's eyes gleamed and the hand that went up to remove his scarf was also momentarily clenched. The hunchback went out, closing the door quietly behind him.

In the Green Monkey, Hambledon and Hyde were finishing their evening meal with a glass of passable brandy and some excellent coffee, when the landlord entered the room.

"If the gentlemen still wish to see my brother, he is here."

"You told him what I wanted, did you?"

"But yes, m'sieu. I will send him up."

The innkeeper's brother was a man of remarkably few words. Yes, he would take the gentleman across the frontier, he suggested tomorrow evening, crossing by night. There would be a moon. Hyde offered to drive both Hambledon and his guide as far as was practicable in the car.

"For M'sieu, yes; for me, no, with thanks. Better that we are not seen together here."

"Where shall I meet you, then?" asked Tommy.

"There is a road which turns off by the church. By the fifth milestone I shall be waiting. At seventeen hours if that is convenient?"

"Perfectly."

"And M'sieu's baggage?"

"I shall not take any."

"It is well," said the guide. "I have the honor to wish the gentlemen a good night's repose." He was gone before Hambledon had time to offer him a drink.

"Not very voluble," said Hyde. "Perhaps he'll open up a bit when you get to know him better."

"I shan't want to talk," said Tommy. "I shall be too busy trying to keep up with him. Oh dear."

"What do you want me to do," said Hyde, "when you are gone?"

"I don't think there'll be anything, thanks. At least, I hope I don't have to bolt back here, though of course one never knows." Hyde looked so like a dog whose master is going for a walk without him that Tommy nearly laughed. "Frankly," he added, "I don't know where I'm going or by what means, but I expect to keep moving. Still, thanks very much; if you would stay on for two or three days just in case—"

When Hyde came back to the Green Monkey on the following evening after conveying Hambledon to the fifth milestone, he found a short stout man awaiting him in the inn yard.

"M'sieu will excuse—"

"Certainly. What can I do for you?"

"A small matter about M'sieu's car."

"Why? Is there anything wrong?" asked Hyde.

"But no. It is a nice car and doubtless of the utmost reliability. I was, however, wondering whether M'sieu was thinking of taking drives in this district."

"I don't know what you're getting at," said Hyde, who was even less at ease than usual in French with this man's southern accent.

"I will be frank with M'sieu. I have a client who has commissioned me to obtain for him an Austin saloon in exchange for his Bugatti. Austins are scarce in France today, I have been searching for one for many weeks. Accordingly, when I heard that M'sieu had an Austin I took the unpardonable liberty of coming here to speak to him about it. My name is Jules Arcache."

"My car is not for sale," said Hyde slowly, but there was no conviction in his tone. The fact was that he had always wanted to own a Bugatti, which stood in his mind for distinction, daring and emancipation ever since he had read, twenty years earlier, a story in the *Strand* magazine about a man who drove a Bugatti—

"No, no. M'sieu is not a dealer, naturally. But I am. One has experience. There are men of different kinds and there are cars of different kinds. A man should have a car which assimilates itself to his personality. The moment I saw M'sieu I said to myself: 'That is a Bugatti man, why is he driving an Austin?' Asking pardon for my freedom of speech, that is what I said."

"Er—I suppose—"

"And my client of whom I spoke is an Austin man driving a Bugatti. Figure yourself that he changes down whenever he sees a farm cart coming. Whereas M'sieu—I have seen him drive—"

"Come and have a glass of wine," said Hyde, "why are we standing out here?" The fact was that he wanted time to think. One must not be rash or allow oneself to be hustled. But a Bugatti . . . He led the way into the bar.

"This car of which you speak," said Hyde when they were served, "where is it?"

"Here in Haut Vannes, m'sieu. My friend who has the garage opposite is housing it at the moment." This happened to be perfectly true. There was a Bugatti there whose owner had died; his widow was finding some difficulty in disposing of a high-powered car in a small place like Haut Vannes and might be expected to accept a reasonable offer. Arcache knew perfectly well that no tourist would wish to be suddenly without a car in the middle of a tour; he had looked for a substitute for the Austin before trying to approach Hyde.

"I should have to give the car a thorough test before even considering the exchange," said Hyde. "What date is it and how much running has it done?"

"But of course, every test. End of 1937, in perfect condition, only done a few thousand kilometers. It is a wonderful bargain," urged Arcache.

"How much does he want for it?" asked Hyde bluntly.

"A straight exchange, m'sieu. Your Austin for his Bugatti."

Hyde had been tempted before but this almost decided him. He was a business-man and knew that if the Bugatti was anything near so good as it was described it was worth a lot more than his Austin.

"Very well," he said. "I will see it in the morning and try it out too, if I may? At half past nine? At the garage across the road; will you be there, Mr.—I beg your pardon—"

"Arcache. Jules Arcache at your service. At nine thirty I will be there. I shall look forward with pleasure to the delight which the sight of the Bugatti will give M'sieu. And to drive it! Ah! Until tomorrow, then, my compliments, m'sieu. Good night."

Chapter Twelve
The Disappointed Taxi Driver

Arcache walked away from the Green Monkey very pleased with himself. Wenezky could be induced to give him three times what the Austin was worth, he had bar-gained for the Bugatti at a third of its value, and the difference would go into his pocket besides—one hoped—a gift from Wenezky for finding the Austin, another from Hyde for finding the Bugatti, and a percentage of the Bugatti's price from the garage proprietor. Very, very good. His heart sang and he dropped into a homely brasserie to stand himself another one or two on the strength of it. Then he went along to the Horn of Roland to tell Wenezky that matters were in train.

"The guest is out," said the hunchback behind the bar.

"Out! So late in the evening? With his delicacy of the chest!"

The hunchback looked faintly amused but said nothing and went on polishing glasses.

"Very few patrons here tonight," said Arcache amiably.

"Presently, perhaps," said the landlord. "What will you take?"

"A small glass of something until the guest returns."

The landlord served him and turned away to attend to one or two customers who had come in. They stood together at the far end of the bar and talked in low tones; Arcache took his glass to a small table, rolled himself a cigarette and waited. Time passed; the clock struck eight; more time passed. Customers, in twos and threes, came and went, but no Wenezky. Arcache got up suddenly and went back to the bar.

"I am uneasy about my patron," he said. "He has been ill, this place is strange to him, it is now dark, and the night air is dangerous."

"No need," said the hunchback. "The guest is among friends."

"But he knows no one here, he told me so."

"He is among friends," repeated the landlord.

"But two days ago he would not venture out in the midday sun without scarves in profusion and gloves upon his hands," objected Arcache. "Now, upon the mountains, he goes out in the middle of the night!" The prospect of his golden deal disappearing in an attack of pneumonia was almost more than he could bear.

"Be at ease," said the hunchback coldly. "Twenty-one hours is not the middle of the night by any reckoning."

"But the night—"

"But—but—" mimicked the hunchback. "Go and sit down or go home to bed!"

Arcache blinked, hesitated and ordered another glass. He retired to his table again and prepared to wait indefinitely.

At a quarter to ten there were footsteps outside, the door opened and most of the men who had been there the night before streamed in together. In the midst of them came Wenezky, hatless, with his black hair falling into his eyes, his face flushed and animated, his coat unbuttoned and his shirt open at the throat. Arcache stared; it was no exaggeration to say that he hardly recognized the man. Wenezky, however, was talking, and there was no mistaking that extraordinary accent. "Thus we did in Warsaw," he was saying, when he caught sight of Arcache and stopped. "What are you doing here?"

"I came—I came to see you. To—to tell you about the business—about the car—"

"Oh, that! Not tonight, my good fellow. Tomorrow, come and tell me tomorrow. I am busy tonight. Tomorrow at noon."

He turned away; Arcache mumbled agreement but stood there gaping until another member of the party touched him on the arm and indicated the street door. Another opened it, the taxi driver stumbled out into the dark street and made his way towards his lodging, stopping every few yards to shake his head.

"The drink," he decided finally. "These foreigners. It must be the drink. Just Heaven, let him live at least until he has bought the Austin."

Hyde saw the Bugatti next morning, tried it out and fell in love with it.

"I'll have it," he said. "You can have the Austin."

"Very good, m'sieu," said Arcache.

"What's the matter? You don't seem very bright this morning. Anything wrong?" asked James Hyde kindly.

"It is nothing, m'sieu, only the headache. I have the migraine."

"Take three aspirins and a cup of strong tea. Oh, of course, you don't drink tea in these parts. Well, take three aspirins and lie down in a dark room for an hour. About the transfer of the car, whom do I see, the police?"

"The garage proprietor will advise M'sieu. If he will excuse me I will take his advice."

"Do, there's a good chap. Come and see me when you feel better."

Arcache smiled wanly and ambled away. He had spent a restless night persuading himself that Wenezky had merely been on the drink and that as soon as he had slept it off he would become again just an invalidish eccentric with more money than wisdom. But doubts haunted him. That eager manner, those flashing dark eyes, that look of youth and energy; Arcache had never known a mere binge to work such a miracle. "It never does with me," he said sorrowfully. He was nearly an hour too soon for his appointment with Wenezky, but his feet took him to the Horn of Roland by the nearest way. He pushed the door open and went in.

The place seemed empty, he walked wearily up to the bar and leaned against it, looking idly out of the dusty window at a clump of gillyflowers growing in a crevice of the wall opposite. Wonderful how those things kept alive with no earth to speak of. He yawned.

A voice spoke within a foot of his ear and Arcache sprang round as though he had been stung. The hunchback was behind the bar looking at him with that faintly amused expression which Arcache had found so unpleasant the night before.

"What—what did you say?"

"I only said 'What will you take?' "

"A glass of wine. I didn't hear you come in."

"I didn't come in. I was here all the time."

Arcache's dislike grew to superstitious dread. Everyone knew that hunchbacks were unlucky unless you could touch their humps, and he knew he could never endure to touch this one.

"I came also," said the taxi driver, "to ask after the health of my patron."

"The guest is well," said the landlord, and pushed the full glass across the counter. Arcache drank it straight off, asked for another, and drank that.

"You seem nervous this morning," said the hunchback. "When you are restored, the guest wishes to see you."

Arcache wiped his mouth, twisted up his mustaches and said: "It is well, I also wish to see him if convenient."

"I will take you up," said the landlord. He led the way upstairs to Wenezky's room and announced Arcache. Wenezky was sitting with his long arms laid out straight upon the table before him; a favorite pose with him. It seemed to Arcache that it had something animal about it, reminding him of the way a cat will lie with front legs straight out and claws faintly twitching, a very big cat; a tiger, for instance. Also there was nothing elderly or invalidish about Wenezky this morning, he was evidently a man between thirty and forty years old, haggard and grim indeed but certainly not decrepit. Arcache stood and stared, and the door shut behind him.

"Tell me," said Wenezky abruptly, "where has the Englishman gone?"

"The Englishman? He has not gone anywhere. I saw him this morning."

"This morning? When?"

"But half an hour ago. I arranged with him about selling you his car—"

"Not that one, fool! His passenger."

"As to his passenger, m'sieu, I do not know. I did not—"

"Did you see him this morning?"

"Neither this morning nor last night."

"So you don't even know whether he is still at the inn."

"No, m'sieu. I did not know that you took any interest in him."

"I heard that an Englishman was conducted across the frontier this morning, I want to know whether it was that one or another. These English," said Wenezky irritably, "they are everywhere."

Arcache did not answer. He was torn between justifiable annoyance at being bullied and a desire to keep Wenezky sweet for business purposes.

"You can go back to the Green Monkey and find out. The landlord will know, it is his brother who is the guide. No, better not ask him, he will not talk. Make some excuse to speak to the other Englishman, they—no, perhaps not. I will find out some other way. You may go."

"But the car," began Arcache.

"Car? What car?"

"The Austin saloon you commissioned me to buy."

"Oh, that one. I don't want it."

"You don't want it, m'sieu?" stammered Arcache. "But you came here on purpose to buy it—"

"I have changed my mind."

Arcache raised his arms to heaven. "But I have arranged it all! And I have bought a Bugatti for the gentleman in exchange, and the man at the garage will—"

"Get out."

"But, m'sieu—"

"Get out!" snarled Wenezky, and his lip lifted like a wolf's. Arcache turned and went out without another word, stumbled down the dark stairs and out through the bar, with the hunchback's sardonic smile annoying him as he went.

Arcache was almost in tears with rage and disappointment. All that good money gone, and the sale of the Bugatti to be canceled, and standing in that upstairs room to be insulted by that species of animal, that— He would get out his taxi, drive straight back to Auch and never return to Haut Vannes as long as he lived. No, he would go to the police and complain. There rose before his mind the memory of James Hyde's pleasant voice telling him to go and lie down and come back when he felt better. He didn't feel better, he felt ten thousand times worse, but he would go to the Englishman who was a Christian and a gentleman (unlike that illegal offspring of a diseased camel at the Horn of Roland), and tell him all his troubles.

Hyde was standing outside the garage horribly and happily entangled in the proprietor's technical phrases. He was giving Hyde some good advice about advancing and retarding the ignition on the Bugatti; the Englishman, with the help of a small pocket dictionary, thought he was talking about adjusting the headlamps, and both men were enjoying themselves. The miserable Arcache tottered up to them and the laughter ceased abruptly.

"Heavens, man, what's the matter with you?" asked Hyde in English, and translated the remark. Arcache, in a voice trembling with emotion, gave a description of Wenezky which would have aroused the envy of a Thames bargee; unfortunately most of it was wasted upon Hyde, who had not heard those words before. However, he understood the general gist of it.

"I gather you're annoyed with somebody," he said, when Arcache stopped to breathe. Hyde used the word *"ennuyé,"* which means "bored with" somebody; the taxi driver found it inadequate, and said so. The garage owner courteously suppressed his amusement and intervened, after which the matter became clearer.

"He says," the garage owner explained in slow and simple phrases, "that the man who was to buy your car does not now want to buy it."

"Well, we can sell it to somebody else, can't we?" said James simply.

Arcache's face cleared up like sunshine after storm. He said that if the world were entirely composed of persons resembling Hyde in every respect, heaven would already be attained. He wept.

"Nonsense," said the embarrassed James. "Matter of business. I want the Bugatti, I sell the Austin. Simple. Why the fuss?"

Arcache said that it was not only the business side of the affair which worried him, but being also insulted by that species of pig after all the trouble he, Jules Arcache, had taken to trace the Austin from Auch to Haut Vannes and—

"Here," said Hyde sharply, "what's all this?"

"From Auch," said Arcache. "I live there."

"Does your—your client live there too?"

"Heaven forbid. Auch is a respectable town. Who knows where he comes from? He is a foreigner, a Bulgarian, a Czechoslovakian, a—what do I know? His French is of a barbarity of the most unendurable. It is of the utmost difficulty to understand."

"I think you could do with a drink," said Hyde. "So could I. Come across to the Green Monkey." He took Arcache by the elbow and fairly dragged him across the road and into his private sitting room. Drinks having been provided, Hyde settled himself in his chair, laid his dictionary at the ready in case it was wanted, and said: "Now then. Why did this man want the Austin traced from Auch?"

"He saw it, m'sieu, and desired to buy it, or so he said."

"Where did he see it?"

"At the inn at Ste.-Marie-en-Marais, the day after the bandit was shot there. I drove him to the scene, there were many who desired to see it. You also, m'sieu, you were standing by your gray car talking to another man; we were pulled up just behind. He saw your car then and desired it."

"Just a minute," said James. "I want to think." He took a turn or two about the room. Hambledon had given him a very particular description of Wenezky including several samples of his peculiar accent, but surely even Wenezky would not have had the impudence to return to Ste.-Marie the day after the shooting. Hyde sat down again.

"Describe this man," he said. "What did he look like?"

Illumination dawned as Arcache described the muffled invalid in the dark glasses, and the identification was completed when the taxi driver talked about Wenezky without his wraps at the Horn of Roland. "But young, m'sieu, a little more than thirty years; but virile, but active, but"—Arcache's voice dropped—"but evil." He added full if unflattering particulars and no doubt was left in Hyde's mind, though how Wenezky had connected him with Hambledon was still a mystery. However, the point was unimportant.

"Tell me the whole story in detail," said Hyde, and Arcache did so, ending with: ". . . and at the last, this morning, it is not the Austin in which he is interested, nor even in you, m'sieu, but in your friend who is gone across the frontier."

"Eh?"

"I ask pardon, this two-tailed goat said that he thought your friend had been taken across the frontier but he was not sure."

That settled it, to Hyde's mind. This was Wenezky chasing Hambledon; it was much more probable than that a lunatic should chase a gray Austin more than a hundred miles and then refuse to buy it.

"How did he know my friend had been taken across the frontier?"

Arcache shrugged. "These villages—is anything hid from them? His friends told him."

"Who are his friends?"

"I do not know any of them, m'sieu, but the type, we all know it. The anarchist, the communist, what you please. They swarm on this frontier, everybody knows it, the mountains are full of them. On the Spanish side they are in their thousands, they are banditti, they are guerrillas. They hold up convoys—"

"Ha," said Hyde thoughtfully.

"They raid country houses, they terrorize lonely villages, they steal arms and food and money and women. This man I drove, he is such another when I see him as he is. He was at Warsaw, I heard him say so."

"Oh dear," said Hyde. "This inn at which he is staying, did he know it before? He told you to drive him there, did he?"

"But no, m'sieu, I take him there myself, imbecile that I am. He would not come here; I do not know this village well, I have been here once—twice before. Once I stay a night at the Horn of Roland, that was before the war, it was a quiet place then run by decent quiet people, not that hunchback." Arcache shivered. "So when he say: 'Not the Green Monkey, some other inn,' I take him there. Why not?"

"Hunchback? Is he the landlord?"

Arcache nodded. "You do not see him coming and then there he is, smiling, just behind you."

"Doesn't sound very nice to me. Look here, what were you thinking of doing now?"

"I had not considered it, m'sieu. Return to Auch, I think."

"Could you stay on for two or three days? You shall not be the loser by it, I promise you. You see, my friend has made this passenger of yours his enemy, but my friend does not know the man has followed him here. I must find out what he is going to do and perhaps warn my friend, but what can I do? You see how badly I speak the language."

"And M'sieu wishes?"

"I want you to hang round, pick up any items of information you can and bring them to me. Can I trust you, Arcache?"

"M'sieu, you have acted like a Christian to me and for that I would delight to serve you. Again, that species of bestial insults me, Jules Arcache. I am a poor man, m'sieu, but I would work for weeks without pay to be revenged on him."

"And as it won't be without pay, Arcache?"

"M'sieu can count on me."

"Very well. Go now, then, and see what you can do, for I think this man, when he acts, will act quickly."

"I go," said Arcache, rising to his feet, "and I will come again, preferably after dark. Au revoir, m'sieu."

When the taxi driver had gone, Hyde sat down with rather a bump, for his knees were unsteady. He thought of a friend of his, one Hugh Selkirk, now dead, who had propounded a theory that the presence of imminent danger was necessary to bring out in a man that little something extra he didn't know he'd got. That might well be, but Hyde was not yet conscious of any access of moral force, quite the contrary. He was very severely frightened and felt far from home and much alone. What was worse, something might have to be done to help Hambledon; Hyde doubted if he were the man to do it, for he was essentially modest. Reinforcements were obviously called for, and Hugh's brother Adam Selkirk was the first choice. But Adam was on the move and not to be found at a moment's notice. Charles Denton, Hambledon's constant associate—Hyde did not know his telephone number and he would not trust a telegram to a village post office in that part of France. As Arcache had said, these villages—

Hyde's face cleared suddenly, for he had thought of the right men. He went to find the landlord of the Green Monkey and asked him to put a call through for him to London. The call was to a modelmaker's shop in the Clerkenwell Road.

Chapter Thirteen
Jeannot of the Goats

When the landlord of the Green Monkey brought in the supper that night, Hyde asked how soon the guide might be expected to return.

"Not for three days, m'sieu, or possibly four. He told me that he had also a small matter of business to attend to on the other side. Did you wish to see him particularly?"

"Not urgently, no. I only wanted news of my friend."

The landlord nodded. "My brother is in request tonight," he remarked. "One enquired for him but half an hour ago."

"Someone else wishing to go across?"

"So I suppose. He did not say so and I did not ask. I told him my brother was away for a few days, and the man said, 'Down yonder?' like that. Do I babble about my brother's affairs? No. I said that he had gone to a wedding at Ostabat of a war comrade of his who was marrying the twin daughter of the baker there, a nice girl but cross-eyed."

"Did he believe you?"

"He would not believe the blessed Archangel Gabriel, that one, if I am any judge of men."

"Oh. So it was someone you didn't know personally," said Hyde.

"He was a stranger, m'sieu, and I would prefer that he should remain one. I asked Jeannot of the Goats who that one might be and Jeannot said he was at the Horn of Roland. Jeannot is an innocent, but he knows all who come and go."

Hyde's toes curled up without consulting him, but he remarked in a perfectly casual tone that he supposed the man was a visitor. The landlord agreed; not only a visitor but a foreigner, for he spoke the French of a talking tomcat, not of a Christian. The spasmodic contraction in Hyde's toes extended to his spine. Wenezky in the next room—

"And then he went away, did he?"

"Yes, m'sieu." The landlord gathered up plates and prepared to leave the room, but Hyde felt that his society for a little longer would be a comfort.

"I miss my friend tonight," he said. "Will you not take a glass of wine with me if you are not too busy?"

"It will be an honor. Excuse me one moment while I fetch a glass." Hyde got up hastily and closed the shutters; he felt naked to the world within the lighted windows.

"This Horn of Roland," he said, when the landlord returned, "it is kept by a hunchback, is it not?" He filled the glasses.

"Your health, m'sieu. Yes. It is a pity. It was a small inferior house, but respectable, when the old Père Perritet kept it. Then he died and his widow went to her married daughter who keeps a *confiserie* in Oloron, and this man came. Who knows who he is? He paid the money, so he took the house. I do not know what it is like now, we of the town do not go there."

"Then how does he make it pay?"

"He has his clientele, m'sieu. The *comunistos.*"

"The which?"

"*Comunistos*. The communists who escaped over the frontier from Spain when

Franco pursued them. There is a camp where they live, it is over the bridge as you come into the town and two kilometers up the lane which turns off there. It is a terrible place."

"They are Spaniards, then? Let me refill your glass."

"I thank M'sieu. Your health. They were all Spaniards at first, that is why we call them 'comunistos,' but now they are of all nations, French, Italian, Russian, what do I know? Germans too. Anyone who is bad enough is welcome there, fugitives from justice, all kinds."

"But the police?" suggested Hyde.

The landlord made a contemptuous noise. "The gendarmes? They are but few, they have wisdom. So long as the comunistos do not behave themselves too outrageously, they let them alone. Why not? What would a few gendarmes do with that mob? It is a couple of regiments with artillery which would be needed. Besides, they are quiet enough, on the whole."

" 'Let sleeping dogs lie' is a saying in my country," said Hyde.

"It is a good saying. If M'sieu has everything he wishes I will ask his permission to retire. The bar fills up at this time of the night and my wife has but one pair of hands."

"I am inconsiderate," said Hyde quickly, "I should have remembered that. Ask my pardon from Madame your wife."

"I am sure it is already granted," said the innkeeper.

When Hyde was alone he poured himself one more glass for a nightcap and thought over what he had heard. Wenezky had come to the Green Monkey to look for Hambledon and no doubt knew that Hyde was there. "He knows me because he saw me at Ste.-Marie-en-Marais. I should recognize him if I saw him, I think; certainly I should know him if I heard him speak. Tomcat's French is rather good." Hyde had one hold over Wenezky, the police were after him and Hyde could tell them where he was on second thoughts, not much of a hold, since at the first sign of imminent arrest Wenezky would no doubt take refuge with his friends in the communists' camp, and the police were not at all likely to stir up that hornets' nest for the sake of arresting one man. The third thought was even worse; if Wenezky realized that Hyde knew him and was likely to inform the police, he—Wenezky— would probably take immediate steps to silence him—Hyde. James got up hastily and pegged the shutters more securely; when he went upstairs he pushed a heavy settle against the bedroom door to reinforce the bolt and slept, for the first time in his life, with a revolver under his pillow. He did not sleep well, a revolver is an uncomfortable bedfellow.

The morning was bright and sunny and life looked more promising. James whistled as he shaved. A telegram awaited him on the breakfast table, it said that the reinforcements for which he had telephoned would be there by noon next day; only another day and night to get through and he would no longer be alone. In the meantime there was the Bugatti and he could leave Haut Vannes for the day. He attacked his coffee and rolls with a good appetite.

He had hardly finished when the landlord came in, shutting the door behind him.

"There is news," he said gravely. "My brother has returned."

"Already?" said Hyde, and saw that the man was disquieted. "Send him in, please, at once."

When the guide came in James was standing by the window; he turned as the man entered.

"Well? What has happened?"

"The gentleman has been arrested."

"Arrested! By whom?"

"A Spanish patrol, m'sieu. He is in the prison at Torida."

"How did this happen?"

"We crossed in safety. I met a man I knew, he said the patrols were out. We went on. There was a road through a wood, I heard horses coming and took the gentleman a little way into the wood. We crouched down, the horses came near, it was the patrol. When they were very near the gentleman rose to his feet and went into the road. They asked him many questions, I could hear what was said. He said he had a passport but they said it had no Spanish visa. He expressed surprise at finding himself in Spain. He said he had gone for a walk on the mountains alone, lost his way and wandered across the frontier. He apologized and said he would go back. They said that was not permitted, they would take him to the military governor at Torida. They mounted him on a spare horse and all rode away. Later, I went to Torida and made enquiries. It was said that an Englishman had been found wandering and the governor had sent him to prison."

James passed through bewilderment to reassurance. Obviously Hambledon had intended the patrol to take him, though why on earth anybody should want to land himself in a Spanish prison was quite beyond Hyde. Hambledon knew best, of course, and no doubt it was all part of the plan, whatever that was.

"It was not my fault, m'sieu," added the guide.

"Evidently not," said Hyde. "I do not blame you in the least. No doubt my friend had some purpose in what he did. In any case, he has influential friends who will help him to get out again. These patrols, who were they looking for?"

"The *comunistos*, m'sieu."

"I see. Friends of these people at the camp here?"

"That is so, m'sieu."

That made it clear to Hyde, or comparatively clear. Hambledon was acting against the *comunistos*, therefore the patrol was on the side of his friends. He went out, whistling, and took the Bugatti for a test run with a mechanic from the garage for company. Wenezky seemed suddenly to have become unimportant, Hambledon was out of his reach and all was well. Hyde rather regretted, in the confident sunshine of a Pyrenean morning, having sent for his friends in the Clerkenwell Road. Never mind, a short holiday would do them good.

After dark that night the taxi driver was shown into James's sitting room. Arcache had the air of a conspirator, he wore a cloak which he had borrowed from somebody and a broad-brimmed hat pulled over his eyes. He removed the hat with a flourish, advanced to the table, leaned upon it and spoke in a hoarse whisper.

"I have news. Grave news."

"Really?" said James. "Won't you sit down?"

"I thank M'sieu. The communists are going to attack the jail."

"Really," said Hyde again. "I didn't know there was a jail here."

"Not here, m'sieu. The jail at Torida, where the friend of M'sieu is incarcerated."

"Now, how the devil did they know that? Or you either, for that matter?"

"It is all over the village, m'sieu. Myself, I heard the women talking about it at the fountain before noon today."

"Good gracious. But why are they going to attack the prison?"

"They say it is to rescue the Englishman."

"Rescue? Has Wenez—has your late passenger got anything to do with it?"

"But everything, m'sieu. At the house where I live there is a young man who is affianced to a girl whose father gets up barrels from the cellar and does other heavy work for the hunchback at the Horn of Roland. He is not there at all times, you understand, he goes for an hour in the afternoon to get the place ready for the evening. As a rule there are but few customers there at the hour when he goes, today it was full, and the men were talking. He was in the cellar with the flap open; this flap, it is behind the bar. They speak of a jail attack, he does not know what jail. Then the guest, as they call him, comes in, that is my passenger, m'sieu. He talks much. He says that this man they call 'the Englishman' is his comrade, his more than brother. Shall he languish in jail, he says, or shall he be rescued for the honor of the Cause? One says one thing and one another, and he says it is necessary he should be rescued, he carries something indispensable for the success of the Cause. Then one says at least there will be some throat slitting, which is always good practice, and another that there will be loot in the jail, arms and ammunition, of which they are short. Then they all say it shall be done but it must be kept secret, and at that the father of my friend's girl is so frightened that he shuts down the flap as softly as a feather settling upon a pile of hay and creeps out by the way that they carry the barrels in, and he runs home by the back lanes, m'sieu, not to be seen leaving. When he gets home he tells his daughter and she tells her young fiancé and he tells me, so as soon as it is dark I disguise myself and come to tell you, m'sieu. For I remember that you tell me this man is your friend's enemy and now he calls him comrade and brother, so I know there is a mischief brewing. Have I done well, m'sieu?"

James emerged slowly, like a waterlogged plank, from this flood of words. He had missed bits here and there but he got the gist of it very well.

"You have done excellently," he said slowly. "When do they mean to do this?"

"I could not say, m'sieu. It will take them some days to arrange, surely?"

"By which time my friend may have gone from Torida."

"Heaven grant it, especially if you could send him word."

"Yes," said Hyde, "yes. I will see if that can be arranged. In the meantime, go on getting information from any available source. Er—it will involve you in some expense, no doubt. Just a moment."

When financial arrangements had been made to their mutual satisfaction Arcache resumed his hat, pulled the brim down to his eyebrows, flung his cloak about him with a romantic gesture and departed on tiptoe, reminding Hyde of a picture of Sancho Panza in an illustrated *Don Quixote* which had lain upon the drawing-room table at home when he was a boy at Yeovil in Somerset. Upon the same table was also a copy of the *Pilgrim's Progress*, with pictures; the two books were coupled in his mind because he was allowed to look at them on Sundays. Hyde looked back at that small boy from very far off, like one who contemplates his own feet through a telescope. The table was of polished mahogany, the books stood upon a mat crocheted of red-and-white wool with bobbles round the edge, and James had always to wash his hands before he touched them. Now, in middle age, he was contending with brigands on the Spanish frontier. Well, well. He went to the door and called the landlord.

"M'sieu desires?"

"Come in just a moment. Now then. Your brother told me yesterday that after my friend was arrested he—your brother—followed them into Torida and made enquiries. He has friends there, then?"

"Yes, m'sieu. Cousins also."

"Splendid. Now listen. If I wanted to get a message to my friend in the prison there, could your brother arrange to have it delivered?"

"I will ask my brother if he considers the thing possible to be done."

"Thank you, if you would. Tonight?"

"Yes, m'sieu. It will cost money to persuade the prison warders."

"No doubt. Your brother will advise me."

"I will send Jeannot of the Goats to ask him to come here," said the landlord, and went away.

When the guide came in Hyde went to the point at once.

"Etienne. Have you heard that the communists are planning to attack the jail at Torida where M. Hambledon is lodged?"

Etienne's face assumed the expression which meant that he was amused.

"On the way here," he said, "that village innocent called Jeannot told me so."

Hyde was momentarily deflected from his anxieties.

"Tell me," he said, "your word 'innocent' means lacking in wits, does it not? Yet it seems to me that that boy knows everything before anyone else. How on earth does he do it?"

"Those who have had no schooling have good memories, m'sieu. He wanders about, he is silly, nobody notices him, and all the time he is like a record being made for the gramophone. Everything he hears goes in and, for those he likes, comes out again. He does not understand, nor does the gramophone record. He just reproduces words."

"I see," said Hyde. "Very curious. Very interesting. Well, I heard the same story, and I think it is probably true. I want to warn M. Hambledon. Could it be done?"

The guide hesitated.

"Would you require an answer to be brought?"

"No. I don't think so."

"Then it can be done, but it will cost a thousand francs. That is for bribery, mainly, and a little for the man who passes the message. I do not, myself, know the prison guards."

Hyde nodded. "Shall I write the message now?"

"As small as possible, m'sieu, on a piece of thin paper."

Hyde wrote a brief message, put it in an envelope and gave it to the guide.

"Did that boy Jeannot hear when the communists proposed to make the attack?"

"No, m'sieu. It could not be for some days. Nonetheless, the sooner M'sieu Hambledon has this, the better."

"I leave it to you," said Hyde, "with the utmost confidence."

"I will do what I can," said the guide, and went away with his usual suddenness.

Chapter Fourteen
Entry of the Modelmakers

William Forgan and Archibald Henry Campbell kept a small shop in the Clerkenwell Road, London, where they sold, made and repaired models of all kinds but particularly model railways. Earlier in their careers they had been employed on a ranch in the Argentine where they had learned to speak Spanish with fluency and effect, to deal with emergencies promptly and without fuss, and not to be readily intimidated. They were old friends of Hyde's and well disposed towards Hambledon.

When Hyde found that Wenezky was at Haut Vannes, looking for Hambledon, he had a long conversation with them over the telephone and gave them an outline of the story.

"I want you to come out here," he said urgently. "Now, at once. I can't cope with this fellow by myself, I can't, really. Can you fly out tomorrow? Charter a plane."

"It certainly sounds tempting," said Forgan, "and it's a long time since we had a holiday. This sounds as though it ought to be a complete change from the Clerken-well Road. I'll talk it over with Campbell, find out whether we can charter a plane or not, and send you a telegram tomorrow. All right? Good. Keep alive till we get there—if we do. Good-bye."

The partners talked over the matter, closed the shop for a fortnight, and chartered a private airplane to land them as near as possible to Haut Vannes in the Depart-ment of Basses Pyrénées. Considerable excitement was caused in the village when an airplane touched down in Aristide Riquette's meadow, discomposing his cows. Two men got out of the aircraft, which immediately took off again; the men picked up their baggage, which consisted of a leather bag each and a black box measuring fourteen inches by sixteen by eight deep, which they carried alternately. It appeared to be of some weight. They walked towards the village and were at once surrounded by twenty-three children, four old men, five old women, the local policeman, and Jeannot complete with goats. The policeman addressed them.

"Halt, messieurs, if you please."

"He wants us to stop," said Forgan to Campbell.

"Tiresome," said Campbell. "I've only just started. However. *Bonjour, m'sieu de la gendarmerie. Comment vous portez-vous?"*

The policeman said he was in perfect health and hoped that they were. He then became official and asked to see their passports and other evidences of identity and respectability, and asked them where they had come from.

"England," said Forgan. "London." Both men produced documents in every way satisfactory, and the gendarme beamed. The children closed in, asking for chocolate, and Campbell told them that there wasn't any where he came from as the bears had eaten it all. The gendarme shooed the children back and enquired whether the gentlemen had passed the customs.

"Certainly," said Campbell. "At nine thousand feet. A nice man, he keeps rab-bits."

The gendarme gave it up and Forgan asked to be directed to the hotel of the Green Monkey. "Where the so famous editor is filling in his vacancies."

"Pardon?"

Campbell explained that his friend meant "spending his holidays," and the gen-darme thanked him. "This so famous editor," he urged, and the assembly closed in to hear the answer.

"Why, the great James Clarendon Hyde," said Campbell, "of course. Didn't you know? I say, could somebody call off this goat? It's trying to taste me. Here, go and eat hay."

"Jeannot," said the gendarme, "remove the goat. M'sieu Hyde"—he pronounced it Eed—"I know, naturally. I had not heard that he was an editor—"

"Of the *Record,"* said Forgan, nodding his head. "The London *Record*, that great paper. You have heard of it? Yes?"

"I say, Forgan," said Campbell, still speaking French, "do you think we are letting out a secret? He may have wished to remain incognito."

"Merciful heaven," said Forgan, "what have I done?"

"M'sieu can rely upon our discretion," said the gendarme. "I speak for all present who are old enough to understand. The London *Record!* And you gentlemen are doubtless managing directors?"

"No, no," said Campbell humbly. "Mere, mere reporters. He sent for us, we come. Now, may we go to him, by your good leave?"

They went, in a body, Forgan, Campbell and the gendarme in front; the assembly, which now numbered about fivescore, trailing along behind, the children revolving round and walking backwards before them the better to stare, and Jeannot with goats bringing up the rear. Hyde, who had expected them to arrive by car from some convenient aerodrome, saw from his window the procession approaching and took it at first to be some religious rite. When he recognized his friends in the van of the array, he went to the door to meet them.

"What has happened?" he said. "Have you been arrested?"

"No," said Forgan. "At least, I don't think so." He continued in French, "Sir, we have the honor to salute you." He took off his hat, placed it centrally across his person, and bowed deeply, Campbell did the same.

"Accept, messieurs," said the gendarme, "the expression of our sentiments of the most profound respect." He turned to the crowd and waved his arms at it. "Go away, the company. Jeannot, it is prohibited to pasture the goats upon the main road, lead them hence. Messieurs, adieu."

Forgan gave him five francs and shook him warmly by the hand, Campbell gave him two francs and kissed him upon both cheeks. He went away, driving the populace before him, and the three men were left alone upon the doorstep of the Green Monkey except for the hotel staff, peeping round corners.

"In the name of heaven," said James Hyde, "what is all this?"

"Just ground bait," said Forgan.

"Just a bit of extenuating circumstance, as it were," said Campbell.

Hyde broke into a laugh for the first time since he had known Wenezky was also at Haut Vannes.

"You are doing me good already," he said. "Come in and tell me what it's all about, and have a glass of sherry while we wait for lunch, it won't be long."

"It's like this," said Campbell. "We gathered that only Very Important Persons or journalists charter private aircraft these days, so as no one would put us in the VIP class we had to be journalists. It follows that you must be our editor."

"And, obviously, the editor of a paper of which everyone has heard," said Forgan, "even in Haut Vannes. The *Record*, of course."

"You'll get me hanged," said Hyde cheerfully. "Oh, here's the sherry. Landlord, these are my friends who will be staying here for a few days."

The landlord said he was truly honored, and backed out of the room.

"He's heard it already," said Forgan. "He fixed you with his glittering eye, didn't you notice?"

"He's a very good fellow," said Hyde, "it's a shame to deceive him."

"It won't hurt him," said Forgan. "Think what a thrill he's getting."

Over lunch, whenever the landlord was not in the room, Hyde filled in the details of the story he had told them by telephone. "The position now is this," he ended. "Hambledon's in jail at Torida. Wenezky is here, organizing his ruffians for an attack on Hambledon, for that's what it amounts to. Can we do something about it, and if so, what?"

"I wish we knew," said Forgan, "exactly what Hambledon is doing in that jail. According to your guide, he practically asked to be taken prisoner. Why? Is the prison governor a friend of his and was it just a method of getting to him quickly? And how long is he going to stay there?"

"I don't know any of the answers," said Hyde. "I think this. So far as being in jail is concerned, Hambledon can probably look after himself. As you say, he went there deliberately and he's no fool. But this *comunistos* business is another matter. It's an open secret that in certain parts of Spain—that is, in the hill country of Andalusia and also in an area west of Madrid, and most particularly in the foothills of the Pyrenees—the anti-Franco movement is practically in control. The government forces in the towns are like garrisons in enemy country, so long as the insurgent forces are scattered they can hold out all right, but if there was a serious attack on a small place like Torida they'd be in an awkward position. Hambledon may be staying in the governor's palace as an honored guest for all I know, he's quite capable of it. But if the governor can't protect him it won't matter whether he's in the best bedroom or in a dungeon. Wenezky's my headache, not the governor."

"It seems to me," said Forgan after a short pause, "that there's only one thing for us to do and that is to go there and see for ourselves. It certainly seems quite easy to get there, all you have to do is to meet a patrol."

"But," began Hyde.

"Yes," interrupted Campbell. "I agree. Besides, it's so simple. You heard that there was to be an attack on the jail so with the true journalistic flair for a scoop, you sent for us to go over and report it. That's what you tell Haut Vannes and of course Wenezky will hear it. It may put him off, you don't know, these conspirators don't like publicity as a rule. By the way, I'd like to have a look at Wenezky before we go."

"We might go and interview him," said Forgan. "Why not? 'Off the record, sir, is it true that you are the justly famous Señor Zero?' Can the blighter talk Spanish?"

"If I might suggest," said Hyde, "are you sure it would be wise to do that? We don't know how things will turn out, and it may be an advantage in Torida if he doesn't recognize you as having been here with me."

"I dare say you're right," said Forgan. "In any case, as our true object is not really to see him but to annoy him I expect it will keep. We might be able to annoy him to some purpose later on."

"Besides," said Campbell, "it's wasting time. I think we should get to Torida as soon as possible. How silly we should look if we missed Hambledon altogether and only got there in time to be besieged."

"You could always write an article for the *Record* about it, couldn't you?" said Hyde.

Tommy Hambledon obeyed Rougetel's instructions to the letter. "Once across the frontier," he had said, "all you have to do is to get yourself arrested. Everything has been arranged." Accordingly, when Etienne the guide dragged him into the wood because the frontier patrol was coming, Tommy disengaged himself casually and strolled into the road. He was immediately stopped and questioned, his papers were examined; finally he was arrested, mounted on a horse and escorted to Torida. He was very pleased about it; in that wild country it might have taken him hours to find somebody to arrest him; also, these men had horses and he felt he had walked far enough for one night. They clattered through the narrow streets of Torida with harness jingling and the tramp of their horses' feet thrown back at them by the stone-walled houses. The place was beautiful in a grim El Greco manner; tall narrow houses with steeply pitched roofs, secretive alleys dark in the blaze of the morning sunlight, and an ancient church, flat-fronted, heavy and austere, with the leather curtain swinging slowly in the open doorway and one cracked bell jangling from the belfry high above. Tommy straightened his tired back and looked kindly about him; this would be a nice place if breakfast were promptly served.

The escort turned up a road so steep that the houses were one above another rather than side by side; Hambledon glanced up and saw the prison directly before him, it looked like a castle. It was, in fact, a castle which had been adapted for the purpose with as little expenditure as possible. High walls glowered down upon the little town and a great door opened slowly to admit the party. They rode into a courtyard with buildings upon the other three sides; one side consisted of a house of several stories and some evidences of comfort in the way of curtains at the windows, flowers upon stone balconies and smoke ascending from chimneys. Hambledon correctly guessed it to be the governor's house. On the other two sides of the square were continuous buildings only two stories high, originally kitchens and stabling but now subdivided into cells for the accommodation of prisoners. The great door closed behind them, the party dismounted and the horses were led away.

Hambledon looked about him with an expression of pleased interest and asked innocently what castle this was. The sergeant of the patrol answered him with grave courtesy, for the arrest had not yet been confirmed.

"This is the prison of Torida, señor, though it is true that it was once a castle. Follow me, if you please."

Hambledon was shown into a cell furnished as cells are furnished all the world over with the addition of a crucifix upon one wall. Tommy said that he was hungry, not having yet breakfasted, and absentmindedly jingled coins in his pocket. The sergeant nodded and went out, presently another soldier came with coffee in a jug, a roll of rye bread and butter. He was suitably thanked and appeared pleased about it. Tommy guessed that prisoners who were prepared to pay for small attentions were rare in the Castillo Torida.

"And when do I see the governor?"

"In an hour's time."

Two hours later the sergeant returned and took his prisoner into a large room with a bar right across it and behind the bar a table and some chairs on a dais. Here they waited for some time longer till Tommy felt that unless something interesting happened soon he would fall asleep. "The air of your mountains," he said, by way of apologizing to the sergeant for yawning. Finally, just as the sergeant had retreated into the far distance and acquired two heads a door opened sharply and Tommy woke up. The door which had opened was behind the biggest chair on the dais; two soldiers came in followed by two men in black gowns, one carrying papers and the other a wand of office. The procession opened out to right and left and the governor entered.

He was a short man whose smart tunic strained at its buttons across his chest, he had an egg-shaped head upon which stiff bristles of black hair fought a rear-guard action with baldness. He wore gold-rimmed pince-nez upon a nose which started broad and narrowed to a sharp point, a small petulant mouth and a buttonlike chin. He stopped as soon as he was fairly through the doorway and froze into the fascist salute, arm raised, chin up, lowered eyelids and a blank expression. Every man in the courtroom assumed the same pose except Tommy, who waved his hat gracefully through the air, brought it to rest over his heart and bowed deeply in imitation of Douglas Fairbanks in *The Three Musketeers.* The governor's eyes opened widely and his wooden expression relaxed. He dropped his arm and sat down in the big chair with his two legal advisers on either side of him.

"Is this the prisoner?" he asked.

"I have the honor to wish Your Excellency good day," said Tommy politely. "It is an honor to me to be brought before you."

"It is, at least, a convenience to find that you can speak Spanish," said the governor drily. "Let the officer commanding the patrol describe the arrest."

Hambledon's friend the sergeant did so, adding kindly that the prisoner had been dignified and amiable throughout and given no trouble.

"And what excuse did he give for being found upon Spanish territory without proper authorization?"

The sergeant said that apparently the prisoner had been for a walk and lost his way.

"Where were you staying?" asked the governor, addressing Hambledon directly.

"At Haut Vannes, Excellency, just a stone's throw across the frontier."

"A stone's throw! It is at least twenty kilometers," said the governor. "And across the mountains, too. And in the night, if your story is to be credited."

"Moonlight, Excellency, broad moonlight. I went out for a stroll after dinner, with my cigar, and your wonderful mountains tempted me on. The air—the moonlight—the solitude drew me imperceptibly forward. Your Excellency knows how it is," said Tommy, warming to his subject. "One says to oneself: 'Just to that rock,'" and then one hears a waterfall. 'Just to that waterfall,' and so the kilometers flow beneath one's feet. The night passed like a beautiful dream, I awoke (as it were) in the dawn to find I was far from my starting place. These good men of yours came along the road, I stepped out from the wood in which I had been resting, intending to ask my way. They told me, to my utter stupefaction, that I was in Spain."

"I don't believe a word of it," said the governor. "Twenty kilometers?"

"I am an Englishman, Excellency," said Tommy proudly. "We English think nothing of walking twenty kilometers before breakfast, especially when pursuing the deer upon the mountains."

The governor shuddered. "It is well known that all Englishmen are mentally afflicted by Heaven in all matters connected with fogs," he said.

"Fogs?" said Tommy. "Fogs?"

"That is the name for what takes the place of air in Britain," said the governor. "I know, because I had a relation who was for a time on the staff of the Spanish Embassy in London. He told me they would frequently say: 'I am going out to take the fresh air.' And it is all fog."

"Oh, surely not," said Hambledon.

"So it is just conceivable, just conceivable I say, that with pure air to breathe for the first time in your life you might have walked twenty kilometers without realizing it. Spain is just and merciful, Englishman. In spite of the trouble we have had with your miserable countrymen slipping across our frontier to spy and report untruths, I will give you the benefit of the doubt. I will not sentence you at once to the term of imprisonment your folly has deserved. I will merely keep you in custody until the will of the government in Madrid is known. Sergeant, remove the prisoner."

"I thank Your Excellency," said Tommy solemnly, and was removed. As he went out at the door he heard the governor's comment to those about him.

"Mad, no doubt, but civil. Unexpectedly civil," he said.

Hambledon was satisfied with the course of events. The governor was sending his name to Madrid, where it would be recognized by the man who was waiting to see it. In the meantime his cell was cool and airy, the food was good and sufficient and he was allowed to walk upon the terrace to admire a quite magnificent view. In the words of the well-known Spanish proverb: "Patience, fleas, the night is long." There was no hurry.

He changed his mind abruptly three days later when the soldier who brought his dinner glanced meaningly at him and slipped a letter under his plate. Tommy read it the moment the man's back was turned; it ran: "Look out. The communist bands are going to force the jail to get you for Wenezky." It was signed J.C. Hyde.

Hambledon was perfectly well aware of the state of affairs in that part of Spain and that, if the insurgent bands really gathered their strength and made a determined attack, the situation might be nasty. He had also seen enough of the military regime in the prison to have very little confidence in it. The governor was a carpet soldier who had never seen active service, even in the Civil War his services had wisely been used in an administrative capacity only. The garrison was not nearly large enough and composed entirely of men from distant parts of Spain. This was done with the idea that if they had no local connections they were less likely to be infected with the local communism, but the result was that they were homesick, bored and discontented. Besides, soldiers always form local connections. Hambledon said to himself that the sergeant, Cortado, who had arrested him, was the only real soldier of the lot. The outlook was not pleasant. On the other hand, it would be difficult to warn the governor effectively without revealing that a letter had come in, which would get his own soldier attendant into trouble and probably Cortado too. Still, something must at least be attempted. Hambledon asked to be allowed to speak to the governor upon an urgent security matter, two hours later an answer came saying that the governor would give him ten minutes.

He was taken across to the governor's house this time and kept waiting for nearly an hour in a dusty little room with walls painted green and smelling of onions. At last the governor came in, nodded curtly to Hambledon, sat down abruptly and said: "Well? What is it?"

"Is your jail safe?" asked Tommy.

"Safe? This jail?" The governor laughed shortly. "I suppose this is an English joke."

"No joke at all, Excellency, I am deeply serious."

"So am I. Much too serious to waste my time with such nonsense. You will find the jail safe enough so far as you are concerned, believe me."

"But if you are attacked by the *comunistos*—"

The governor snorted, but Cortado, at Hambledon's elbow, moved slightly.

"A contemptible handful of rabble," said the governor.

"Not so contemptible if there are enough of them," said Tommy. "And they are well armed, as Your Excellency knows."

"They will not dare," said the governor, but his voice was less confident. "They will not dare," he repeated in a louder tone. "And as for you, do you think you can frighten me with bogy stories? You have been reading the lies about Spain that are published in your rotten press. There are no communists in Spain, or so few that they dare not even speak. The government is in complete control and I represent the government." He paused and added abruptly: "What proof have you?"

"None. Only my word that I heard an attack being discussed on the other side of the frontier."

"Bah!" said the governor.

"Not 'Bah!' at all. Very serious," said Tommy.

"Remove the prisoner," said the governor, and stalked out.

On the way back across the yard Cortado took Hambledon's elbow as though to steer him away from a pile of stores which were being unpacked.

"Was that what was in the note?" asked the sergeant in a low tone.

"Yes," said Tommy. "Don't know when, but soon."

"Thank you," said Cortado, and returned the prisoner to his cell.

Early the following morning Hambledon heard the patrol come in as usual from the night's duties and presently the voice of the governor uplifted in lamentation upon the terrace.

"Mother of God," it said, "not two more Englishmen?"

Chapter Fifteen
The Gatecrashers

The governor held another court of enquiry in the same room in which Hambledon had been interrogated, only this time the guard was doubled because there were two prisoners. Their passports lay on the table before him so he knew their names and which was which. He addressed them separately.

"Forgan. *Sabe usted hablar español?*"

Forgan shook his head.

"Camp-a-bell. *Sabe usted hablar español?*"

Campbell shook his head, shrugged his shoulders, raised his hands and said: "No spicka da *español.*"

"They do not speak Spanish," said the governor resignedly. "Well, at least they will not lecture me on how to protect these premises. Let the officer commanding the patrol describe the arrest."

While this was going on the prisoners stared about them as men do who cannot understand what is said until Forgan had a bright idea. He pulled a small booklet from his pocket and nudged Campbell, who nodded eagerly. Together they turned over the pages, penciled a mark in the margin and made signs for the book to be handed up to the dais.

"What is it that they have there?" asked the governor.

"It is a phrase book, Excellency, such as tourists use. They have marked a sentence."

"What is it?"

The official with the wand of office read it out. "Do us the favor to direct us to the railway station."

The governor took the book into his own hands and glanced through it. "This has possibilities," he said. He marked the phrase "There is no occasion for it," and passed it back.

Campbell and Forgan came back with: "I must go away at once."

The governor hunted wildly through the book for some equivalent of "Not if I know it," but the nearest he could find was: "The children would not dare to go into the garden without permission."

"Blimey!" said Campbell, and marked: "These children will not be quiet."

The governor ground his teeth and indicated two consecutive sentences. "It is neither good for you nor me. She died next morning."

Forgan: "How lovely these flowers are!"

The governor, with menace: "They appear to be a long way from here, but they are not."

"Sinister, what?" said Campbell, and marked: "With regard to the assertion he made, we must see whether it can be proved."

The governor really wished to ask them why they had crossed the frontier, but the phrase book did not provide for gatecrashers. What he wanted was an interpreter; he thought of Hambledon and hesitated. He did not wish to see any more of Hambledon on any account, he did not want to be under any obligation to him, and finally it might be a very serious mistake to let the three Englishmen meet. However, there seemed no ready alternative and he ordered Hambledon to be brought in. He came at once and only his habitual self-control prevented his mouth from falling open when he saw who was there. Forgan and Campbell looked at him with polite indifference.

The governor addressed Hambledon. "These are two more of your crazy compatriots who have entered Spain irregularly. Please ask them why they did so."

Hambledon realized that among the dozen or so Spaniards in the room there might be one who understood some English even if he could not speak it. He translated the governor's words without addition or comment.

"Just shut our eyes and sleepwalked," said Forgan.

"Excellency, they say they walked here in their sleep."

The governor said he didn't believe it, and used such energy in saying so that no translation was necessary.

"I think the gentleman is being rude," said Forgan plaintively.

"Ask them once more," said the governor, "and tell them that unless they give a civil answer this time they shall be chained in a dungeon till they mend their manners."

Tommy did so, adding: "He probably will, too."

"It's like this," said Campbell. "Why don't they mark their frontiers? We thought frontiers had tall wooden posts painted in colored stripes, and electrified wire netting topped off with barbed wire with bells hanging on it. Was there? Was there heck! There was nothing, I tell you, nothing to show which was France and which was Spain." He paused to allow Tommy to translate, and added: "They aren't even different colors as they show you on the map. It isn't fair."

The governor raised his eyes to heaven and waited while the scribe at his left hand wrote it all down. Then he asked what their profession was at home in England.

"We are journalists," said Forgan.

The governor said what he thought of journalists.

"Oh no," said Campbell gently. "Not that kind at all. We are reporters for the *Record* of London."

Tommy controlled himself and passed on the news.

"But the *Record* is a reputable paper," said the governor. "For an English paper, that is."

"It is without exception the greatest paper in the whole world," said Forgan.

"And the *Record* sent you two out here?"

"Certainly."

"What for?"

"Oh, just to see what things are really like on the Franco-Spanish frontier," said Forgan. "The situation certainly has possibilities. Interesting possibilities."

Tommy took the liberty of translating "interesting" as "dangerous" and the governor recoiled.

"Enough," he said. "Tell these men that I will communicate with Madrid regarding their fate. In the meantime they will be kept in custody. Remove the prisoners." When they were out of earshot he added: "Let them be well fed and civilly treated. I do not like Englishmen, but the *Record* after all—they might write an article about me."

Hambledon was allowed to go out on the terrace every day after the hour of the afternoon siesta; as a rule he spent his time smoking cigarettes kindly provided by the guard at three times their normal price, looking at the view and talking to any soldiers who might be lounging about. Discipline was not usually severe in the castle prison of Torida. On this day he noticed that things were different. Rifles were being cleaned and boxes of ammunition carried out; from the yard on the farther side of the prison buildings came words of command suggesting that drill was in progress, and at the far end of the terrace a group of men were practicing taking down and reassembling a machine gun under the direction of Sergeant Cortado. No one took much notice of Tommy and he strolled carelessly away in the hope of being able to locate Forgan and Campbell.

Presently from the window of one of the cells came the sound of a loud and careful voice teaching Spanish. "These are the numerals," it said. *"Uno, dos, tres, cuatro, cinco, seis, siete, ocho, nueve, diez."*

The voice stopped and immediately started again in the middle a of word. "—umerals, *uno, dos, tres—*"

"I've got it," said Tommy to himself. "Spanish on gramophone records."

The record stopped again and Forgan's voice followed. "You know, Campbell, we ought to practice these numbers."

"Let's count sheep," said Campbell. "Make it more interesting."

"What's the Spanish for 'sheep'?"

"Don't know. There's a soldier, let's ask him." They came to their window, barred but without glass, and beckoned urgently to a soldier who was staggering along with a heavy box of ammunition.

"Ho! *Soldado! Soldado!*"

Anything being better than carrying heavy boxes, the fellow put it down at once and approached the window. Campbell, prompted by Forgan, addressed him.

"What is—*qué es*—the Spanish for—*el español por*—'sheep'?"

"*Perdone?*" said the man, grinning.

"There you are, it's *perdone,*" said Campbell.

"No, no, that means 'I beg your pardon.' He doesn't understand. Sheep, man, sheep. Listen. Baa, baa."

"Baa, baa," they chanted in varying tones together. The soldier started to speak but laughter overcame him, he rocked on his feet and his comrades came to join him. There was a group of them together, with grinning faces turned up to the window from whence came the sound of a whole flock protesting, when the governor came round the corner.

"What the devil is all this?"

The soldiers immediately busied themselves with their duties and the mutton duet ceased.

"Excellency," said Forgan.

"Go to Gehenna," said the governor.

"*Prefero requiescat in pace ici,*" said Forgan.

"What dog's talk is this?"

"*Requiescat*—let them remain—*in pace*—in peace—*in hoc*—in this—*castrum*—castle. No wanchee Gehenna—is that your home town?"

The governor gathered that they would rather stay where they were. Dignity suggested that it would be better to walk away, curiosity detained him beneath their window. He half turned to go when Campbell had the right idea.

"*Viva Franco,*" he said. "*Viva España.*"

"Ah!" said the governor, and beamed upon them. "You are on the right side, after all. We must find some means of converse." He looked about him and saw Hambledon at a little distance elaborately pretending not to hear what was said. "Come here, you, and interpret. It now seems possible I may have mistaken these gentlemen's intentions. Tell them so."

Before Tommy could speak Campbell had started the gramophone record at another point. "The ship is now approaching the quayside," it said in Spanish. "Those are the customhouses on your left hand. What a beautiful city is Barcelona!"

"What is all this?" said the governor. "Do they think they are in Barcelona?"

"I don't think so, Excellency. That which you hear is a Spanish language record, I think they are trying to learn the language."

"Very praiseworthy," said the gratified governor. "Very creditable. It would have been better still if they had learned it before they came here. Ask them why they came over the frontier in that manner instead of obtaining visas and entering Spain correctly."

As this was exactly what Hambledon was wondering himself, he obeyed at once.

"The old boy wants to know why you sneaked over the frontier like that but it's nothing to the things I want to know. Did Hyde bring you out?" Forgan nodded. "Why on earth?"

"Because Wenezky was a bit more than he could tackle alone. Tell the old boy the *Record* wanted to know if a man could slip across the frontier so we came and slipped."

"They were instructed by their paper to do so in order to see if it were possible," translated Tommy.

"How many soldiers are there in this place?" asked Campbell.

"Fifteen, and eight armed warders," said Tommy. "Where is Wenezky now?"

"On his way here with an unknown number of pals. He started with fifty, but he is meeting a lot more on his way here. Couple of hundred, maybe."

"Sounds sticky," said Tommy.

"What are they saying?" asked the governor.

"They were asking whether Your Excellency was a personal friend of General Franco's."

"I should not presume to say that. I have had the honor of being presented to him."

"Franco seems to have thrown him back again, doesn't he?" said Forgan. "I mean, you wouldn't make a man governor of a place like this if you wanted to see much of him, would you?"

"But why did you come here and get yourselves jugged?"

"Oh, just to see the fun. Things have been quiet lately in Clerkenwell Road."

"I always thought you two were a bit mad," said Hambledon, "and now I'm sure of it. They say," he added to the governor, "that they hope, now they are here, to see some of the beauties of this famous and ancient land."

"But not ancient beauties," said Campbell. "Impress that upon him."

The governor said that he would present their case to the Madrid authorities in the most favorable light possible, and Campbell asked if they couldn't have a few pinup girls to go on with. "To warm this cell up a bit, you know."

"Ask him if we can come out of here," said Forgan. "This place smells of mice that have been eating onions."

But the governor said that, to his deep regret, it was not possible until tomorrow, it being against regulations for prisoners to leave their cells during the first twenty-four hours of their confinement. "Tomorrow," he repeated to Tommy. *"Mañana,* tell them, *mañana."*

"He's great on regulations," explained Tommy. "He looks them up in a book. When are we to expect Wenezky and party? Tonight?"

"Might be, we don't know for certain. Tonight or tomorrow. Can you let us out when the time comes, or do we just kick the door down?"

"I'll see to it," said Hambledon. "The sergeant over there is a good man, his name is Cortado."

The governor caught the name and asked what it was about Cortado.

"I told them that Cortado is a disciplinarian and if he gave an order they'd better jump to it."

The governor smiled kindly and said that firmness was an essential ingredient of discipline. He added that he had given himself this pleasure long enough, and must go and attend to his duties. He wished them *"buenas noches"* and departed, shooing Hambledon in front of him and finally handing him over to Cortado to be locked up again. "I shall require your services as interpreter again tomorrow," he said. "If you are diligent and attentive, certain indulgences will be granted."

Hambledon thanked him and turned to Cortado as soon as the governor was out of earshot. "Tonight or tomorrow the attack may be expected," he said.

"Is it known how many?" asked the sergeant.

"Not definitely. Possibly a couple of hundred."

Cortado raised his eyebrows. "And we are twenty-three, counting the warders."

"Twenty-four, counting me," said Hambledon.

The sergeant nodded as though he had expected that answer.

"And twenty-six, counting the other Englishmen," added Tommy.

"I will bring the rifles to you myself," said Cortado, preparing to lock the cell door.

"What about the other prisoners?" asked Tommy. "We aren't the only ones."

"No good," said Cortado. *"Comunistos.* Also one dishonest clerk aged seventy." He locked the door and went away.

"If words were money," said Tommy, "you'd be a miser. Good chap, though."

The twilight deepened until night had completely fallen. There was a tiny oil lamp in Hambledon's cell but he did not light it, partly because it was easier to see out of the barred window if it was dark within and partly because he did not wish to make a target of himself. He went to the window and looked out; there was a pale streak across the sky against which was silhouetted the figure of a sentry marching up and down the terrace and, every so often, pausing to look over the wall which was low there since the ground fell precipitously away on that side. There came the sound of someone singing, not any of the garrison since the words were English and were accompanied by a band. Forgan's gramophone, obviously. Tommy listened and caught the words.

"In a little Spanish town,
'Twas on a night like this—
Stars were peek-a-booing down . . ."

Forgan appeared to be short of records, for he played this one many times over till it ran round and round in Tommy's head and, when at last it stopped, the sentry was whistling it.

An hour later, just when Tommy was expecting supper, his cell door was flung open and the governor entered hastily, hands outstretched.

"My dear fellow—most worthy señor—how can I sufficiently apologize—"

"Why worry?" said Hambledon lazily.

"I took you for an Englishman, sheep's head that I am—I have just heard from Madrid by telephone—"

"They have taken a long time about it," said Tommy coldly.

"I beg that you will overlook this unfortunate misunderstanding. I beg that you will come out from this miserable cell and honor my poor house with your presence. This man will carry your luggage—ah, I see, you have none. We old campaigners know how to travel light, do we not? This way, pray precede me. If only I had known—if your honor had but given me the smallest hint——"

"Would you have believed me?" asked Tommy, but the agitated governor let the matter pass.

"They are sending a plane from Madrid to fetch you, it will arrive tonight. We have an emergency landing ground, señor, and I am to light up the flare path. Be welcome to my poor house, the private rooms are upon the first floor."

The governor babbled on but Hambledon scarcely heeded him. Very awkward, Forgan and Campbell being here. If the plane arrived before the attack started he would have to go in it and leave them here to see the business through without him. Well, it could not be helped and it wasn't his fault they were there, they had come of their own accord even if it was with the idea of helping him. Hyde's idea, probably, these zealous helpers . . .

"What time do you expect the plane to arrive, Excellency?"

"Not for two hours or more yet. We have plenty of time for dinner and, indeed, I was wondering whether it would really be necessary for you to leave before morning. I am convinced it would not. So much pleasanter to travel by day and see the country after the benefit of a good night's rest in a soft bed instead of the penitential palliasse to which my stupidity consigned you. I still wish that you had given me one little hint—just a few words in German, I speak a little German—"

"So do many other people who are not Germans," said Tommy shortly, and went on eating his dinner and listening till his ears ached for some sound outside—a rifle shot or a series of yells or a few hand grenades at the gate. "I am not responsible for Forgan and Campbell," he told himself firmly. This was the kind of thing that happened when one worked with amateurs.

"In my native Andalusia," said the governor, toying with his wineglass, "the most beautiful time of the year is the—"

There came a dull thud, not loud, but everything leapt upon the table and the windows shook as though they had been kicked. There followed a piercing scream in a man's voice, shouted orders and the sound of small-arms fire. The governor clutched the arms of his chair and Hambledon rose slowly to his feet.

"Well," he said. "It's begun."

Chapter Sixteen
Castle in Spain

Tommy ran down the stairs and the governor followed him more slowly. When Hambledon reached the door leading into the prison yard he paused and peered carefully round the doorpost. The yard was as light as day, for there were floodlights trained upon it and upon the gate, and Cortado had turned them all on. The gate was actually a huge wooden door opening in two halves; one half was flat upon the ground, and splintered pieces of the other half were still hanging crookedly from its hinges. The yard itself was quite empty except for a dead man who had been the sentry at the gate when it was blown in. From where Tommy stood he could see at a slant through the gateway where crouching forms moved stealthily about. As he looked there was the red flash of a rifle and a bullet hit the doorpost just above his head; he dodged hastily back and cannoned into the governor.

"Put this light out," said Tommy, referring to the passage light above their heads, "where's the switch?"

"There," said the governor, and pointed at it with the revolver he held in his hand. The hand was very unsteady and the revolver wavered like reflections in water.

"Better give me that," said Hambledon, and took it from him. "A Luger, eh? Good. Ammunition? Give it to me, that's right. Now I'll switch out the light, they won't see us so well and I shall see a lot better."

"The confidential papers," bleated the governor.

"Damn the confidential papers," said Tommy, and turned out the light. "Now, where's that blighter who potted at me?" He fired four shots rapidly and jumped across the passage into cover; there was a yelp from beyond the gate and a bullet hit the opposite wall. Flashes came from the cell windows facing the gate as the garrison replied.

"I wish I had a rifle," said Tommy.

"The situation looks extremely dangerous," said the governor, and his voice retreated down the dark passage.

"Here, I want you. How does one get round the prison without crossing the yard?"

"Follow me, I am leading the way," said the governor. Tommy shut the front door and bolted it; the ground-floor windows were heavily barred. He turned and followed the governor down the passage, through a room on the left and out through a door onto the terrace.

"Where's Cortado?" asked Tommy.

"Along to your left, señor, if you pass along the terrace you will find him."

"Come on," said Hambledon, and started at a run with the governor tagging behind. "Have you got your master key to the cells?"

"Yes, but what—what—the prisoners are all rebels—"

"Give it to me," said Tommy, and stopped at the door of Forgan's cell. He flung it open and the horrified governor observed the two Englishmen smashing up their portable gramophone.

"What—why—"

"The party has begun," said Tommy.

"So we noticed," said Forgan.

"We were just unpacking the fireworks," said Campbell. The box finally fell to pieces and disclosed beneath an oddly small gramophone motor two large revolvers and numerous packets of ammunition. "We thought these might be helpful."

The governor was so agitated that he did not realize that both men were talking fluent Spanish. "To bring firearms into the prison, it is unheard of, it is—"

"Against the regulations," said Forgan, loading rapidly.

There were furious yells from the courtyard upon the further side and the firing increased to violence.

"Sounds as though the blighters have got in," said Campbell, for their cell had no window towards the courtyard. "How do we get at 'em?"

"Alternate cells face that way," said Tommy. "I'll unlock them, they're all empty along here." He dodged round the governor and collided with a man in the doorway.

"The rifles, gentlemen," said Cortado quietly. "The rebels are in the courtyard and are trying to release the *comunisto* prisoners."

"Cortado, have you gone mad?" asked the governor.

"Oh, go and comb the canary," said Forgan, pushing past him. "Gentlemen, to the barricades!" He added a rifle to his armory and disappeared, followed by Campbell and the sergeant. The governor trotted after them.

"Cortado!"

"Sir?" said the sergeant, slipping another clip into his magazine.

"I am going to place the confidential papers in safety. I hand over the command to you during my absence."

"Very good, sir."

"Sergeant, can one get up on the roof?" asked Hambledon.

"I have some men up there, señor. With machine guns."

"Well done."

The governor clapped his hands to his head and trotted back along the terrace followed by a burst of melody from Campbell, in English this time, punctuated by shots from his revolver.

"In enterprise of martial kind when there was any fighting
He led his regiment from behind, he found it less exciting,

But when away his regiment ran, his place was at the fore-O
That celebrated, cultivated, adulated warrior,
The Duke of Plaza-Toro!"

Cortado disappeared and Tommy found himself a window looking upon the courtyard, no longer empty but occupied by fighting men, some firing at the windows,
some attacking the side of the yard to the wall, the wing where the convicted
prisoners were kept. These men were shrieking encouragement to the attackers
and thrusting clenched fists through the bars of their windows in the communist
salute. "If they get through there," said Tommy, "they'll come round behind and
we're *alles gesunken.*" He cuddled his rifle to his shoulder and began to pick off
the men attacking the doors. He could not distinguish, at such close range and in
such an uproar, where most of the shooting was coming from, but men in the yard
were falling fast, the defense was doing pretty well. A little later there came a burst
of machine-gun fire from the roof and the effect was dramatic. The attackers broke
and ran for the gate, those, that is, who could still run; the courtyard was dotted
with the bodies of those who could not, and the prisoners in the cells howled like
wolves. Tommy amused himself by firing at the bars of their windows and produc-
ing a satisfying "Whang!" every time till the howls were hushed.

The firing stopped suddenly for lack of targets and the sudden silence was so
disconcerting that Hambledon started violently when a quiet voice spoke behind
him.

"It is well so far, señor."

"Cortado—I am glad you're all right. What will they do now?"

"Attack somewhere else, señor. There are many ladders in the town. If I blow
my whistle three long blasts, retire to the governor's house, it is easier to hold than
these long buildings. I have told your friends."

"Very well."

"I am going up on the roof again to see—"

"Hush!" said Tommy. "What are they shouting?"

Someone outside the wall was hailing the leader of the *comunistos. "Fuego!"*
the voice cried. *"Fuego al—"*

"Fire at what? I can't hear," said Tommy.

"Fire at the convoy," said Cortado, bending his head to listen, "the convoy is on
fire, he says. Their convoy? Follow me to the roof, señor."

Tommy rushed upstairs at the sergeant's heels, up a ladder to a trap door and out
upon the leaded roof where two men with a machine gun were staring and pointing
away to the north. A couple of miles away there was a line of fires blazing, plainly
a convoy of vehicles drawn up close together against a wood and burning furiously.
Even as they looked another burst into flame, and another as dark gaps in the line
were filled with fire, and the trees caught also.

From outside the gate there rose an agitated babble of many voices exclaiming and arguing, and Cortado recognized his moment.

"I am going to attack," he said to Hambledon, and called orders to the other men on the roof to go down at once. "Stay here, señor, we are enough," he added, and dropped down the ladder after his men. Tommy stayed; if the sortie were beaten back he might be useful where he was. In the quiet which followed he heard a distant drone, at first barely audible and growing louder with every moment.

"Aircraft," he thought. "One, only. Dear me, I suppose that's my plane. What a moment to arrive."

Sudden darkness blinded him, Cortado had turned off the floodlights. The next moment there was the sound of running feet across the yard, somebody tripped over something and fell with a crash, but the rest of the sortie burst out of the gateway and fell upon the *comunistos* outside. Instantly uproar broke out again only to be almost drowned in the roar of the aircraft passing low overhead.

As the sound of its engines diminished Tommy could hear the course of the battle outside and it was obvious that the sortie was successful. Cries and shots receded and scattered and the sounds of conflict gradually died away.

"I shall go down and congratulate the victors," said Tommy, easing himself carefully through the trap door. "By heck, that fellow Cortado deserves a decoration. I wonder whether Wenezky is among the jetsam in the courtyard?"

He went first to look for Campbell and Forgan and found them in their cell applying first aid to each other with iodine and strips of elastoplast.

"Hullo! Casualties?"

"Not to speak of," said Campbell cheerfully. "Forgan's got a nick out of his ear—it always did stick out—and the wretched thing won't stop bleeding. Here, hold your head still, can't you? Mine's nothing, a clout on the knuckles from a splinter of stone."

"Glad it's no worse," said Tommy. "I say, did you hear someone had set fire to their convoy? I saw it from the roof. A lovely blaze, I wonder who did it."

"I don't know, of course," said Forgan, peeling off his coat, "but Hyde's out there somewhere. It seems a pity to waste all this blood, doesn't it? If I send this coat to a blood bank they could wring it out, couldn't they? Messy things, ears."

"Hyde?" said Tommy. "What the devil's he doing in Spain? I thought I told him to go home."

"Why should he?" said Forgan. "Spain's big enough for both of you, surely. He's only touring. His papers are all in order and he came in quite legally."

"I beg your pardon," said Hambledon instantly. "Why not, as you say? But what's he doing out there? This isn't on the main road to anywhere."

"Waiting for us," said Forgan. "We arranged to join him for a short trip as soon as this was over."

"We are going to look at the ancient beauties of Spain," said Campbell solemnly.

"Tell me," said Hambledon, "why did you pretend you couldn't speak Spanish?"

"To make questioning more difficult, of course," said Forgan. "Or was it just perversity?" He opened a suitcase, took out a suit and began to put it on; it was of noticeably foreign cut and so, Hambledon noticed, was the one into which Campbell had changed.

"Can we give you a lift anywhere?" asked Campbell politely.

"Thank you, but that airplane has come to take me away," said Tommy.

"Would you mind telling us where you're going," said Forgan, "as experience suggests to us that it might be more peaceful elsewhere?"

Hambledon laughed. "To Madrid, for a start," he said. "I don't know where I shall go after that. Let's go out and acclaim Cortado, shall we? Also I want to have a look at the debris in the courtyard."

"Wenezky isn't there," said Forgan. "I saw him run out. Unless, of course, he was pipped in the sortie, but he looked to me as though he wasn't stopping."

"You know him, do you?" said Hambledon carelessly, and Campbell laughed.

"He was the showpiece at Haut Vannes, wasn't he? Tourists always inspect local objects of interest such as ruins, freaks and curiosities. He didn't see us, or Hyde."

"We wanted to go and interview him on behalf of the *Record,*" said Forgan. "But Hyde dissuaded us."

"Hyde was right," said Tommy rather shortly. "Well, shall we go and greet Cortado?"

"By all means," said Forgan. "You lead the way, will you?"

Hambledon went ahead and eventually found Cortado superintending the temporary repair of the gate. He said, in reply to Hambledon's compliments, that the sortie was a foregone conclusion. The *comunistos* thought that the airplane had come to machine-gun them from the air and they had had experience of that before. "They were already running, señor, it was but to push a falling tree."

"Where's the airplane now, d'you know?"

"Landed in the meadows by the river, señor, below the town. The landing lights were on, I saw them from the roof."

Hambledon looked about him and could not see either Forgan, Campbell or the governor. He ought to speak to the governor, it would be only civil. He asked Cortado where His Excellency might be.

"In his house, señor. He may be still engaged with the confidential papers in the strong room."

Hambledon shook hands with the sergeant, went across to the governor's house and looked for a stair down to the cellars. He was right, there were cellars, he found the stair and met the governor coming up. There was an exchange of courtesies, very formal on Hambledon's part, and he took his leave.

"Say to them in Madrid," urged the governor, "that the garrison of Torida are men who know their duty and do it."

"I will insist upon their hearing every detail," said Tommy, and went off to have a final word with Forgan and Campbell and to send a message to Hyde. He felt a certain compunction, they had come here to help him and he had not shown much appreciation. The fact was that the two modelmakers rather exasperated him; they always, as it were, backed away and disengaged themselves behind a smoke screen of words. He remembered with annoyance that he had told them where he was going but had no idea where they were bound.

They were not in the courtyard. While he was looking about a soldier came up to him and said that the plane was ready and the pilot would like to take off as soon as convenient.

"Yes, in just a moment," said Hambledon, and went round to the cell where Forgan and Campbell had been imprisoned. They were not there and he could not wait. He met Cortado on his way out.

"I am going now. I shall hope to see you again someday."

"And I your honor. *Adiós, señor.*"

"When you see the other two Englishmen, do me the favor to tell them that I looked for them at the last moment and could not find them."

"It shall be done."

A quarter of an hour later the plane took off, circled the town and turned away southward for Madrid.

Forgan helped two of the warders to carry a balk of timber for the repair of the shattered gate, he went outside to help them lift it into place and slipped away under cover of the wall where Campbell joined him and they walked away together. It was dark in the narrow streets once they were beyond the influence of Cortado's floodlights; the two men kept close together down the middle of the road with their revolvers in their hands, for though there was nothing to be seen in that obscurity small noises in the deeper shadows suggested that the alleys were not so empty as they seemed. In ten minutes they had passed beyond the houses and were walking along a country road. Forgan spoke for the first time and even then his voice was low.

"Well, we got out of there without having our throats cut," he said.

"It may happen yet," said Campbell cheerfully. "Our late antagonists are doubt- less all over the countryside on their way home."

"I am hoping we may be mistaken for one of them, they can't all know each other."

"The idea is sound, especially if we appear nervous," said Campbell. "Leap away from shadows every now and then."

Forgan did so at the moment when they passed a clump of bushes and the partners ran for thirty yards before they slowed.

"Was there really anything there?" asked Campbell.

"Oh yes, a man with a gun. I saw the starlight run along the barrel. I think we'd better not talk."

Half an hour's fast walking brought them to a deserted farm with two tall trees by the broken gate. The sight appeared to cheer Campbell, for he began to whistle as they approached it and the tune was "The Campbells Are Coming." When they came level with the gateway two men stepped out from the shadow of the trees.

"Good evening," said James Hyde. "How are you both?"

"Quite well, thank you," said Forgan. "A little in need of refreshment, perhaps. Good evening, Etienne."

"Good evening, messieurs," answered the guide.

"Come along to the car," said Hyde. "I've got a picnic meal of sorts there, I thought you might be hungry. We put her in the barn. We can switch on the side-lights, I think."

"Much more private," said Campbell.

Etienne laughed. "This privacy, it is wise. We have been too much in the lime-light tonight."

"Was it you, then, who set fire to those lorries?"

"Assuredly. M'sieu here enjoyed himself, I think."

"It was rather fun," said Hyde. "They were all parked together, nose to tail, and the front and rear ones immobilized. Actually, we saw them from miles away, they came along to that wood and then all turned round facing the way they'd come for a quick escape, no doubt. You could see the headlights swinging as they turned. So we gave them plenty of time to get well away and then came along to see if we could do anything. We didn't really begin till we heard the first bang up at Torida. This is tongue, Forgan, and these are a couple of cold chickens, help yourselves while I draw this cork. I can't find the corkscrew—here it is. How is Hambledon since he hasn't come with you?"

"Quite all right. He's gone to Madrid by air."

"What, before the attack?"

"No, afterwards."

"We heard an *avion*, m'sieu," said Etienne with the leg of a chicken in his hand.

"So we did. Hambledon must have a pull. Much excitement at your end?" asked Hyde.

"Lively while it lasted," said Campbell. "Tell me, how do you set about igniting a lorry? Fire lighters against the tires?"

"Etienne's the expert," said Hyde with a laugh.

"Strips of rag, messieurs, dipped into the filler of the petrol tank and left trailing out of it. One match, and f-f-f—!" He gestured with the chicken leg. "So did we in the days of the Resistance."

"And then you came away singing," suggested Campbell.

"Well, more or less," said Hyde. "Actually, we stayed a few minutes too long."

Forgan put down his glass and looked at Hyde. "Somebody go for you?"

"Not exactly. I said the lorries were alongside a wood. There was a car in the wood, up a sort of lane, and we hadn't seen it. We were getting into the Bugatti to come away when this car came out just in time—the undergrowth was burning. He had to stop, we were in the way. It was Wenezky."

"He did leave Torida rather early," said Forgan thoughtfully.

"We thought by the way he ran that he wasn't going to return," said Campbell. "We said so at the time, I remember. What happened?"

"I'm afraid I just hopped into the Bugatti and drove like blazes," admitted Hyde. "With a tickling sensation at the back of my neck. We soon lost him, he couldn't hold the pace. I then lost myself; if it hadn't been for Etienne I should never have got here. In fact, we hadn't been here long when you arrived."

"So you don't know which way he went," said Forgan.

"No idea," said Hyde. "I'm sorry, ought I to have done something about it?"

"Short of shooting him," said Campbell, "I don't quite see what you could have done. He recognized you, did he?"

"Must have done. He turned on his headlights and there was I in the middle of the road ten yards away."

"Let us clear our minds," said Forgan. "Wenezky is after Hambledon whom he knew to be at Torida. He must know Hambledon wouldn't stay at Torida long; where will he go and how? At this juncture he sees you, and you were driving Hambledon before. Presumably you have come to pick him up again, I don't suppose Wenezky knows he has gone by air. So if Wenezky can hang onto you, you will lead him to Hambledon, I imagine that was why he chased you so earnestly. Am I right so far?"

"I suppose so," said Hyde. "But we got away."

"Yes," said Forgan. "All the same, I don't think we ought to hang about here till daylight, there aren't so many passable roads in this neighborhood and if we give him time he might arrange to have them watched. I think, if you agree, we should push off soon."

"I agree," said Hyde.

The guide Etienne put down his glass.

"The gentlemen are speaking of avoiding one man only," he said. "Without wishing to intrude my unasked opinion—"

"Go on, Etienne, please."

"It will be all over the district in a few hours that it was you who burned the convoy. The district will therefore be unhealthy for M'sieu."

"Etienne, what about you? I dragged you into this," said Hyde anxiously.

"I was not seen," said the guide, "I was already in the Bugatti when the other car came out of the wood. Have no fear for me, I have friends who will prove I was miles away at the time. It is M'sieu who should remove himself, forgive me."

"He's right," said Campbell. "Every *comunisto* for miles will be sharpening a knife to cut your throat withal. A Marked Man is what you are."

"I expect you're right," said Hyde. "Incidentally, are we going to Madrid?"

"It seems a good place," said Forgan. "We may see Hambledon there or we may not. If we do, it might be rewarding; it usually is, I notice. If we don't, we can potter along somewhere else and be real tourists for once. I've always wanted to see Granada."

"There is still five hours of darkness," said Etienne, rising. "If M'sieu has no further need of me, I should be on my way."

"I owe you more than I can ever repay," said Hyde. "Some day we shall meet again."

"Till then, m'sieu, remember me."

Chapter Seventeen
A Present for Wenezky

Wenezky was much happier and more confident the moment he crossed the border into Spain, for he had been there before. In the days when the Spanish Civil War was burning up the country he had gone there with a contingent from Russia to fight on the side of the *Frente Popular;* he had been in Madrid when a man could look out of the upper windows of the tall post office and see Franco's trenches little more than a mile distant. He knew the city well, he even thought he could still find friends there if need be. France was strange to him, for he had traveled to Spain by the Mediterranean and gone back the same way when all was lost. France he did not like and rightly accounted himself fortunate when the luck of the chase took him to the Horn of Roland at Haut Vannes where the landlord greeted him with the sign of the clenched fist and the *comunistos* from the nearby camp dropped in for thick glasses of red wine and a lot of windy talk. Among them were many men who also had fought Franco and some who had even defended Madrid; though there were none whom he had actually known it was not long before they were comparing memories and there was no doubt that he was one of them. He was accepted and welcomed, not only as an old comrade but as a traveled man who had seen much to interest men who had been drearily interned for years and who were not so much ageing as rotting in inactivity. He sat round their campfires and told them stories, mainly about Poland and East Prussia, in a Spanish as fluent as his French was obstructed. When he offered them an adventure in the attack on the Torida prison, they seized upon the idea and discussed it at great length in every detail. It was, at least, action instead of dry rot. Strategy, tactics, transport, reinforcements from the Spanish side, the time and place of meeting, routes and methods, arms and munitions; these men had not been so happy for years nor so busy. He told them that Hambledon was a comrade to be rescued because he and Wenezky had a mission for the Cause.

"When it is all over," they said, "when the place is in our hands and your friend is freed, where will you go?"

"That is for him to decide," said Wenezky, who had not the faintest idea. "He will, by then, have his orders."

They were impressed and looked it. "Have you a passport, comrade? If you should wish to remain in Spain, papers will be necessary."

Wenezky admitted that his passport had no visa for Spain, nor stamp of the place of entry.

"Here is one which came into our hands," they said, and gave him a passport which had once belonged to one Erich Sachsen, attached to the German Embassy in Madrid.

"A filthy German," said Wenezky distastefully. "A fascist reactionary."

"That is so, but it is all duly stamped, visaed and authorized. Further, it bears the official permit of the Madrid police."

"Suppose I meet him," said Wenezky doubtfully.

"Not this side hell, comrade, for that is where he is now. It is but to transfer your photograph, we have a man who is clever at that. He worked at one time in a passport office."

"Let it be done," said Wenezky casually.

The time drew near for the attack on Torida. Wenezky and some fifty of his friends crossed the frontier and met other comrades as arranged. Four lorries moved off together on the appointed night and drove towards Torida, seven more joined the convoy en route. Wenezky was not in command; the leader was a local hero who knew his men, the surrounding country, the town and even the prison, having served a sentence there. He led the procession in a small car of his own and parked it inside the wood. Wenezky made his own intentions quite clear.

"All I want out of that place is my friend," he said nobly. "The rest is yours."

"Tomorrow morning you shall breakfast with him at the governor's table while the governor hangs by the neck from the balcony outside," said the leader. "He insulted me and I wash out insults with blood."

But Tommy Hambledon shot him through the head as he was attacking the door of the cell where once he unwillingly resided and the governor remained unhanged. When the machine guns opened up from the prison roof and the communist attack broke up, Wenezky ran with the rest. He paused in a doorway at a safe distance in case the attack reformed and saw with his own eyes the glare of the burning convoy. The *comunistos* were visibly disheartened and when, five minutes later, Cortado's counterattack burst upon them Wenezky did not hesitate. There was the small car which perhaps was not burning with the rest and he needed it. He was a long-legged man in good condition, he passed other fugitives as though they were merely walking, dodged through the wood, started up the small car and drove out into the road to see, only ten yards ahead in the full light of the fire, the neat respectable figure of that other Englishman who had driven Hambledon from Auch to Haut Vannes in the gray Austin.

Wenezky was so surprised that he stopped the car; the Englishman's expression changed abruptly from pleased excitement to extreme dismay, he leapt into his car and instantly drove away. Unfortunately he was no longer driving the Austin but a Bugatti, and the Englishman could drive. At the end of seven miles he was beyond pursuit and not even the lights of any car were to be seen anywhere in the dark uneasy countryside.

Wenezky pulled into the side of the road, lit a cigarette and settled down to think.

In the first place, this Englishman—Hyde, that was the name, Hyde—must have come there to meet Hambledon, presumably to drive him somewhere else. Therefore Hambledon must have arranged to leave the prison that night and, unless he had been shot in the attack, the confusion would make it easier to escape. Therefore it was no use looking for Hambledon at Torida, he wouldn't be there.

In the second place, this countryside would be unsafe for communists and their friends for some time to come. Smuggling, a little quiet looting and an occasional murder were one thing; a full-scale attack on a town was quite another. The government would act, troops would arrive in force, there would be hunting, questioning, searching, arresting and shooting. Wenezky had seen it all before several times; it was great fun to be on the side of the hunters, but on that of the hunted, no. Definitely not. Therefore Wenezky also had better depart, and with Hambledon gone from Torida there was nothing to keep him.

Wenezky stretched, yawned and lit another cigarette, for he was not a quick thinker. The next problem was where to go, and that brought in the question of where Hambledon was going. This was more debatable, but on the whole Madrid seemed the most probable answer. Hambledon was certainly working with the Germans and though the German Embassy in Madrid was no longer what it had been it was probably still the center of German influence. In any case Madrid would suit Wenezky very well; there were almost certainly a few people still there who would help him, there was that Erich Sachsen passport endorsed by the Madrid police, and finally it was always safest under the lamp.

He threw away the end of his sixth cigarette, started up the car and drove off in a southerly direction. He crossed the Ebro at Castajo at dawn; Hyde, Forgan and Campbell had crossed by the same bridge two hours earlier.

Hyde, Forgan and Campbell stayed at the same hotel in Madrid and even had rooms along the same corridor, but in public they did not know each other. Hyde was openly an English tourist with an expensive car, plenty of money and all his papers in order. He spoke Spanish after a fashion whenever he could not make himself understood in English, he was friendly without intrusion and guileless without folly. He also professed himself a great admirer of the Franco regime; though Englishmen are not officially popular in Spain he made himself liked wherever he went.

Forgan and Campbell were entirely Spanish in spite of Campbell's red hair,

Spanish in dress, speech and manners. They told anyone who appeared interested that they had come over from the Argentine in the matter of a legacy from their mutual grandfather—they were cousins, they said—and the legacy was a matter for litigation in the appropriate courts. They were awaiting the outcome of this litigation, and in the meantime having a holiday in the land of their ancestors. To those who told them that if they waited for Spanish litigation to have an outcome their holiday looked like lasting for years, they replied cheerfully that if their money ran short they could always go back to the Argentine, couldn't they?

They used to go along to Hyde's bedroom when the hotel had settled down for the night, or meet as casual strangers in a café or on some seat in the Prado to compare notes about their doings. Several days passed without event, they had neither seen nor heard of Hambledon nor of Wenezky either, and Forgan was getting restive.

"Campbell and I," he said, "have practically exhausted the more reputable amusements of this historic city. Haven't we, Campbell?"

"Very quiet and seemly," said Campbell. "Highly respectable, Madrid. We've been here nearly a week now and nobody has even tried to murder us."

"Do they generally?" asked Hyde.

"It has occurred," said Forgan, "though not always within so short a time as a week." They were sitting under the awning of a street café in the morning sunshine, sipping glasses of Malaga and watching the passersby.

"That's a pretty girl," said Campbell. "Do you think that if I gracefully pursued her something would happen to break the monotony?"

"She's got thick ankles," said Forgan.

"Oh, has she? Pass, Thick Ankles, all's well."

"If nothing's going to happen," said Hyde, "we may as well push off. Heaven knows where Hambledon is, he may have merely come here to meet somebody and gone straight on somewhere else. Where did you want to go to, Forgan? Seville?"

"No, Granada," began Forgan, but Hyde interrupted him.

"Look who's going past! On the other side, by that hat-shop. It's Wenezky." Hyde snatched up a newspaper in readiness to hold it before his face if the passerby should look their way.

"So it is," said Forgan. "Very interesting." He picked up his hat and rose leisurely to his feet. "He does not know us. You sit tight."

"Life begins anew," said Campbell. "Good-bye, till we see you again."

They lounged out and drifted along with the crowd till Hyde lost sight of them. The streets were full at that hour and they had no difficulty in keeping Wenezky in sight without attracting his notice; eventually he went into a small hotel in a side street. There was a man standing in the doorway who was apparently one of the staff; he greeted Wenezky as he entered.

"Looks as though our friend lives there," said Forgan.

"How fortunate that there is a café opposite," said Campbell. "I find the pavements of Madrid tire the feet, don't you? I hope it's a nice café, we may have to wait some time.''

The café was not particularly nice but at least it was not busy and the proprietor had no objection to two gentlemen spending an hour or so over wine, thin black cigars and a chessboard. When Wenezky came out again and went away down the street the two men finished their game quickly.

"A small parcel is, I think, the best idea," said Forgan. "There are some shops at the end of this street."

"What shall we buy him? A nice funeral wreath? Too large, you wouldn't drop that without noticing it."

"A shilling's worth of rope," said Forgan, "labeled 'For Personal Use Only.' "

But the first shop they came to was a chemist's so they bought a bottle of deodorant—"Do not offend your friend"—had it neatly packed and returned in haste to Wenezky's hotel.

"There was a gentleman who came out from here ten minutes ago," said Forgan to the hall porter. "It so chanced that we were behind him and followed him along the street. He dropped this packet when he was in the act of boarding a tram, we tried to attract his attention but we were unsuccessful."

"So we brought it here," said Campbell. "It might be valuable to him."

The porter thanked them and wondered which gentleman it might be. Forgan described Wenezky in sufficient detail.

"The Señor Sachsen," said the porter, nodding his head. "There is no room for doubt."

"Sachsen," said Campbell thoughtfully.

"A foreign visitor," said the porter. "Erich Sachsen."

"It is a good thing that foreign visitors are once more coming to the country," said Forgan. "They bring money with them."

"May I tell him the names of the excellent señores who have done him this courtesy in order that he may—"

"By no means," said Forgan hastily. "The most insignificant act of social duty—come, Miguel. The señora awaits us."

"And she does not like to wait," said Campbell gloomily.

When they told Hyde the name under which Wenezky was passing he looked thoughtful.

"Sachsen. I've seen that name somewhere within the last day or so. Sachsen, Erich."

"Sounds like a list of some sort if the surname was put first," said Forgan.

"Perhaps it was in the newspaper," said Campbell. "Life is full of silly little coincidences. Are you sure he hasn't had twins or won a lottery prize?"

"It was on a list," said Hyde. "Typewritten, and pinned up somewhere. No, not typewritten, printed. I have it! It was in the police station."

"What sort of a list? Heroes of the Spanish Republic, or Wanted for Bigamy?"

"Shut up, Campbell," said Forgan, "you'll put him off."

"When I went to the police station to report and get my passport stamped," said Hyde slowly, "I had to wait, so I read some notices stuck on a board. This was an old one, it was dusty and faded. It was headed *Criminales extranjeros de guerra*, that means—"

"Foreign war criminals," said Forgan. "Are you sure?"

Hyde wasn't, he went back to look and returned in triumph.

"Yes, that's right. He is a foreign war criminal, anyone knowing his whereabouts must inform the police at once and there is a penalty for anyone who harbors him—them, rather. There are about thirty names on the list. He is a German, or so they say. Yet, you say, he is openly staying at a hotel under that name?"

"I expect he's acquired the passport," said Forgan, "without knowing the owner."

"How careful one ought to be when borrowing another man's name," said Campbell, "to pick somebody respectable."

"What do we do," said Hyde, "send an anonymous letter to the police?"

"We could, of course. They'll take about three months to act on it if I know Spain," said Forgan. "I wonder whether he knows where Hambledon is."

"If only we knew," said Hyde, "we could warn Hambledon that Wenezky's in Madrid."

"But we don't. I think," said Forgan, "that you might as well write your letter to the police, at least it won't do any harm—"

"You'll have to write it, my Spanish isn't adequate."

"But I don't suppose it'll do much good. In the meantime Campbell and I will keep an eye on the foreign war criminal."

"Something interesting might happen," said Campbell cheerfully.

For three days Campbell and Forgan took it in turns to follow Wenezky about the city and found themselves in some very queer places in consequence. Wenezky was visiting old friends and trying to obtain information. Eventually it appeared that he was interested in a small but select hotel in the government quarter of Madrid. It was called simply the Aranjuez after its proprietor, who was a man of the utmost discretion; enquiry produced the interesting fact that this hotel was often used by the government to house guests whom they desired to honor but not to advertise.

"Sounds like Hambledon to me," said Hyde thoughtfully.

"It does," said Forgan, "but why haven't we seen him? Wenezky may be looking for somebody else."

"Can't you make an excuse to walk in and ask for Hambledon?" said Hyde.

"I tried that and they said they'd never heard of him. May be true or just natural cussedness. I think we'd better just hang on."

On the following morning it was Campbell's turn to shadow Wenezky and he dared not get too near. Wenezky hung about in the public garden opposite the Aranjuez for about half an hour and then started to walk away so suddenly that

Campbell was almost left behind. It is very difficult to trail a man through crowded streets without losing him especially when the trailed man walks fast. Campbell missed him altogether at one point and hurried round a corner to find Wenezky looking into a tobacconist's window. As Campbell drew near, Wenezky, who was looking the other way, suddenly dived into the shop. Campbell walked past without slackening speed and crossed the road to shelter himself behind a van parked opposite. He looked across from behind the van and saw Hambledon coming towards him on the other side of the road. Tommy passed the tobacco shop; a moment later Wenezky came out and followed him and Campbell fell in behind. In that order they returned to the Aranjuez.

What had actually happened was that Wenezky had been quite unable to get any news of Hambledon among his friends. Wenezky had learned, however, that the Aranjuez was the most likely place to find him if he were not staying in a private house, and the only hopeful course appeared to be to haunt the Aranjuez in the hope of seeing him. Wenezky, like Forgan, found that the Aranjuez staff were not giving information away. Hambledon had been found accommodation there while transport was being arranged for him, and had been told to lie low and not show himself in the streets until the time came for him to leave. Boredom was his lot, not mitigated by his fellow guests, who were either so busy bewaring of indiscretions that they hardly spoke at all, or who tried so earnestly to pump him that he fled when he saw them coming. Eventually he ran out of collars and handkerchiefs, cocked a snook at warnings and went shopping. A man must blow his nose.

The procession returned to the hotel, Hambledon went straight in and the swing door closed behind him. Wenezky immediately quickened his pace and followed in only a few yards behind.

Campbell broke into a run.

Chapter Eighteen
Distinguished Caballero

Tommy Hambledon walked hastily through the lounge to the stairs, for one of his pet aversions was waiting near the lift—a large dowager who had, it appeared, near relations in practically every ministry in the Spanish government. Tommy bowed politely from a distance and galloped up the stairs two at a time before she could stop him. Nor did he look round, she might be beckoning. On the first floor he slacked off, merely walked up the next flight and down a short corridor to his room. He shut the door with a sense of sanctuary and unwrapped his parcel. Collars in the left-hand top drawer, handkerchiefs in the right. He still had his hand in this drawer when he heard the bedroom door behind him open; someone came in quickly and the door shut again. A servant or an acquaintance would knock; when

Hambledon spun round he had already an automatic in his hand.

Wenezky was standing inside the door with another automatic which was leveled at Hambledon's head; his eyebrows went up when he saw that he also was covered.

"Get out of my room, Wenezky," said Tommy.

"When I get what I came for. Or when I shoot you and take it."

"My good fool," said Hambledon contemptuously, "people don't shoot each other in this hotel. There's a notice about it in the bathroom."

"Where is that packet?"

"Packet? My handkerchiefs?"

Wenezky snarled. "The packet you took from the man Goertz outside Stockholm. It is of no use to pretend you don't know," he added irritably. "He died, and you took the packet—"

"Oh, that packet. I didn't keep it, I thought it would be safer elsewhere, so I posted it in Stockholm," said Tommy with perfect truth.

"You lie. You either gave it to the man Rougetel in Paris or brought it here yourself. You—"

"That was another packet and it was burnt with Rougetel. You should have been more careful, you know," said Tommy reproachfully. "I think that was quite the clumsiest murder I've ever seen. You are a bungler, Wenezky, you are really."

"You would not come here empty-handed," said Wenezky with some logic. "Therefore you must have the packet or you would not be here. I do not believe your story."

"That's why I told it to you, of course. You dogtoothed half-witted codfish," said Tommy, losing patience, "get out of my room before I lose my temper."

"I shall kill you," began Wenezky.

"Of course you can since you've got a gun. In my death agony my finger will jerk and I shall plug you in the stomach. You won't die, Wenezky, unless they kill you in a Spanish hospital, but you'll wish you had, believe me. I know, I've done it—"

The door opened abruptly and two civil guards swept in with drawn revolvers.

"Drop your guns, señores! At once!"

There being no doubt about their intentions, both Hambledon and Wenezky obeyed instantly.

"Delighted to see you, señores," said Hambleton. "As a favor, be so good as to remove that brigand."

"This man is an impostor," said Wenezky loftily. "The passport he carries was stolen from an Englishman in Rotterdam."

He waited with a triumphant grin while the senior of the two *guardas civiles* asked for Hambledon's passport, received it and looked at it carefully. The grin wavered and faded out when the man closed the passport with a professional snap and handed it back to Tommy with a polite bow.

"But," said Wenezky.

"Now your papers, please."

"You'll find mine are all right," said Wenezky, and brought it out with a flourish while Tommy Hambledon picked up his automatic from the carpet.

"That man has rearmed himself," protested Wenezky, but the guards took no notice.

"You are Erich Sachsen?"

"I am."

"Formerly attached to the German Legation in Barcelona?"

"That is so."

"It is well. We have been looking for you. You are arrested as a war criminal demanded by the Allied Military Tribunal on the application of the French authorities."

"What?"

"You are also—"

"But," said Wenezky, "I am a German. Spain does not treat Germans in that uncivilized manner."

"You are also," continued the guard, "wanted by the Spanish police for large-scale frauds in connection with a lottery, and by the Mediterranean Sea Haulage Company of Barcelona for the illegal sale to a foreign buyer of three ocean-going tugs chartered from the company by you acting on behalf of the German Legation."

Hambledon managed to turn a laugh into an outburst of coughing, but Wenezky lost his head.

"I am not that man," he said.

"Not who?"

"I am not Erich Sachsen, I did not—"

"But you have just said you were."

"I know I did, but there was a reason for it. I will explain. I—"

"Explain it to the examining magistrate," said the guard curtly. "About turn. March!" They removed him as far as the door and opened it.

"Just a moment," said the second guard, "there is his gun." He picked up Wenezky's automatic from the carpet and examined it with interest. "A valuable weapon, this. Compact. Well designed. I have never seen an automatic I liked so much as this."

The better to examine his new treasure he thrust his own revolver, still cocked, carelessly into its holster with the butt sticking out. His senior made a move to reprimand him but Wenezky was quicker. He snatched the revolver out of the holster, shot one guard and turned like a flash to deal with the other, but two sharp cracks came almost simultaneously. The surviving guard's shiny cocked hat flew off but Wenezky sagged at the knees and dropped to the floor. Tommy Hambledon had put a bullet into his head.

The *guarda civil* looked down at the floor and crossed himself, then over his shoulder at Hambledon, saying: *"Muy obligado, señor."*

"Don't mention it," said Hambledon politely. "Is that another corpse outside the door?"

There was, in fact, another body in the passage outside but it was in the act of rising. Hambledon recognized Campbell, who had sensibly thrown himself flat when the shooting started.

"Señor," said the guard simply, "what are you lying there for? Are you, then, wounded?"

"Not at all, thank you. No, I thought an escape was being attempted and if I threw myself down the fugitive might fall over me. Good idea, no?"

Doors opened along the passage and heads were cautiously poked out. Aranjuez the manager desisted from a frantic attempt to get underneath an ornate sofa with insufficient clearance to admit him, rose to his feet and signaled to the heads to retire. Doors closed without a word and the corridor was silent except for the manager, who was appealing to a whole potency of saints.

"Be quiet," said the guard. "These bodies will shortly be removed and all will be as it was. They are neither guests nor on your staff."

The manager nodded shakily.

"An ambulance will come," said the guard, "with stretchers."

"To the back door," said Aranjuez, "after dark if you please. In the meantime I will send up the divan."

"Divan?"

"Box divan. To convey the bodies downstairs. My guests must not be distressed with corpses."

"You always arrive," said Hambledon quietly to Campbell, "when the party's getting rough. Did you send up the gendarmerie?"

"Well, yes. I thought you might find a use for them."

"I am extremely obliged to you. So much better for me to shoot him for shooting a policeman than for somebody else to shoot him for shooting me. Selfish, but there it is."

"I couldn't agree more," said Campbell.

"I should like another room, please," said Tommy to the manager. "Corpses are all very well in their place but not beside my bed."

"It proclaims itself," said the manager. "Do me the favor to follow me—there is a room at the head of the stairs which is larger and better appointed than this—the Duque de Valleverde only vacated it this morning—" He trotted off.

"This room must be locked," said the *guarda civil*, and the manager rushed back.

"At once, señor, I will do it at once."

"And I will take the key," said the guard.

"My clothes," said Tommy, "my sponge, my toothbrush—"

"They shall be brought to this room," said Aranjuez, starting down the passage again. "Follow me, señor, follow me—"

He showed Hambledon into the room at the head of the stairs and immediately rushed away to fetch his possessions before the guard locked them all up. Campbell drifted into the room at a sign from Hambledon, sniffing as he did so.

"The duke used scent," he said. "Gardenia? *Nuit en Paris?*"

"Some muck," said Tommy bluntly and threw the windows wider open. "Look here, are you tired of excitements yet?"

"No. Where do we go from here?"

"Las Palmas, I think. I'm almost sure but not quite. Would you care to come on there?"

"Delightful resort," said Campbell lazily. "Been ashore there several times on the passage to B.A."

"Know anyone there? Or rather, anyone know you?"

"No. Oh no. Just passersby."

"Good. If I am going there I'll put an advertisement in the principal Cadiz paper saying that there are two horses, one bulldog and a grand piano for sale because the owner is going to Las Palmas or wherever it is. I gather one sails from Cadiz. All right?"

"We shall be there, if possible," said Campbell, "and it usually is."

"You and your partner do seem to me to be the sort of people it's nice to have about one," said Tommy handsomely. "I shall probably want all the help I can get."

"There's a tobacco kiosk just by the Santa Catalina Mole, leave a note there addressed to Enrico Campo Campana, I'll call for it, here's your luggage coming," said Campbell all in one breath. As the manager entered the room he was regretting in voluble Spanish—and how voluble Spanish can be—that the excellent caballero (Hambledon) did not wish to buy his horse, a superlative horse, brave as a lion, active as a cat, gentle as a maiden, enduring as——

Tommy cut him short, Campbell bowed himself out. The guard was waiting to speak to him, after which he left the hotel and found Forgan waiting outside to relieve him.

"We may go," said Campbell. " 'The strife is o'er, the battle done.' "

"So Wenezky's dead?"

"Completely," said Campbell, and told his friend about the morning's events. "We threaded our way through the crowds back to the hotel like three pearls upon a single string. Hambledon went in, Wenezky went in and I also. I was just in time to see Wenezky running up the stairs so I pursued him with the manager pursuing me in a dignified manner."

"Thus providing the fourth pearl."

"I only wanted to see which room Hambledon was in. Wenezky went far enough up the second flight to get his eyes above floor level and watched somebody while I came steadily on. A door shut and Wenezky advanced. I also, manager coming up on the wing. Wenezky took something out of his pocket, hesitated a moment—"

"Pushing the safety catch off," suggested Forgan.

"Probably. He then opened the door suddenly and walked straight in. I stopped and the manager attained me. He said it was strictly forbidden for unauthorized strangers to wander about the passages, I should have told my business to the porter. He took another look at me and added 'at the back door.' "

"Very disrating," said Forgan.

"I said that the distinguished caballero in Room 73 had told me to call and see him about a horse of mine he thought of buying, but as another visitor had just entered his room I would go away and come back later. I left without delay and made a beeline for a couple of *guardas civiles* who were standing looking handsome by the fountain in the garden opposite."

"They're usually there. At least there are usually two there."

"I went up to them and asked whether it was a fact that there was a reward out for one Erich Sachsen, a foreign war criminal. One said 'Why?' but the other said 'Ah. Erich Sachsen,' nodding to himself. I again mentioned the reward and they both returned to a bit more consciousness and said 'Why?' together. I told them that I used to know him and he owed me some money and he'd just gone into Room 73 second floor of the Aranjuez yonder. They told me I'd better come along too because if I'd deceived them I should regret it, and we formed threes and proceeded into the hotel. I thought the manager would have had a stroke when he saw me again but the *guardas* were very short with him and we all went up in the lift. They told us to wait in the passage; they went into Hambledon's room and shut the door behind them. Whoever Erich Sachsen is they weren't taking any chances, they had their guns out. The manager twittered about and kept on asking me if I'd been arrested and if not, why not, till the door opened again and there were the two *guardas* with Wenezky in tow. Then the shooting started, I went down flat and the surviving *guarda* thought I'd stopped one. Very respectful he was, and called me 'señor.'" Campbell finished the story and added: "The *guarda* was waiting for me, there will be an enquiry and I must give evidence."

"That won't do at all," said Forgan.

"Of course not. They'll hang us up for weeks and we'll never get to Las Palmas."

"Not only that. Our papers are all right for ordinary use but they won't stand a real scrutiny."

"Then we'd better go to Cadiz," said Campbell. "At once."

"Hyde had better go home," said Forgan seriously. "If they find we're English with forged passports staying at his hotel he'll get dragged in and we shall all go to jail. In earnest this time."

"Convince him that his company is a danger to us and you won't see his heels for dust."

"You gave the address of our hotel, did you?"

Campbell nodded. "I thought I'd better, they may be following us."

"You did quite right. Well, we'll talk to Hyde tonight and tomorrow the party will split up," said Forgan. "We'll go to Cadiz and stroll on the Alameda in the intervals of reading advertisements in the papers."

Hyde agreed at once that it was wiser to part company. "I'm afraid I am rather conspicuously English," he said. "Besides, I don't think I like Spain, the way they treat their animals makes me sick and I will not, under any circumstances, go to see a bullfight."

"Well, you needn't," said Forgan reasonably. "There's no law to compel it."

"I know, but if I stayed long in Spain I should. Like a street accident, you know, it's very difficult not to look at it. Never mind, it's of no importance. So you're going to Cadiz, are you? Do you know the place?"

"Not very well," said Campbell, "but we do know a man who lives there and that's far more useful. He was the head cattle man on Selkirk's ranch at Carmen de las Flores when we worked there; he went home to Cadiz when he retired. Man named Domingo Savedra, not a bad *hombre.*"

Hyde stayed on in Madrid for a day or two longer and then took the Bugatti home by easy stages; Forgan and his partner left unostentatiously for Cadiz early the next morning. Domingo Savedra owned a small house on the Isla de Leon, south of the city and looking across the bay to La Carraca; he was among his vines when the two Englishmen pushed open the white gate and walked up the drive to the house but Señora Savedra recognized them at once and greeted them with shrill cries and hospitable babble. A small boy was sent to fetch Savedra, who came, running.

"This is a joyful day for my house," he said. "The hour is good that brings you here. A glass of something to relieve your weariness—Anita! She is gone for it already. This house is yours, my friends. What news of the caballero Adam Selkirk?"

They sat on the terrace in the shade of a great magnolia as big as a forest tree and looked across the blue bay to the white houses of La Carraca and the sunburnt country behind climbing up to the heights of the Andalusian Sierras inland. "This is better than Madrid," said Forgan contentedly. "Much better."

"You have just come from Madrid?"

"In rather a hurry," said Campbell. "There was a little matter of a *guarda civil* who got himself shot. Oh no, we didn't shoot him, but I was there and they want me to give evidence. I did not want to give evidence—our papers, you see, are not all they might be—and anyway we'd seen Madrid. So we came away."

"It is under the direction of Heaven," said Savedra. "You stay here with me six months—a year—they will forget. A *guarda civil*, what is he? There are plenty more of them. Too many, among friends in the privacy of my own garden. He is dead, let him go."

"Is that today's paper? May I look at it?" asked Forgan, and ran his eyes down the advertisement columns. "Nothing here yet."

"Good," said Campbell lazily. "I could bear to look at this view quite a lot more."

Savedra, with instinctive good manners, rose with an excuse, but Forgan said: "No, don't go. It is only that we have to meet a friend and he will put an advertisement in the paper to tell us where to go."

"If it is not an inconvenience to you, may it be long delayed," said Savedra. "There is a gap of many years to be filled with talk between us three."

"It is the truth of God," said Forgan, "but before we start, a small matter of business. From here to Las Palmas how would a man go who did not wish to add to the burdens of the port authorities?"

"You have not changed," said Savedra, with a flash of white teeth in his sunburnt face. "These authorities, they get thin if they look to feed on you. Such a man would go in a small ship as one of the crew perhaps, at least in appearance. One of the wine boats, I suggest, such as that one yonder." He pointed out a tubby steamer of about three hundred tons making her slow way out to sea. "They go out with grain and mixed cargoes and come back with wine, they are always going and coming and who notices what he sees every day? Do the port authorities count the number of the crew every time the *Maria Perez* or the *Inocente Gomez* puts to sea? No. They are sensible men and life is not all work. Another glass of wine, *amigos.*"

Five days went by in the sunshine of the Villa Savedra till a day came when the paper carried an advertisement: "For Sale. Two good riding horses, a bulldog and a grand piano by Steinway, owner going to Las Palmas, write . . ." There followed a box number.

"This is it," said Campbell and showed it to his partner.

"Good," said Forgan. "I was beginning to wonder. We will now talk definitely to Savedra about wine boats." He stretched out his legs comfortably and began to read items of news in the paper; the Caudillo had made a speech condemning the attitude of Russia on the problem of Trieste, there was a triple murder in Puerto Real, a calf with six legs had been born on a farm near Morón de la Frontera, a transport plane had crashed on the south side of San Cristobal, the first prize in a lottery had been won by the newborn son of a baker at San Fernando, the police were seeking information—

"Here," said Forgan sharply, "look at this."

The police were seeking information, particularly in seaport towns, regarding the whereabouts of one Manuel Rodriguez, so called, who had disappeared from Madrid after being summoned to appear as a witness in a case of murder at the Aranjuez Hotel. There followed an accurate description of Campbell. "The name of Manuel Rodriguez is probably assumed."

"Too right," murmured Campbell. "How did they guess?"

The wanted man had been accompanied by another calling himself Benito Torre, and the description was that of Forgan. "These men may be attempting to leave the country by sea, and the attention of port officials, dock police, seamen's employment bureaux and others is drawn to this notice."

"But why all this fuss?" asked Campbell indignantly. "I didn't shoot anybody."

"They probably think you were some kind of stooge for Wenezky," said Forgan. "You follow him into the hotel, he finish, you vanish. Too bad."

"Oh gosh," said Campbell, and went to look for their host, taking the paper with him. Savedra read the notice carefully.

"All this fuss about one *guarda civil,*" grumbled Campbell. "All the same, we'd better leave as soon as possible. We might get you into trouble."

Savedra scorned the idea. "For one thing, the local *policía* is the nephew of my sister-in-law's brother," he said. "For another, we of Andalusia are not lackeys to Madrid. What, shall that overblown village of yesterday dictate to Cadiz, which was a city in the days of Tyre and Sidon?" He applied an epithet to Madrid.

"Oh, quite," said Campbell. "I absolutely agree. But in any case we should have to go, because the advertisement for which we were waiting is also in this paper. Our friend is going to Las Palmas, as we thought he probably would."

"That is quite another matter. To go because you wish to go, *bueno*. To run at the bidding of Madrid, not so. After Señor Forgan spoke to me the other day about a passage to Las Palmas, I made a few enquiries. There is one of the wine boats which sails on Thursday, that is the day after tomorrow, she is the *Perla del Mar* and her captain is the husband of a cousin of my wife's. Carlos Diaz. He will want payment for the passage and the risk, but not too much, he is a Christian."

"Bueno. Where can I see him?"

"Here at my house, I will ask him to eat with us tonight, thus everything can be discreetly arranged."

"I am immensely obliged to you," said Campbell.

Captain Carlos Diaz came to supper, a tall thin man whose high-bridged nose and salient jawbone suggested the Moorish ancestry so common in Andalusia. He was a silent man compared with Savedra, he listened to the story without interruption and nodded when it was done.

"Certainly I can take the señores," he said, "once they are safely on board. It will not, however, be wise for the señores to come to the docks. Copies of this notice"—he tapped the newspaper with a lean forefinger—"are affixed today to the notice board of the dock police."

Campbell said: "Quite like old times," to Savedra, and Forgan asked Diaz what course he would recommend.

"The señores will hire a boat. A rowing boat. Domingo here will know a reliable man. He will row a mile straight out from this house at twenty hours tomorrow, with a small lantern in the bows. I will come along inshore and pick you up. It is agreed?"

"It is only to avoid being arrested until then," said Forgan.

"It is only one day," said Campbell. "Twenty-four hours from now."

The following morning Savedra's sister-in-law's brother's nephew, who was the local policeman, came up to the house and produced a paper from his wallet.

"Not to incommode you," he said, "there is a ridiculous notice."

He spread it out; it began: "The police are seeking information," and Campbell already knew it by heart.

"Information has already been brought to the police station," he continued, "by that warty-nosed elder son of the postmaster who fancies himself a Falangist, that there are two strangers staying in this house." The policeman looked everywhere except at Forgan and Campbell. "I am a policeman, I do my duty. I said I would come here and search the house. At what time would it be convenient, brother-in-law of my aunt, for me to search your house?"

"Tonight after dark," said Savedra, "would be the most sensible time, for at that hour guests would most naturally be within doors."

"It is true," said the policeman. "I come here this morning and see no one who is a stranger." Again his eyes avoided Forgan and Campbell. "Tonight at twenty-two hours I will come again. I have the honor to wish the company *buenos días."* He bowed politely and went away without looking back.

"Charming fellow," said Forgan.

"Quite the nicest policeman I ever met," said Campbell.

"He has had education," said Savedra, meaning that he had been well brought up. "Nevertheless, when he comes again tonight he will search the house with his eyes open. Why not? He does not wish to be dismissed the service, there is a pension, and we all wish to live as God permits."

"By that time, if all goes well, we shall be out of the bay," said Forgan.

At ten o'clock that night Forgan and Campbell leaned over the stern rail of the *Perla del Mar* to watch the jeweled lights of Cadiz grow dim and sink below the horizon. Campbell looked at his watch.

"The policeman is just arriving," he said.

Chapter Nineteen
Santa Brigida

Hambledon came to Grand Canary in a Spanish-owned steamer conveying general cargo and about fifty assorted passengers. The sea was rough and Tommy had little opportunity of becoming acquainted with the other passengers, few of whom could accurately be numbered among nature's sea dogs. Besides, they did not look particularly interesting.

They were taken ashore in a tender at Puerto de la Luz and passed in single file through an office where a man sat at a desk to examine their papers and stamp their passports. There was another man standing by the further door which led out to the Parque de Santa Catalina and the main road; this man was dressed in a gray linen dust coat and wore a peaked cap, Tommy correctly guessed him to be a chauffeur. When it was Hambledon's turn to have his passport stamped the customs officer nodded to the man by the door, who came forward and took Hambledon's luggage.

"There is an automobile, señor," he said. "Permit me—come this way."

"I think I am being a fool," said Hambledon to himself. "It is not yet too late to detach myself from this expedition, make a bolt to the British consul and refuse to let go of his hand even at mealtimes until I am put aboard a steamer bound for London." However, he suppressed his instinct of self-preservation and followed the chauffeur to a car which was waiting outside. There was a cast-iron kiosk of Moorish design at the point where they turned into the main road and Tommy saw that newspapers were sold there; no doubt it was here that the note for Campbell was to be left. The car passed through the port area and along the coast road to Las Palmas with fine buildings at intervals and between them slopes and dunes of dry yellow sand. The chauffeur did the honors of the route, pointing out places as they passed, "the Metropole Hotel, very smart," the palace of the military governor "where our Caudillo Franco lived when he was here." They drove right into the town and over a great stone bridge with thick balustrades into the Plaza Santa Ana—"our cathedral, señor"—and then turned right; almost at once the road began to climb through groves of palms and past stone-walled gardens where bananas grew in terraces. At one sharp corner the chauffeur braked suddenly and a long silly face with a bored expression looked down upon Tommy from the end of a long sway-ing neck—a camel, loaded with bunches of green bananas. The road climbed up and up, leaving the palm groves behind and running through clumps of eucalyptus and chestnut. They passed through a village, "Tafira," said the driver, and on into country which to Tommy's mind was an improvement on Surrey except that in Surrey there are no vineyards in terraces nor queer ugly cacti in odd corners. A couple of miles farther on another village came into view; Tommy leaned forward and said: "What place is that?"

"Santa Brigida, señor."

"Indeed," said Tommy faintly, and leaned back.

They did not enter the village but turned off about half a mile before they reached it. There was a big notice board by the roadside, "Hotel Bienvenida," and a glimpse of a long white house between the trees.

The car pulled up at the front door and the chauffeur leapt out to open the door for Hambledon and carry his luggage. The entrance hall was large and cool with palms and ferns in pots and a fountain playing in the middle, there were several people sitting about looking perfectly ordinary, and one enormous yellow Canary dog as big as a calf who lumbered up to push his nose into Tommy's hand and wave a languid tail before flopping down again in the coolest place.

"Nice dog," said Tommy.

"But lazy," said the chauffeur. "There's so much of him it's too much trouble to move it. This way to the office, señor."

There was a clerk in the office busy entering up items in ledgers; he looked up as Hambledon went in and wished him good morning.

"Good morning," said Tommy.

"This is the Señor Hambledon," said the chauffeur.

"Ah yes," said the clerk. "We have a room reserved for you, señor." He ran his finger down the page of a book. "Here it is. Room 36, Enrico, tell the porter to take up the luggage, will you?" The chauffeur went out, shutting the door behind him.

"Your full name, señor?"

"Thomas Elphinstone Hambledon. E-l-p-h-i—here, you'd better copy it from my passport."

"Thank you," said the clerk. "I have it, yes. British nationality, thank you. May I see your *permis de séjour?* Thank you, all in order, I see. Now, if you would please sign the visitors' book when you go out, you will find it on a desk to the left of this door, outside."

"Is that all?" asked Hambledon.

"That is all, señor. We have to be particular about these tiresome formalities," he added, with a sidelong glance.

"When visiting a country not one's own," said Tommy sententiously, "the least one can do is to comply with the law."

"Decidedly, señor," said the clerk with a smirk.

"When will lunch be served? In an hour from now? I have time, then, for a stroll," said Tommy, half expecting to be told it was not allowed.

"But certainly. This district is renowned for its delightful walks and, indeed, outings of all kinds. Let me give you a small handbook," said the clerk, and did so. " 'Walks, Rides, and Drives about Santa Brigida.' It is fully illustrated and I shall be pleased to advise and help at any time."

Tommy took it and went out, feeling slightly dazed. He had expected to be taken to some house which looked like a house but was really more like a prison, where earnest plotters conferred behind locked doors, exchanged passwords and distrusted each other. This place appeared to be a perfectly normal hotel. Very odd. He walked out of the front door and down the drive, still expecting some man to step out from behind a bush and tell him to go back, but one or two guests who were strolling in the grounds merely glanced at him; a gardener, working in one of the flowerbeds, did not even look up. Hambledon passed through the gate into the main road and took off his hat to a young priest riding past on a bicycle, his soutane flapping awkwardly round his thin legs. Cars went by at intervals, a farm cart, a man and a girl on horseback with a dog trotting behind, then, with a notable rattle as of many loose parts, the country bus with a nameboard along the roof, "San Mateo. Santa Brigida. Tafira. Las Palmas."

"Oh, really," said Tommy, who disliked being puzzled. He returned to the grounds by a small gate farther down the road and sat on a seat in the gardens beside a thin old man with a white goatee who said that he was a retired bank manager from Avignon. He was, he added, an enthusiastic amateur anthropologist and had come to the Canary Isles to make a study of the primitive Guanche civilization. Hambledon was rash enough to remark that the subject was interesting, whereupon the old gentleman delivered a lecture upon the prehistoric remains at the Montaña de las Cuatro Puertas, with special reference to a parallel between the *harimaguadas*—"the consecrated daughters, m'sieu"—and the Vestal Virgins. At last a deep-toned gong within the hotel announced lunch and Hambledon expressed his grateful thanks, though whether he was grateful for the lecture or the gong was not at all clear.

"I will take you to the caves myself," said M. Paul Duvallet kindly, "we will make a little anthropological expedition together, shall we not?"

Hambledon sat down at a table some distance from M. Duvallet's. At the same table were three Americans, very American indeed, two men in Palm Beach suits and a woman in the early thirties in a cotton dress of vivid stripes; all three had sunglasses with thick tortoiseshell rims parked at the side of their plates. They greeted him with some exuberance and very strong Middle Western accents.

"Say, it's a real pleasure to meet a guy who can talk English. It sure is an education to travel in foreign parts and pick up bits of foreign languages, but I'll say it's a rest to get out of the schoolroom sometimes. Yes, sir."

"You, sir," said the other man, "are a Britisher, I take it?"

"I am," said Tommy.

"It is an honor and a privilege to meet you and with your permission I will shake you by the hand. I am Ezra Blenkinsop van Houten of New York and this little girl is my wife Elvira. My brother, Hiram Biggs van Houten."

"My name's Hambledon," said Tommy, and they all rose from the table, clutching table napkins, ceremonially shook hands and sat down again. Hambledon did not know much about America but he did know that people from New York with a name like Van Houten would certainly not speak with a Middle Western accent, and in any case nobody could possibly be so American as these three. They were too vivid to be real, they were too gloriously Technicolor, in short they were phony. He beamed shyly upon them and prepared to enact the complete Britisher.

"I couldn't begin to tell you," said Elvira, bright-eyed, "what England means to us Yanks."

"Oh, I say, you know," burbled Tommy, "too frightfully good of you, what?"

"I always say," pursued Elvira, "now don't I, Ezra? I always say that nothing's too good for—"

"You certainly do always say, girly," said Ezra.

"Oh, you horrible man! Say, isn't my husband a horrible man, Mr. Hambledon?"

"I don't know him as well as you do, Mrs. Van Houten."

"Don't you take no notice of them two kids," said Hiram. "They'll squabble to everlasting. Say now, what's your views on this Trieste problem?"

"Now, you lay off the Trieste problem, Hiram, and let poor Mr. Hambledon eat his fish."

"I don't go much on the fish here," said Ezra. "All bones laid together cockeyed, as a rule."

"For cryin' out loud," said Elvira, "mine's legs on it. Mr. Hambledon, tell a poor girl, what is it?"

"Octopus," said Hambledon. "Little baby ones. Very nice."

But Elvira shrieked and insisted that her plate be removed.

After lunch Hambledon strolled about or sat in the palm court near the fountain and made acquaintance with any guest who came within reach. There was a forest officer from the Belgian Congo and a friend of his who came from Charleroi; a Dutchman and wife from Amsterdam with a cousin who said they were wine importers; a short square man from Malmédy; five Swedes, four men and a woman; no less than seven Swiss; three Greeks, beautiful but dumb; four more Americans, all men, who went about together and did not talk much to anybody else—Tommy caught snatches of their conversation and thought their accent quite the oddest he'd ever heard. A short study of the visitors' book added a contingent of six from South America who were out for the day and did not return till after dark, a Frenchman who was something important in a silk factory at Lyons and his wife who spent the day doing a circular tour of the mountain roads and came back in time for apéritifs before dinner, and one untidy fat man with a ragged beard who said he was a professor of applied science in the University of Milan though Austrian by birth.

That made thirty-eight in all, not counting Tommy, and the hotel had fifty-four bedrooms according to its own advertisements. It was a little curious, therefore, that when a car drove up to the hotel the following afternoon with three people requesting accommodation, they were told with polite regrets that the hotel was completely full and was booked right up for the next three months.

Next day Tommy approached the clerk again to ask at what times the Las Palmas bus passed the gate. "It is hot," said Hambledon, "I desire to bathe. I see in your excellent booklet that the sands of Confital Bay are recommended for bathing."

"That is so, señor, the bathing in Confital Bay is superlative," said the clerk. "There is an electric tram from Las Palmas to the Puerto de la Luz, if you alight near the spot where you came ashore any of the roads leading west will take you to the bay." He gave Tommy a bus timetable and wished him a pleasant morning. Hambledon walked down the drive accompanied as far as the gate by the Canary dog, who answered, when he felt like it, to the name of Tonio. The bus came along, Hambledon hailed it and got in.

"Just as easy as that," said Tommy to himself. "I wish I knew where the catch is."

He bought a swimming suit and a towel in the town and took the tram along to the Parque de Santa Catalina. Here was the kiosk, Tommy bought a newspaper and a Maurice Dekobra in a paper cover and unostentatiously left a letter for Señor Campo Campana, to be called for. He added a couple of bars of chocolate to his purchases, walked across to Confital Bay and swam most luxuriously. He was lying on the sands in the sun, nibbling chocolate and watching the bathers, when he realized that three of them were familiar figures. They were the three alleged Americans who called themselves Van Houten.

"I thought something like this might happen," said Tommy to himself. "Of course it may be coincidence; anybody might want to bathe this morning and this is the best place."

He waited till they came out of the sea and waved to them, they galloped up to him with cries of joy.

"Well, if it isn't Mr. Hambledon!" and so on.

"And tell me, how did you get here, Mr. Hambledon?"

"Bus and tram, don't you know," said Tommy.

"Oh, you can't ride in that horrible autobus," said Elvira. "We rode down in it just the one time when we first arrived and I declare my teeth aren't settled in again yet. I said to Ezra here, I said, 'Ezra, if there isn't an automobile to be bought or hired in Las Palmas——' "

"So he bought one," said Hiram simply.

"And of course you'll ride back with us, for I won't take 'no.' "

"But I'd adore to," said Tommy, "thanks frightfully."

"Next item, boys and girl," said Ezra, "the drinks are on me."

"When I'm dressed," said Hambledon firmly, "I haven't got a coat with me."

"Meet us at the Towers in ten minutes, brother," said Ezra. "Over yonder."

They drank cocktails in the bar of the Towers Hotel, played with the gray-and-pink cockatoo who waddled up to ask for biscuits, and drove back to the Bienvenida in perfect accord.

In some such manner Hambledon passed a week during which nothing in particular happened, but small things here and there lifted the curtain of mystery a little. Hambledon noticed that whenever members of one nationality were together, all the Swiss for example, or all the Swedes, they became much less Swiss or Swede as the case might be instead of more so as might be expected. Their national characteristics subsided instead of sticking out like the knobs on a wart hog and there emerged a curious likeness between them all, even to the Belgians and the Greeks. Not a physical likeness, but something which they held psychologically in common; they were a type, as are clergymen and naval officers, they had a certain stamp, and Hambledon recognized it. As for their aggressive nationalism, he saw at last what they were doing. They were showing off to each other, displaying like peacocks their Frenchness or their Americanisms. Hambledon realized with amusement that he also was doing the same thing, being not only more English than the English but positively Bertie Wooster. Well, it seemed to go down very well.

At the end of the week the porter came to Hambledon and said that if it was convenient for the señor to spare a few moments the hotel manager would like to speak to him.

"Certainly," said Hambledon cheerfully, "lead the way, will you?" To himself he added: "This is it."

The manager's office was just like any other hotel manager's office but the man himself was unlike any hotel manager he had ever met. Hambledon had thought it odd that he had never seen him about the place until that moment, he had been merely a name on notice boards, "W. Martin." Very un-informing, since Martin is a name common to most European languages. He rose from his chair as Hambledon came into the room; Tommy had a momentary spasm of panic because he recognized him. A tall lean figure, square-shouldered, upright and soldierly to the point of stiffness, with hard pale eyes, hair cut very short and dueling scars across his right cheek. Martin be hanged, this was Torgius, Colonel Leonhard Torgius of the Afrika Korps, seriously wounded when Tobruk fell, invalided out of the army and subsequently lost although diligently sought for. They had met once or twice in Berlin in 1941; if Hambledon had not reminded himself firmly that then he had been hidden like an owl in an ivy bush behind shaggy hair and luxuriant whiskers he would have turned and fled.

Torgius held out his hand. "Mr. Hambledon, I believe," he said, with a smile. "A daring impersonation, Herr Henochsberg, but it seems to have been successful."

Hambledon shook hands with him and dropped into a chair. "Actually, I deserve no credit for that," he said, "the Fates offered and I accepted. It was Kenrade at Rotterdam who produced the Hambledon passport, it was stolen at the docks there, I believe. This fellow Hambledon must be something of a personage, I had but to display his papers and all doors flew open. Wonderful."

"You came through without too much trouble?"

"Oh yes. I took a few simple precautions."

"Yes, we heard about those," said Torgius. "You must have had an amusing trip."

"I am sorry," said Hambledon, "that I failed in the most important part of my mission. That packet—poor Rougetel wished to carry it himself and it seemed just as safe with him as with me. He had it with him when the lorry crashed near Auch and he was killed, you probably know all about that."

"Yes, I heard a general account of it, you must tell me the details sometime. Poor Rougetel, he was an able technician and we miss him, but I cannot see that it was in the faintest degree your fault. He was primarily responsible and it cannot be helped."

"The two men who did it are now both dead," said Tommy quietly. "Not that that helps in the least, of course."

"No. Happily the accident can be made up, at least in part. You were not the only messenger, the other is due to arrive here shortly."

"I am glad to hear it," said Hambledon solemnly.

"Yes. Well now, till he comes I hope you are comfortable? It will not be much longer to wait, and an occasional holiday is beneficial."

"I am extremely comfortable, thank you, and having a simply wonderful time. What a beautiful place this is! And what a delightful house. The gardens—"

"It serves," said Torgius. "When I was crippled and left the army I had time to think and plan. Later, when things were obviously going wrong—tell me," he burst out, "did ever any man since the world began make so many mistakes as that maniac Hitler? I was saying, I gathered together all the money I could, and I am a rich man, Herr Henochsberg, got out of the country and came here and bought this place. We must have a center for the rebirth of our Germany and I am honored beyond my deserving to be able to provide it. Here meet together the devoted nucleus of a new Germany, the faithful dreamers who act, as in the days of old—"

Hambledon sat back and listened while Torgius limped round the room and unrolled his vision of rebirth, new growth and future conquest. Another fanatic, thought Tommy wearily. Why in the name of heaven or of common sense can't these people see that they are barking up the wrong tree, exploring the wrong avenues and turning all the wrong stones? What do they hope for, anyway, more wars and more misery? This fellow hasn't learned one little fact since 1914. Gosh, these Germans . . .

Torgius stopped abruptly and said: "I talk too much, forgive me. Soon, we act instead. In the meantime I am a hotelkeeper and you are my guest. Tell me, how are you as regards money?"

Hambledon was so surprised that he stared. "Why, I can manage, I think—I haven't too much—why do you ask?"

"There will tomorrow be an account in your name—I mean Hambledon, of course—let me see. You are English, it must be a bank with English connections." Torgius named one and added: "If you will go there tomorrow and introduce yourself they will give you a checkbook."

"I don't know how to thank you," began Tommy, but Torgius stopped him.

"It is nothing, this money, do not thank me; it is not personal but to serve Germany. About your fellow guests, have you met the Herr Professor Schlagel?"

"Isn't he the stout gentleman with the windswept beard? He isn't about so much as the others, I don't think I've actually spoken to him."

"No. He is working very hard." Torgius uttered a laugh, it was more like a bark. "He is really a very brilliant chemist, but in everything else he is a simple soul. Childlike. Practical jokes amuse him beyond measure—I had to put my foot down. He has but one weakness, he tipples when he can get it. I have given orders that he is not to be served."

"Poor old boy," said Tommy impulsively, and Torgius stiffened.

"Not at all. Beware of pity, it is enfeebling as well as useless. He must find his happiness in serving Germany and in nothing else. My orders forbidding him to be supplied with drink are irrevocable and apply to everyone here. You will re-member, please."

"Oh, certainly," said Hambledon. "I didn't mean—I shouldn't think of such a thing."

"It is well. I think that is all, Herr Henochsberg, I will not detain you longer from your friends."

Hambledon got up at once. "It was good of you to give me so much of your time."

"Not at all," said Torgius mechanically, "a pleasure." He came to the door with Hambledon; when it was opened there was Tonio the dog waiting patiently outside. When he saw Hambledon he waved his huge tail, yawned loudly, and stood ready as one who would say: "Now that's over where do we go from here?"

"Hullo, Tonio," said Tommy. "Nice beast, this."

"A stupid lazy brute," said Torgius. "I only keep him as a bit of local color. This was a real hotel, you see, until recently. The dog seems to have formed a curious attachment to you, by the way."

"They generally do," said Tommy lightly. "I like dogs. So English, you know."

Torgius uttered his short laugh, went back into the room and shut the door.

"Come on, Tonio," said Hambledon, "let's go out for a walk and get some nice fresh air, for it is written: 'The more I see of men the more I like dogs.' "

He left the house by a door near the kitchen premises since it happened to be the nearest; as he strode down the drive with Tonio wallowing behind he passed an ancient Ford van on its way to the back door. In front were sitting two shabby men in faded blue berets; on the side of the van was painted the words: "Benito Torre. Pescadero," which is to say "Fishmonger."

Chapter 20
Howl to St. Thomas

Campbell and Forgan found their paths smoothed for them at Las Palmas. Domingo Savedra, their host at Cadiz, told the captain of the *Perla del Mar*, who informed the mate, who passed the word to the crew that "the gentlemen had been in a little trouble." Some small matter of a *guarda civil*, it was understood. The tiresome fellow had died. No comment was ever made on the matter but small courtesies were offered beyond what was absolutely necessary; once or twice the travelers were addressed as "comrade" and a change of clothes was found for them less conspicuous than the town suits they had worn in Madrid. When the *Perla del Mar* tied up alongside the mole of Santa Caterina to unload, two willing men in faded blue overalls with faded blue berets on their heads lent a hand with the unloading of cases and barrels out of the hold. When the sun went down and work stopped for the day, these two slipped on shabby serge jackets over their dungarees and went ashore with the mate.

"You want somewhere quiet to stay and no questions asked," said the mate. "You come with me."

They were found lodgings in the house of a widow woman in the fishermen's quarter of Puerto de la Luz, between the docks and the Isleta with its barbed wire and sentries. Campbell collected Hambledon's note from the newspaper kiosk and plans were made. A small Ford van was rescued from the brink of the scrap yard and renovated with a coat of paint, several pieces of angle iron, numerous screws and some wire. The engine was overhauled as only trained engineers could have done it, and a name painted along the side. "Benito Torre. Pescadero."

"Let me see," said Campbell. "Does Hambledon know that you're Benito Torre?"

"No. We didn't change our names till we got to Madrid. Unless you told him at the hotel?"

"No. For one thing, there wasn't time."

"It doesn't matter," said Forgan.

Accordingly, when the Ford van passed Hambledon in the drive of the Bienvenida Hotel the name of Benito Torre conveyed nothing to him and the men in the front seats were looking the other way. Hambledon and dog passed on and the van drove up to the tradesmen's door.

Forgan rang the bell; when one of the scullery maids answered it he said: *"Bue' días, señorita.* Fish. Fresh fish. As good and beautiful as you are."

She giggled and said she would tell the cook. The chef came, looked distrustfully at Forgan and said they already had a fishmonger who called.

"But he is not reliable," said Forgan. "His fish is not always fresh and sometimes he does not come at all."

"Who told you that?"

"You did. If he had been satisfactory you would not have come out to see me. You would have sent a message telling me to go away."

"You are at least intelligent," said the chef.

"Give me a trial," pleaded Forgan. "Every day we come up here. One day you give the orders, next day we bring the fish. Good fish, so fresh you'd think St. Peter himself had just caught them, they are still flapping, *por Dios!* Do me the favor but to look at them. I will bring them to you. Manuel!"

"Eh?"

"Get out the best tray, I will help you."

Between them they carried a wicker tray to the door and it was plainly true that the fish were fresh. One of them fell off and flapped helplessly upon the doorstep.

"Look at the beauty," said Forgan. "He flaps his tail like a dog to attract your favorable notice."

"I will buy," said the chef, and bought largely. He added an order for the next day, Forgan called down blessings on his head and the van drove away. The next day it came again and the partners carried the fish into the scullery and talked to the same maid while they waited for their money. Torgius passed through and glanced at them but did not speak.

"Your friend," said the scullery maid when Campbell was out of earshot, "what is his name?"

"Manuel Rodriguez, my pretty. Why? Do you fancy his looks?"

"He is a Spaniard, then?"

"Of a certainty. He comes from Algeciras in Andalusia."

"He has not the coloring for a Spaniard," she said doubtfully. "Red hair and blue eyes—"

"Hush!" said Forgan imperatively. "Do not mention it—it is a matter of delicacy. These seaport towns—you would not understand, little one."

Steps were heard just behind Forgan, he turned round to see a fat bearded man in a white coat come hurrying up some stairs, he passed them and went into another part of the house.

"Who's that?" asked Forgan. "The wine waiter?"

The girl giggled. "Wine waiter, indeed! That is a very famous professor, I can't pronounce his funny name."

"But what's he doing in the cellar?"

"I don't know. He works, he told me so. He's a nice old gentleman, but they aren't very kind to him."

"How? Who aren't?"

"Señor Torgius, the manager, he who came through here just now. He won't let him—"

The chef came bustling back. "Here is your money. Anita! Get on with your work, you are not paid to chatter. Here is the list for tomorrow, Torre. Do not fail me."

"Before doing that, I would first die," said Forgan, and went away.

Next day when they came with the fish Anita was kept too busy to speak and there was no delay about the money; the partners drove off again at once. Halfway down the drive they saw a spare figure in gray flannels and a broad-brimmed straw hat of local manufacture; he was kneeling upon one knee extracting a thorn from the paw of the dog Tonio.

"There he is," said Campbell.

"Ah," said Forgan. He adjusted levers with some care and the elderly van began to cough, splutter and hesitate, there was one beautiful backfire and the engine stopped. Forgan got out and looked inside the bonnet; what he saw apparently did not please him, for he snatched off his blue beret, cast it violently to the ground and jumped on it, calling upon San Tomaso to give him patience. Hambledon, having extracted the thorn, strolled casually towards the van; if he recognized the agitated driver he naturally did not show it. By the time he reached the spot Campbell was leaning over the open bonnet while Forgan wound the starting handle furiously but quite without result. Tommy stood on the top of a bank just above them while Tonio sat down and leaned heavily against his legs.

"A little trouble, evidently," said Hambledon in Spanish.

Forgan outlined what he thought was the matter in terms which were more anatomical than mechanical, and a gardener who happened to be passing grinned broadly and paused to look on.

"Is there a spark?" said Forgan to Campbell.

"Santa Ana, how should I know? Am I, then, a motor mechanic or a fisherman?"

"Put your finger there, look. Now, when I pull the handle—"

Campbell uttered a yelp and sprang into the air.

"It is evident that there is a spark," said Forgan gravely.

"Possibly an obstruction in the fuel pipe," suggested Hambledon.

"Myself," said the gardener, "I offer, with apologies, the opinion that it is natural death. That van, she was not new when I was a *niño* too young to go to school."

Torgius crossed the drive lower down and glanced towards them as he did so; the gardener excused himself hastily and went about his business. For the moment there was no one within earshot, Hambledon upon his bank could see all round him.

"Glad to see you," he remarked.

"If you would walk along the road towards Las Palmas we will overtake you," said Forgan.

"Good," said Hambledon. He wished them better luck and strolled away with Tonio ambling behind. A quarter of an hour later, as he was striding along with his hat in his hand, there came a rattling sound behind him and the fish van pulled up alongside.

"I congratulate you on the camouflage," said Tommy. "If you hadn't been howling to St. Thomas just now I should never have looked at you."

"What are they doing up at that place?" asked Forgan.

"Experimenting with nuclear fission, that's all I know. Another secret weapon, believe it or not."

"Who's doing it, the fat man with the beard?"

Tommy nodded. "Professor Schlagel. Not a bad old boy, I was talking to him this morning. A simple soul, likes practical jokes and brandy, and both are denied him."

"Oh, really," said Forgan. "What happens next?"

"We are all waiting for another traveler in synthetic thorium since I was careless enough to lose my packet. When he comes the professor can make a lot more bombs and the rebirth of the New Germany can get cracking."

"In the name of heaven," said Campbell, "what is the idea? Haven't they had enough of bombs yet?"

"It isn't really quite so silly as it sounds," said Hambledon. Torgius unfolded a bit more of the great Scheme last night. The idea is: tiny but immensely powerful bombs—for their size, that is, only about as big as a packet of a dozen boxes of matches. These people in the hotel come from practically all over the world though they are all Germans. They go back home and plant these bombs in power stations, railway left-luggage offices, postal main sorting offices and so on."

"Reminds me of the I.R.A.," said Campbell.

"Yes, similar idea. Only the Western Powers will think it's the Russians doing it and the Russians will think it's the Anglo-Saxon plutocracies doing it. Then we'll all get so annoyed that war will break out again and when we've all fought ourselves to a standstill Germany will rise up again and scoop the pool. That's what they think."

"It would at least make a frightful amount of trouble," said Forgan, "they're right so far."

"And it all depends on a funny fat scientist with a taste for brandy," said Tommy. "I daren't give him any, it's as much as my life's worth."

"And practical jokes," said Campbell. "Don't forget the practical jokes. How long have we got?"

"About another week, I gather. Our friend was delayed in transit," said Hambledon.

"Pity we can't find out what boat he's coming by and just throw him overboard," said Forgan.

"Even Torgius doesn't know that."

"Oh. Well, I don't think we'd better talk any longer, somebody might notice us," said Forgan. "By the way, our address," and he told Hambledon where they were living.

"Thank you," said Hambledon. "My name, in case you ever want it, is Henochsberg."

"Well, it's better than Guggleheimer," said Campbell. "Good-bye. We'll be seeing you."

On the following day there was again no luck for the fishmongers at the Hotel Bienvenida, no Anita appeared and no Professor Schlagel. The next day promised better; Anita was in the scullery exchanging badinage with Campbell when steps were once more heard coming up the cellar stairs.

"Sacramento, it's hot today," said Forgan, intruding into the conversation. "My pretty one, don't they ever serve drinks in this hotel?"

Anita giggled. "A *limonada* perhaps, or a nice drink of cold water."

"I don't want just wetness," said Forgan. "I mean wine, red wine for preference. A real drink." He mimed the movements of one drinking from a glass. "Glug, glug, glug. Ah, that's better."

The footsteps on the stairs slowed down, Anita tittered again and uttered the Spanish equivalent for "What a hope!"

"Go and drink the brandy in the van," said Campbell and the footsteps stopped altogether.

"Brandy," said Forgan scornfully, "brandy isn't a drink, it's a medicine. I don't drink that for fun."

"Why do you drink it, then?" asked Anita. "Are you an invalid? You don't look like one."

"I am not an invalid, but if you must know, saucy, I have spasms at the heart. Ever since I was ill when I was a boy, I have them, not often, sometimes. I am well, I am strong, I am fine, and all of a sudden—garrh!" Forgan clutched at his heart. "So I carry brandy in a little bottle—so big"—he indicated a very small flask indeed—"and when the pain comes on, down it goes. But it is medicine, not a drink. I have had it too often. Wine is a drink—"

The stairs door behind them, which was ajar, was pushed open suddenly. The professor came out hastily, glanced round to see who was speaking, and grabbed Forgan by the arm.

"That brandy," he whispered, "will you sell it me? What will you take for it?"

"But—" began Forgan, but the professor shook him.

"Go and get it," he said urgently, "quickly, before anyone can come! I will pay you well."

Forgan went. The van was close to the door and he was back in a moment with a small bottle containing two fluid ounces. Schlagel snatched it from him.

"How much?"

"One *peseta.*"

Schlagel paid. "Listen," he said. "You come again? When?"

"Every day, señor, at this hour."

"Good! Good! Bring me some more tomorrow—"

A door opened from the kitchen and the chef appeared. Schlagel turned and pattered down the cellar stairs like a rabbit into its bury.

After this it was easy. Schlagel met them every day when they came; if they did not have to wait in the scullery he strolled outside and spoke to them behind a convenient clump of arbutus.

Tommy Hambledon walked down the road one morning to meet them.

"I thought you'd better know," he said. "There is going to be a board meeting the day after tomorrow in the long saloon. We shall all be there."

"What time?" asked Forgan.

"After siesta, at four in the afternoon."

"What is this," said Campbell, "a breaking-up party, do you suppose?"

"I don't know. Torgius did say it was very important and we were to get our instructions, but the other fellow, whoever he is, hasn't arrived."

"Except for him, the vultures will be gathered about the carcass," said Campbell.

"My carcass?" said Tommy without enthusiasm.

"Only metaphorically speaking," said Forgan, "I hope."

Before the van reached the kitchen door the professor stepped out from his accustomed arbutus and stopped it.

"But, señor," said Forgan reproachfully, "this is unwise. More, it is rash. One day, you will be seen doing this."

"There are people in the scullery today," said the professor. "Have you got it?

What, only a tiny bottle today again? I told you to bring me a big one."

"Señor, it is the desire of my heart at all costs to be obliging. But if you have a big bottle and get—and it is too much for you, all this will be discovered and we shall be forbidden to return."

"Are you suggesting I should get drunk?" said the professor indignantly.

"No, no," said Forgan. *"Por San Antonio,* no."

"If I had a big bottle it would last longer, I should not have to meet you every day and thus the risk would be reduced."

"There is reason in what the señor has said," remarked Campbell.

"There may be," said Forgan doubtfully.

"You get me a big bottle," said the professor, addressing Campbell.

"Listen," said Forgan, as one suddenly making up his mind. "If you will do something for us I will bring you a big bottle."

"What do you want me to do?"

"We—Manuel and I—are going to a meeting of *comunistos* the day after tomorrow. We are not *comunistos,* no! We play a joke on them."

"Ha," said the professor. "When I was a student at Heidelberg—"

"Can you make a gas that will make people sneeze?"

"Of course I can. Nothing simpler. When I was a boy at Klagenfurt—"

"Yes, yes. If we fix up a fish with a rubber container inside, will you fill it with sneezing gas for us?"

"But certainly. On condition that you bring me the big—"

"On the honor of my mother," said Forgan emotionally.

"You will come for it—when?"

"In the morning, the day after tomorrow. Where shall we find you, do we walk down the cellar stairs?"

"Yes, yes. Just walk down and I shall be there. Today and tomorrow I make the gas and you bring your fish the morning after. It will be a good joke. I remember when I was a young man in Vienna—"

There was a quick step on the drive and Torgius came suddenly upon them.

"Schlagel—what is all this? Return to the house at once. Torre—"

"Perdone, señor," said Forgan. "The Señor Profesor was but asking us to bring lobster tomorrow, today we have only crab—"

"Yes, yes," said Schlagel. "I like lobster, you know I do."

"Then why not ask the chef?" said Torgius reasonably.

"Don't like the man," grumbled the professor, and ambled away.

"Bring lobster tomorrow," said Torgius, and went on down the drive.

"I don't think we see the professor tomorrow, do you?" said Campbell.

"No. We'll come a bit earlier and miss him. I don't like that Torgius."

"He looks capable," said Campbell gloomily.

On the morning of the day appointed for Torgius's meeting the fishmongers arrived late, exhibiting distress and fatigue and carrying a basket of fish between them.

They said their diabolical chariot had broken down two miles back along the road and after spending too much time trying to repair it they had given it up and run all the rest of the way uphill carrying the basket themselves. "But how we ran so far, señor," said Forgan to the chef, "I know not. Only our sense of our duty—"

"Give me the fish," snapped the chef, and took it from them in haste. Even Anita seemed thoroughly cross.

"Of course you would select today to break down," she said, flying round the scullery like a miniature hurricane, "and make lunch late just when we all want to get off early—"

"Why?" said Campbell in an exhausted voice. Forgan was leaning against the wall with his eyes half closed and taking no notice.

"If you were not a heathen you would know it is the festival of San Mateo, and the *patrono* has said we may all have the day off after lunch and go to the fiesta at San Mateo, all the staff together, and now you've made us late and we shall miss the bus—"

The fishmongers drooped more dejectedly than before.

"Is it permitted that we rest a moment before we go back to—"

"So long as you keep out of my way I don't care where you are!" She flounced out of the room and when she came back they were gone.

Schlagel was waiting impatiently for them at the foot of the cellar stairs.

"You are late, I thought you were not coming—have you brought it?"

"*Sí, señor,*" said Campbell, and gave him a full-sized bottle of brandy.

"Also the fish," said Forgan, but the professor was not at the moment interested in the fish. Forgan waited until Schlagel was prepared to notice him, and repeated: "Also the fish."

It was a gaily colored fish with a sneering expression and a large mouth wide open, it had a broad thick body which ended unexpectedly in a thin whiplike tail. Forgan laid it carefully upon the table and it sagged oddly in the middle. The professor put down his glass and prodded the fish with his finger.

"What have you done to it?"

"Taken out the insides, señor, and fitted a rubber hot-water bottle instead. He has a good thick skin, our fish. When we filled the bottle with very hot water the skin stuck tight to it all over. He is as shapely as in life, señor, is he not?"

"Better," said Schlagel happily, "much better. Where is the opening? In his mouth? I give you much honour, you are artists. Even I might not have thought of that. You make a hole in it, do you, and leave your meeting with excuses? Yes. Your *comunistos* will be surprised."

"Is the gas all ready for him?"

"Yes, yes. I wish I could be at your meeting, it will be funny. Very funny. I should prefer, however, to wear a gas mask."

"I think that also might surprise the *comunistos,*" said Campbell. "Of course, you could say it was to protect you from the effects of their poisonous opinions."

The professor laughed until he choked and Forgan kindly replenished his glass.

"Now," said Schlagel, "we prepare your joke."

He picked up the fish and noticed a strip of adhesive plaster sticking to it. "What is this?" he asked, and picked at it idly.

"Don't do that!" said Forgan sharply. "That's our—that's where the gas comes out. It covers a cut."

"I see. Most ingenious. It saves your being observed in the act of prodding him with a pin, eh? Very good indeed. We shall get on well together, I think." He made a connection between the fish and a sort of rubber balloon with tubes leading from it, and pressed upon the balloon; as it decreased in size the fish expanded visibly, and Schlagel watched it with delight.

"I hope I have made enough," he said. "The pressure is not great enough to expand your hot-water bottle beyond its normal dimensions, but if it is comfortably full there will be enough to affect everyone in any ordinary hall."

"How big a room," asked Campbell, "will this amount of your gas affect?"

"Oh, quite big," said Schlagel, watching the fish. "He raises his head, look! One would think he were about to sneeze."

"Yes, but how big?" persisted Campbell.

"Oh, bigger than what they call the long saloon here. Do you know it? It looks out on the terrace beyond the front door. Now, to cork him up. You have the stopper, Torre? When I pull the tube off, hold your breath and screw it in quickly."

It was done quickly, but even so enough gas escaped to make Campbell sneeze till tears ran down his face and he held to the table for support.

"Good gas, eh?" said Schlagel proudly. "Have a little brandy, to sneeze so much is a strain. The ventilation in this place is defective, it affects me at times."

They had a drink, very small ones on the part of Forgan and Campbell.

"Will it disturb your studies," said Forgan anxiously, "if we wait here for a little until the servants have all gone? There will be trouble if we are seen coming up your stairs."

"Oh, by—by all means," said Schlagel. "Do not go, I like congenial asso—associates—besides, I want advice. Shkilled advice. There's a Frenchman here and I don't like him. Want to annoy him. Name of Duvallet, Paul Duvallet. Know Duvallet? No. He's a fraud. Says he's an anthropopo—anthro—man who studies races."

"Horse races?" said Campbell.

"No, no. Human races. People. If he's an anthropolist I'm a female impersonator. Gets it out of guidebooks. What's the time?"

"Why?" asked Forgan.

"Got a meeting. In the long saloon. At sixteen hours. Got to explain to a lot of muttonheaded conceited half-witted shelf—self-important—er—"

"Nincompoops?" suggested Campbell.

"That's it. The elementally principles of handling concentrated explosh—explodish—bangs."

Forgan refilled his glass.

"There's plenty of time before your meeting," he said. "What you need is a little stimulant."

"Thank you. Yes. Though I don't care," said the professor with a sweeping gesture which sent his distilling apparatus crashing to the floor, "I don' care if they all blow themselves up."

"I say," said Campbell, exhibiting alarm, "you haven't got any explosives down here, have you?"

The professor laughed so heartily that he sat down upon the floor and Forgan had some difficulty in persuading him to get up again.

"Look out," whispered Campbell, "don't overdose the patient."

"I think he's had about enough," answered Forgan. *"Señor Profesor!* Have you really got explosives down here?"

The professor struggled to his feet, weaved his way across the room and opened a cupboard in the wall. Inside were shelves upon which were ranged boxes of different sizes; most of them were quite small, about, as Hambledon had said, the size of a packet of a dozen boxes of matches. Half a dozen or so were larger, as big as a box of a hundred cigars, and these had dials on one side and a plunger which stood out about an inch.

"Are these all loaded?" asked Campbell in awed tones.

The sight of his masterpieces had a partially sobering effect upon the professor. "These small ones," he explained, "are charged but not fused. They cannot be fused until shortly before they are needed. I say 'shortly,' gentlemen, though the period may be as long as a fortnight or three weeks by arrangement. These large ones, the class will notice, are fitted with dials. You are my class, aren't you?"

"Yes, sir, of course," said Forgan smartly.

"Of course. Only one of the large ones is yet charged owing to the non-arrival of the necessary material. That one," said Schlagel, tapping it with his forefinger. "We will examine the mechanism of one of the uncharged ones since I presume the class desires to survive? Yes. I thought you would. The principle is as follows."

He delivered a lecture which became increasingly technical as it proceeded and ended by being right over the heads of his hearers. On the practical side they gathered that one set the dial to decide the time which should elapse between the pressing of the plunger and the explosion. "Five minutes is the minimum period considered advisable from the point of view of safety," he said. "The cause of science is in all respects paramount, but it is foolish to immolate oneself."

There was an awed silence for a moment.

"With apologies, *Señor Profesor,*" said Forgan, "but did you not say you had a meeting at sixteen hours? It is now upon the hour."

"Good gracious," said Schlagel. He drained his glass and waded, as against a
strong current, up the stairs.

Chapter Twenty One
The Sneezing Fish

As the hour drew on towards four o'clock the various members of the houseparty
began to gather in the long saloon. It had originally been intended for a ballroom
and a number of small gilt chairs still remained. To these had been added a long
table down the middle; the company seated itself on either side with Torgius as
chairman at the head of the table and Tommy modestly near the foot with the door
behind him. Tonio had done his best to come in also but had been firmly pushed
out and left sitting disconsolate in the hall outside. Torgius opened proceedings
with a speech.

"We are gathered here," he said, "to discuss between ourselves the best means
of conducting our campaign for the reestablishment of our Germany in her right-
ful place as leader of the world. I should like first to welcome to our comradeship
our latest arrival, Herr Henochsberg, who has made his way to us through a sea of
obstacles such as would have daunted a less determined man." Tommy bowed. "It
is not his fault that he did not bring that which we hoped he would bring, that was
in the custody of his colleague and was destroyed with him in an attack by Jewish
Bolshevism. A less determined man, I say, would have turned back"—Tommy
bowed again—"but he, having no other orders, completed his journey with credit
to himself and encouragement to us."

"I knew this reminded me of something," said Tommy to himself. "Speech day
at school. Old boy makes good."

"The loss of which I spoke will be restored in part when Herr Borian arrives,
he is bringing a further supply with him to delight the heart of our good Professor
Schlagel. Borian may arrive at any moment."

Schlagel was sitting next but one to Tommy across the corner of the table, and
Hambledon looked at him with some interest. He had come in almost the last, spoken
to no one and slumped down on the nearest vacant chair. He was unusually red in
the face, his eyes were heavy and his breathing audible. He appeared to be taking
no notice at all of the proceedings. "Either he's going to have a stroke," thought
Hambledon, "or Forgan and Campbell have—" At that moment the professor
stirred and frankly regurgitated. "Not a stroke," decided Hambledon. This looked
as though it might be funny.

Torgius said he would first describe the methods of distribution and then call
upon Professor Schlagel to elucidate the—ah!—technical side. Torgius droned on
and Hambledon tried to mitigate his boredom by watching his neighbors, but the
boredom won. The three alleged Americans were sitting together near the head of

the table and Elvira was beginning to fidget. Paul Duvallet was staring out of the window with an absent expression, the man from Malmédy suppressed a yawn. It was very hot.

There came the sound of a car on the graveled drive outside, it stopped, and a horn was blown. Torgius broke off in the middle of a sentence, excused himself, and went out into the hall. The company round the table relaxed their attitudes of polite attention and a little murmur of conversation began. The professor raised his head, looked about him as though he wondered why he was there, and dozed off again.

The car started up, turned, and drove away. Voices were heard in the hall approaching the door, which opened. Torgius's voice telling someone to come in, "please precede me. Not you, dog! Get back." Tonio uttered a muffled yelp and a short sprightly man walked into the room followed by Torgius, who shut the door after him but did not turn the key. The stranger noticed it.

"You do not lock the door, no?"

"Not worthwhile," said Torgius, who did not like being told anything. "The servants are all out, we have the house to ourselves. Ladies and gentlemen, it is my happy privilege to introduce the Herr Lorenz Borian, who has come at exactly the right moment to find us all engaged together in the service of our country." Torgius led his guest to the head of the table. "May I, first of all, introduce those of our company who are as yet strangers to you?"

"Please," said Borian. "Nearly all of them, I think. Ha, Duvallet, I am glad to see you."

"On your right," began Torgius, "the Herren Ezra and Hiram van Houten and the gracious Frau van Houten—"

He named one after another in order as they sat, and each in turn rose, bowed and sat down again, all except Schlagel, who merely grunted. Hambledon's turn came.

"The Herr Ernst Henochsberg from Erfurt."

Hambledon rose, bowed and sat down, but Borian stared at him.

"Who did you say that is?"

Torgius repeated the introduction.

"Nonsense. That isn't Ernst Henochsberg, nothing like him."

"But," said Torgius.

"That isn't Henochsberg," repeated Borian. "He's the only one here I did expect to know. We were next-door neighbors in Erfurt."

There was a stunned silence. Hambledon sat quite still with both hands on the table, eyebrows slightly raised as one who encounters discourtesy, but otherwise apparently calm. Within his mind his thoughts were racing. "At least the door isn't locked, if I can shoot my way out—"

Torgius had an automatic in his hand, it looked much more natural to him than the ornate fountain pen he usually held.

"Did he tell you he was Henochsberg?" asked Borian.

"Of course he did," snapped Torgius. "I—"

"Oh no I didn't," said Hambledon. "You called me Henochsberg and I thought it wouldn't be polite to contradict."

"Who are you?" said Borian, but Hambledon merely smiled.

"He called himself Hambledon," said Torgius, "that was the name on the passport he carried."

"Hambledon?" said Borian. "But is it possible you don't know who Hambledon is?"

"Of course I know, but this isn't that man. He merely had—"

"Isn't it? Are you sure?"

"But he wouldn't come here under his own name," objected Torgius.

"Why not?" said Borian. "If I hadn't come—"

Elvira had been silent too long already.

"Do you mean the British Intelligence Hambledon?" she said. "Do you mean that's really him? Are you, Mr. Hambledon?"

Tommy bowed, and slipped his hand off the table. "I couldn't contradict a lady, don't you know."

"Well," said Elvira in her most violent American, "you may be a spy but I'll tell the world you're a great guy." She turned on Torgius. "Why do you stand there arguing? Why don't you shoot him?"

Tommy dodged back behind his neighbor and his gun was in his hand when the door opened without warning and two fishermen came in. They pulled the door to behind them and stood there blinking.

"With apologies," began Campbell.

"What the devil are you doing here?" roared Torgius. "Get out at once."

One of them staggered back against the door and the key fell out, tinkling on the polished boards; he stooped slowly and picked it up. The other advanced unsteadily towards the table and it was regrettably clear that he was not sober.

"With apologies," he said, "we are doing no wrong. We brought the fish. We can't find anybody. No chef. Not even Anita." He hiccupped and apologized again. "You pay us, we go."

The other came to join him. "Poor fishermen," he whined.

"Get away, go," said Torgius. "You shall have your money tomorrow."

"No," said Forgan loudly. "Now!"

He jerked the fish out from under his coat and sent it spinning along the table. Schlagel awoke with a start, crying, "Not that fish! Herr Gott, not that fish!" and immediately the company threw back their heads and were overcome by the most paralyzing sneezes. Forgan seized one of Hambledon's arms and Campbell the other; they dragged him backwards to the door. Torgius fired one shot which missed them narrowly, others which followed went anywhere, since no man can sneeze and aim. Hambledon, gasping like the rest, was pushed out of the door, which was slammed and locked behind them; he paused and looked through his streaming tears at his rescuers.

"I—ah—ah—atish—"

"Don't stop!" said Forgan. "Run like blazes! Run!"

They hustled him out of the door and dropped down from the terrace. Tonio the dog came—for him—rushing, not sure whether Hambledon was being assaulted.

"What's—hurry? Ah—"

"In two minutes from now this place is going up," said Campbell. "Run!"

Hambledon conquered his mucous membranes. "Tonio! Come on!"

Three men and one huge dog crashed through the flower beds, down the hill, leaping sunk fences, making for an outcrop of rock big enough to shelter them, there it was—

There came a great roaring sound, they threw themselves flat or were thrown by the blast. Tonio crouched in terror. Pieces of stone from the house flew past them with a whistling sound, the air filled with dust and debris and a great beam came down like a javelin and stuck upright in the ground only six feet away. The dog forgot his adult dignity and threw himself into Hambledon's arms, whimpering like a puppy; the effect was to immobilize Hambledon completely since Tonio weighed well over a hundredweight. The ground shook with the concussion; as the column of dust rose and spread even the sunlight was darkened. By degrees the shower of fragments ceased and the three men, white and shaken, looked at each other.

"Forgan," said Hambledon in an awestruck voice, "did you do that?"

"With one of the professor's bombs," said Forgan, "just one."

"He was a nice old boy," said Campbell unsteadily, "but it's as well he's dead. Can't have that kind of thing. Definitely not."

"I think, if we can still walk," said Forgan, "we'd better go. The entire neighborhood will be here in five minutes."

"Tonio," said Hambledon, "could you get off me? I want to sit up."

They kept inside the grounds until they reached the spot where the fish van was standing, and dropped over the wall. There were already men and women coming along the road, running and stopping to point and exclaim. Hambledon and dog got inside the van and the doors were tied together, as usual, with string; Forgan and Campbell, sitting in front, sent the Ford bucketing down the hill. Passing through Tafira they cried the lamentable news to the people standing staring in the street, but did not stop. Presently they arrived at the point where one turns a corner and sees the town of Las Palmas spread out below; out to sea there was a big liner coming slowly in towards the port.

There was a small window without glass in the front of the van, Hambledon kneeled up on the floor and looked out of it. The van was certainly stuffy.

"That's the Highland Chieftain," said Campbell. "She was due in today and sails again early tomorrow—bound for London."

"With us on board," said Tommy firmly, "all four of us. D'you think you'll like

England, Tonio? Tonio! I say, stop, you fellows. Tonio's going to be sick."

Forgan braked, but the road was steep and narrow. "I'll stop at the bottom," he said.

"Don't bother," said Hambledon sadly. "He's been."

"What with one thing and another," said Campbell, "I cannot find it in my heart to blame him."

THE END

About the Rue Morgue Press

"Rue Morgue Press is the old-mystery lover's best friend, reprinting high quality books from the 1930s and '40s."
—*Ellery Queen's Mystery Magazine*

Since 1997, the Rue Morgue Press has reprinted scores of traditional mysteries, the kind of books that were the hallmark of the Golden Age of detective fiction. Authors reprinted or to be reprinted by the Rue Morgue include Catherine Aird, Delano Ames, H. C. Bailey, Morris Bishop, Nicholas Blake, Dorothy Bowers, Pamela Branch, Joanna Cannan, John Dickson Carr, Glyn Carr, Torrey Chanslor, Clyde B. Clason, Joan Coggin, Manning Coles, Lucy Cores, Frances Crane, Norbert Davis, Elizabeth Dean, Carter Dickson, Eilis Dillon, Michael Gilbert, Constance & Gwenyth Little, Marlys Millhiser, Gladys Mitchell, James Norman, Stuart Palmer, Craig Rice, Kelley Roos, Charlotte Murray Russell, Maureen Sarsfield, Margaret Scherf, Juanita Sheridan and Colin Watson..

To suggest titles or to receive a catalog of Rue Morgue Press books write 87 Lone Tree Lane, Lyons, CO 80540, telephone 800-699-6214, or check out our website, www.ruemorguepress.com, which lists complete descriptions of all of our titles, along with lengthy biographies of our writers.